WILDE CARD

IMMORTAL VEGAS, BOOK 2

JENN STARK

ISBN-13: 978-1-943768-07-3

Cover art by Gene Mollica

Photography by Gene Mollica

For Ayn

VI
VII
THE CHARIOT.
XX
JUDGEMENT.

CHAPTER ONE

I couldn't breathe. I couldn't even blink. Six foot two of hard-bodied ex–Special Forces operative was snugged up against my backside, and I was totally falling for him.

For about eight thousand more feet.

My helmet crackled. "You're doing great."

"Unghflun." Worse, we were still spinning. They'd told me the spinning would stop, but it didn't feel like it was stopping. It felt like we were dying. And of all the ways to die, French-kissing a cliff at a hundred miles per hour had not made my short list. It gave a whole new meaning to the phrase "terminal" velocity.

"Right on target."

Something shuddered above us, and I shifted from sprawl to nearly vertical in a sudden blur. I squinted up past the man carabinered to me in not nearly enough places, to see that our parachute had deployed.

That would be the "Low Opening" portion of this joyride into the Siberian mountain range surrounding Lake Baikal. The "High Altitude" section had been covered by our plunging six-mile drop from a souped-up jet now well on its way to Beijing.

Getting off this rock without alerting the local

military would be its own special kind of crazy, but I was down for that. Pretty much any kind of crazy that got me away from Vegas and the Arcana Council for a few days worked for me.

"Drop point," echoed in my ear.

Beside us, two other barely discernible shadows rocketed through the predawn gloom. We were aiming for a strip of gravel tucked between two sheer cliffs where, according to my client, X marked the spot for the ultimate Mongolian treasure: the crown of Genghis Khan. Rumored to give its wearer the Khan's magical mojo for protection, abundance, and crazy long life.

Then again, said crown was apparently resting on the head of a dead guy right now. So there was that.

Another crackle in my helmet. "Bend your knees."

"If I had a dollar..."

My guide's laughter carried through our final several hundred feet of descent, and suddenly we were on the ground, a tumble of arms, legs, and high-tech padding. With impressive military precision, mission leader Zander "Call me Zee" James broke up with me without remorse, thrusting me aside. I lurched drunkenly to my knees as he slowed his run then turned to his parachute and punched it into submission.

The other men landed beside us, neatly outrunning their chutes, and I ducked to avoid a fine spray of rocks stirred up by the movement. Zee stripped off his HALO suit, oxygen mask and gear like he was shimmying out of swim trunks, and shoved them into a we-were-never-here-sized nylon bagel for easy transport out. He flapped his hand at me for mine and I shoved them at him in a big ball. "Report?" he snapped.

Zee's right-hand man squinted down at a device attached to his wrist. "No heat signatures," he said, aiming the thing at the rock wall. "Wall" was being kind. The cliff face surged up as if an angry god had punched through the earth's crust, all crags and fissures and sharp edges. "Seismic activity currently stable."

As if to counter his words, another crackle of falling rocks sounded high above us. "Right." Zee squinted up. "At dawn, this place'll light up like the surface of the sun. We don't want to be here for that. We get in, we get out, we get gone." His gaze shifted to me. "Ready?"

I nodded, then tugged down the zipper of my tech suit to fetch my own tools of the trade, my trusty pack of Tarot cards.

With the deck as my compass, I could find about anything—for a price. As it happened, a hundred G was a heck of a price. That kind of money translated to at least three more Connecteds hidden away from the dark practitioners who wanted to use them for spare parts. Not enough to save them all, no. But enough to count. I had to believe that.

"Sometime today, princess."

Double-tasking one set of fingers to offer Zee my opinion of his people management skills, I used the other to pull a scatter of cards out of the deck.

Here we go.

Four of Cups, the Magician, Eight of Swords, King of Cups. Two that made sense, one that didn't, and one that might make me kill someone. But first things, first.

"Whaddya got?" Zee prompted. I shoved the cards back in place, rezipping my suit.

"We go up." I squinted at the fissure-ridden rock

wall. The Four of Cups typically showed a grumpy young man sitting at the base of a tree, focusing on three cups on the ground, totally missing the cup that floated above him. It could mean lots of things in lots of different scenarios, but in a game of hide and seek…

I peered high. The problem with the client's choice of Mount Swiss Cheese here was there probably *were* a half-dozen holes that legitimately tunneled all the way into the mountain, along with a million and one false starts. Unfortunately, we didn't have time to waste. The place was heavily patrolled, with the next choppers due at dawn.

Fortunately, the cards were pointing the way. I looked yet higher. "Give me a boost?"

Zee moved into position beside me, cupping his hands. He braced me easily as I scrabbled up the side of the wall. I usually preferred to avoid climbing anything more challenging than a mound of pillows, but the tech gloves helped. So did the fact that Zee's arms were solid, even fully outstretched. "You got something?" he asked.

"Hole."

"We got those down here."

"Mine's better." I glanced toward him. "But it's going to be tight. You and Atlas Shrugged will need to suck it in. Boost me the rest of the way."

I knelt on the narrow ledge while Zee free-climbed up behind me, barely grunting with the effort. And… *Bingo.* Half-hidden beneath a rough outcropping, a fissure sank into the side of the mountain, maybe wide enough for a man so long as he wasn't channeling Mr. Potato Head. I picked up a handful of rocks and tossed them into the hole. They skittered a few feet, then fell a fair distance before hitting what I assumed was "bottom."

"Can't see a damned thing," Zee muttered, angling his flashlight beam into the opening. "Blast it bigger?"

Atlas pulled himself up beside us. "That would definitely make the seismic activity unstable. About a fifth of this wall is just itching for a reason to fall down."

"Right." Zee turned toward me and gave me his flashlight, along with a crooked grin. "Ladies first, then."

"Such a gentleman." Still, if anything went wrong, they could haul me out of that hole a lot easier than I could haul them. Sliding the flashlight up my sleeve and manfully resisting the bad joke, I flattened myself on my stomach, then wormed into the tight space.

It was claustrophobic enough to make me panic, but I wriggled ahead anyway, edging deeper and deeper. Using my toes to dig into the loose rocks against the side of the mountain, I snagged an outcropping to haul myself forward and—

Dropped into open space.

"*Jesus!*"

Zee's curse cracked above me, and iron fists clamped down on my ankles as the stone I'd grabbed for crumbled into the cavern below. I hung precariously upside down in full possum for a long, queasy moment, then fumbled the flashlight out of my sleeve.

It only took a second to bring a smile to my face.

Dead bodies did that. Especially when they'd been dead a long time.

I wiggled my ankles to loosen Zee's grip. "All clear!"

"Rolling!" Zee's shout was my sole warning before

he dropped me. I curled into a protective ball and plummeted down several feet, then somersaulted off a mound of scree and rock dust that had accumulated in the center of the room. I landed cheek to jawbone with the nearest skeleton. After an impressive amount of cursing, Zee dropped to the rock pile behind me, followed by his men. The thud of their boots echoed ominously, and I thought I heard the scatter of stones falling deep inside the mountain. The place must be as hollow as a honeycomb.

"Arrows," Zee grunted, poking at the pile of bones and moldy clothes that circled our small mound. "Not friendly fire, I'm thinking. At least they're old as shit." He tossed me one of the long, slender shafts, then fanned his flashlight in a wide arc. "Those bars over there look a bit too solid, though."

I nodded. "Eight of Swords."

The light flared in my face. "Which means?"

"Well, for us it means restrictions we can get around, if we open our eyes."

"That's beautiful." Zee stepped over the mounds of bones and strode forward, then ran a hand over the surface of the bars. "These are embedded in the floor and ceiling. We ain't getting through this way." He flicked his flashlight beam back over me. "What next?"

"Working on it." I pondered the scene in front of me while Zee's men bent over their Techzilla, Inc. readers and muttered observations on psychic energy levels. A few more rocks fell from the ledges above, bouncing lightly off the small mound of gravel in the center of the room. *Magician, Magician, Magician…*

One thing for sure: the Magician *himself* had better not show up here, not while I was on the clock for another client. Mr. Mongol back in Ulaanbaatar had hired me to recover a piece of his heritage, tacking on Team Armor All here for logistics and muscle alone. He would not take kindly to a tagalong, no matter if said tagalong was the leader of the Great and Mighty Arcana Council. The success or failure of this op was all on me.

Fortunately, Armaeus Bertrand did *not* fulfill my worst nightmare by poking his head through the hole in the ceiling, and I dropped my gaze again to take in the small holding cell. Around the rock pile in the center of the room, the remains of bones and clothes hunkered like kids circling a campfire. Something about that…

"Why aren't there any bones in the center? Why just rocks?" I asked aloud. I kicked at the pile of rubble, then brushed more of the dust away as Zee turned his light on me. It didn't take me long to find the reason. "Tool marks. Someone's cut into the floor."

Zee walked over, leaving his men at the bars. "Definitely tool marks." Squatting down, he started chucking rocks toward the larger pile, revealing a graceful arc that had been carved into the stone. We uncovered it bit by bit. The curve met itself in the center, creating a perfect fat teardrop. Zee leaned down and shoved a particularly robust pile forward…and the cavern echoed with a resounding creak.

We all froze.

"What the hell was that?" Zee muttered, but all of us were looking at the same thing, caught in multiple flashlight beams. There was a distinct ridge in the floor right along the carved arc, where our ledge was a millimeter higher than the surface around it.

"Figure Eight," I said suddenly, staring at the design. "We're on half of it." I met Zee's confused gaze. "Infinity sign. It was on one of the cards I pulled. Two sides of equal size, joined in the middle. We're on one side." I pointed. "That pile is on the other. A pile you've made a lot heavier. Maybe it's like a seesaw."

"It's exactly like that, I bet." Zee stood, carefully. "We overload it enough, it goes down, we go up, then everything slides down to whatever's waiting below." He scowled at me. "Trap?"

"I don't think—"

"Zee, we got trouble." The man at the bars peered into the gloom. "No readings on the device, but something's—"

"I hear it." Zee yanked out his gun as a sound from deep in the mountain jolted us. It wasn't shifting rock this time. This was more rhythmic. A *lot* more rhythmic: the sound of running feet.

"Weapons up!" On the heels of Zee's bark, two sturdily built men burst into the room, dressed like desert ninjas in long tunics and trousers, their faces covered with enormous Mongolian death masks—one a dragon, the other a wolf. Zee shouted for them to stand down. Instead, they immediately drew their bows, notching them with arrows. Arrows that looked eerily familiar.

"Fire!" The crack of semiautomatics shattered the silence, but the death-masked men didn't fall. They simply staggered back like they'd been hit with a feisty paintball round, then lifted their bows again. Another crack of gunfire, and more bullets punched through them. This time, though, one of their masks half exploded. That had more effect, and the creature howled, dropping to his knees as he blindly sought to recover his bow.

Zee let fly a third round, then holstered his

weapon. "Keep 'em busy. We'll get this done." He turned to me, clamping his hand on my arm. "I don't want to wait for these guys to call up reinforcements."

He pushed me toward the Crazy 8 in the floor while his men provided covering gunfire. I launched myself onto the rock pile, Zee right behind me, the two of us landing hard. The roar of scraping stone was barely discernible as the floor dipped slowly. Too slowly. We jumped up and down again. The slab wobbled, slipped, then suddenly gained momentum and shot completely vertical, dust and rocks sailing down on us. We dropped down into sheer blackness.

About three point five seconds later, we slammed into a flat surface. The gravel and dust continued falling around us, but not all of it, not completely. My hand connected with a strip of metal even as my knees and feet broke through the floor.

"Iron mesh," Zee barked. "Also old as shit. Get off this thing." We scrambled to the side like startled spiders, then whipped around after we reached solid rock floor. Zee swung his flashlight, the arc of its light barely cutting through the dust. In front of us, a thick mesh of bars crisscrossed the floor, rendering the surface makeshift human net.

I pounded Zee's arm. "*Undead,* Zee*?* Really? nowhere in my contract did it mention undead."

"We didn't know either." He flicked his flashlight around and up. The room emptied into a downward sloping corridor. Above us, the ceiling was easily twelve feet up, once again perfectly sealed. The Magician's infinity symbol glowed in the center of an elaborate scrollwork etched into the stone.

Okey-dokey. That kind of Magician I could handle.

"After the others get clear, they'll assess whether

they come down here or bug out. Let's make that choice easy on them." Zee squinted, leaning forward to tap the wall. "Crypt's gotta be on this level, though. That's hammered gold."

As we pulled ourselves to our feet, the sound of an enormous gong reverberated through the room. Gonging was never good.

Zee apparently agreed. "Move out." We turned and raced down the corridor. The walls were plated with every precious metal of the ancient world—bronze, gold, silver, iron. Then we reached a large center room, with fully a dozen corridors snaking off it. Darkening shadows and various stages of stink indicated that each passageway held its share of crypts.

Zee stopped long enough to fish his Techzilla reader out, pointing it at the open doors. At the third one, it bleated. "Pay dirt."

"Yup." I wasn't perfect at reading energy—that was what I had the cards for. But even I could sense the zing of this last room. The zing…and something else.

"Wait," I said as Zee traded his reader for his gun. "You hear that?" A faint whooshing sound shivered in the distance, almost inaudible, marred briefly by another burst of gunfire far above. "Is that water?"

He shrugged. "We're on a lake, princess. There's water goddamned everywhere."

"King of Cups." I shook my head. "Last card I drew. It was the King of Cups. Cups are water. That's important."

"And Khan was a king. Also important. And my guys will run out of ammo soon. Most important of all. Let's hit this." Without another word, Zee ducked into the low entrance, leaving me to follow behind.

Bodies lined the deep cavern, lying in perfect symmetry and draped in exceptionally well-preserved furs, their heads covered in yet more ritual death masks. Unlike their brothers upstairs, these guys really did look dead.

We didn't stop to make sure.

The shrine in the center of the room was some sort of fancy stone coffin perched on a thick pedestal. With Zee ahead of me, taut as a bowstring, we crept up the small staircase to get a closer peek.

I let out a soft breath when we saw what lay inside the open coffin. "Hey there, old guy."

The corpse was not, as I expected, Mongolian. Granted, he'd probably been dead a long time, and death could really take the stuffing out of a guy. But the cadaver appeared far more Russian than anything else—maybe even European, with pale, papery skin, sunken cheeks and wide-set eyes. He'd not died in a moment of violence either: his features were untroubled, the visible skin of his face and neck unmarked.

But while the dude was a total white guy, the crown was all Mongolia, all the way.

Unlike the spiky-pointed version of its Western European cousins, this headpiece looked more like a helmet, with long metal flaps that came down over the ears and a hardy construction that gave the impression you could wear it into battle. The entire surface of the crown was studded with orange, blue, and green stones, glinting in Zee's flashlight beam. It was pretty enough, but if it followed the pattern of most magical artifacts, the embedded jewels didn't mark its true value.

As I leaned forward to grab it, my glance dropped

to the robes pulled tight over Dead Guy's body. They were made of richly patterned silks, vivid greens flowing into an intricately worked chest patch of red and blue. Zee's flashlight angled, and I froze, mesmerized by the image.

How was that possible? Staring out at me in full embroidered splendor was a blue dragon, its wings outstretched across a field of red. I knew that design. It'd been imprinted on my brain ten years ago on the worst day of my life. But what was it doing on a dead guy's bathrobe?

More concerning, why did it seem so familiar? Like I'd seen it somewhere else, somewhere *recent,* somewhere…

"Princess," Zee hissed.

Reflexively, my fingers closed on the crown, and I jerked it free from the corpse's head.

Its eyes flicked open.

"*Dammit!*" Zee's curse was drowned in the sound of a second massive gong strike, so loud it vibrated the walls. I jammed the helmet into my jacket while Zee thunked his flashlight into the now ex-corpse's skull, which earned him a squawk of outrage. The creature started beating his frail arms against Zee, screaming in a language that sounded shockingly like French. Another slam of Zee's light, and the guy fell back into his coffin, out cold.

Before we could clear the pedestal, however, the skies opened up—or the ceiling, more accurately—and a torrent of water crashed over us. Zee staggered under the deluge. "Son of a—"

"No!" I reached for Zee's arm and yanked him back as he prepared to plunge into the already calf-deep water. "King of Cups—he rules from a platform on water. We need to stay here!"

"Well, it's a popular destination." Zee dashed water from his eyes and pointed, growling in disgust. "Fucking undead."

I followed the direction of his hand. The corpses lining the walls were on the move. They'd sat up straight and were swinging their legs over their pallets. A few of them were already in the water, which was rising fast, cresting the short flight of stairs at the base of our pedestal. More splashes, and Zee cursed again. The walking undead were all heading toward us.

Water cascaded in from all sides, and the platform beneath our feet wobbled, lifting away. I squinted down, surprised at the fact that we were floating, then up again toward the ceiling. Zee squeezed off a few rounds, shooting into the cascade. "Some ideas, here, princess!"

"Working on it—" Then I saw it. "There! Hole!"

"Not going to—fuck!" Zee fired a round point-blank into a death mask that surged out of the water, and the creature spun away, going down beneath the surface. By now the flood was chest-deep, and the platform had broken away, spinning, turning—

"Get into the coffin!" I shouted. "The King rules over the water from his throne. No throne, so hit the coffin."

Zee turned and stared at me, balancing on the shifting platform like a surfer. "What are you *talking* about?"

"Get in!" I threw myself into the coffin, right on top of the spindly former corpse, and Zee gave up trying to understand and clambered in on top of me. Icky White Guy *stunk*. As I shoved him deeper into the coffin, he woke up and hissed at me.

"Whoa! Check your privilege!" I tried to back away, but there was nowhere to go and the old guy started beating at me. Zee's roared curse overrode everything as our stone boat lifted farther, then banged with a gut-wrenching thump against the ceiling. The sound of rushing water pounded our eardrums, and we shifted and bounced along with the current, the rim of the coffin scraping against the ceiling until finally we hung—suspended.

For a long, queasy moment.

Even the ex-corpse shut up, his rheumy eyes going wide in the reflected beam from Zee's flashlight, his mouth with its rotted teeth forming a startled O.

Then we tipped forward, careening out of the room and down what felt like a massive waterfall. Zee braced me while both of us battered the once-again screeching, screaming Skeletor, who grabbed at our arms, our faces, my jacket. One of his finger bones snapped like a twig in his desperate attempt to recapture the crown. He didn't seem to notice.

"...Drop point!" howled Zee in my ear, delivering another punishing blow to the wish-you-were-dead-guy's face.

"What?" I jolted to the side as we raced around another turn in the cavern, then my stomach bottomed out again. Above our coffin, the tunnel's ceiling appeared to lift up and everything was brighter—shockingly so. "Oh—an exit! This must be the exit!"

"Here we go!" bellowed Zee, locking me in an iron grip.

The propulsion force of the water shot us out into blessed open sky. A blur of gray and green streaked past, too fast to identify. The crypt tipped and dropped away, carrying away the ex-corpse as Zee kicked him down again. Brutally cold air ripped through my sodden clothes in stark contrast to the warm body holding me close.

For a breath, all of time stood still, the world too bright and full, the sky too blue and stark, and there was nothing but light and air and the unnervingly close sound of someone screaming bloody murder…

Right before we plunged into the frigid waters of Lake Baikal.

CHAPTER TWO

The trans-dimensional elevator ride up to the Magician's magical lair was shorter than the plane trip to Vegas, but the jet lag sucked just as much.

"You're late." Armaeus Bertrand's voice pushed against my brain.

My brain pushed back. *And you have a stunted appreciation for sleep.*

As my primary client, the Arcana Council had a lot to offer: they paid me well for finding them the magical artifacts they craved. Plus, they were immortal, which had seriously improved my long term cash-flow projections since I'd begun working with them a little over a year ago.

But my work detail with the Council had taken a decidedly nasty turn of late. My most recent assignments hadn't been to find stuff via my traditional Tarot card reads, it'd been to find them via astral travel, a particularly gut-churning, nerve-shredding, head-exploding form of mental projection, for which I'd recently developed an unfortunate proficiency. And while it wasn't this way for everyone I suspected, for me, astral travel *hurt*. It hurt a lot.

It hurt so much, in fact, that getting within two

miles of Council headquarters liquefied my guts and made my heart seize up.

Yet here I was, crawling into the belly of the beast. Again.

Like I said, they paid well.

And after my stopover at Father Jerome's makeshift Connected orphanage in Paris yesterday, I was ready to score more cash. The old priest was doing everything he could to protect the children on the front lines. The least I could do was my job.

With as much swagger as I could manage given that a thousand razor-beaked vultures were taking biggie-sized chomps out of my brain, I strode into the Magician's palatial office. We were at the southern tip of the Strip, soaring above the Vegas skyline, and despite the harsh midmorning light, you could sense the magic in the air of the city, the whirling wheels and snapping cards and the metallic whoosh of slot machines.

It was the sound of madness, but strangely comforting too.

Inside the Magician's office, though, the crazy was kicked up several notches, which was not doing me any favors. Every surface gleamed, glinted, or invited, from the plush couches to the oversized command desk Armaeus favored. Worse, *everything* vibrated with power, be it trinket, tech—or thaumaturge.

"Miss Wilde," Armaeus greeted me, his voice low and resonant, demanding that I look at him. Bracing myself, I did.

Dark, enigmatic, and sinfully sensual, Armaeus Bertrand wrung the most out of his half-French, half-Egyptian birth, never mind that he'd been walking this Earth since the thirteenth century. His face, with its perfect angles and smooth lines, might as well have been a Renaissance masterpiece carved out of bronze. His blue-black hair drifted luxuriously to his shoulders, and his mouth curved in a soft, indulgent smile while his golden eyes swept over me, from my plane-tousled hair to my dusty boots.

He was dressed impeccably, of course, cool and unflappable in a linen suit with a jewel-blue shirt beneath, open at the neck. I, on the other hand, looked like I hadn't showered in days. I was fine with that, though. I believed in truth in advertising.

I shook my head, trying to refocus. I'd had a lot of time to go over the Lake Baikal job as I'd gradually worked my way back to Vegas, after nearly beating Zee to death with the crown once we'd made it to shore and negotiating a postjob undead bonus with my satisfied client. The one piece I couldn't quit thinking about *wasn't* the Mongolian crown, however, nor the near-bout of hypothermia I'd contracted before we'd been scooped out of the ice bucket of Lake Baikal. It wasn't even the relief on Father Jerome's face when I'd given him the money from the job, cash he so desperately needed and deserved.

No. I couldn't get that blasted blue dragon off my mind, the one embroidered into the ex-corpse's robes. I'd seen something like it ten years ago. More importantly, I'd seen something like it two *weeks* ago—an almost identical design on one of Armaeus's planes. And I was almost sure I'd seen a similarly shaped dragon sitting on one of his shelves, too. In this room.

"Where is it," I growled, peering around. "You've got it here, don't you?"

"You forget, I don't have the luxury of knowing your innermost thoughts, Miss Wilde." Armaeus's clipped voice pulled my attention back to the present with a hard thump.

I'd been in business long enough to recognize the sound of pissed-off client. And though I liked to push Armaeus's buttons, I liked getting paid more. "You should not have left Las Vegas," he continued.

"Couldn't be helped."

"I see. Then shall we discuss your experience in Siberia? Or shall I rely on my contacts to give me the full report?"

I regarded my broken-off nails. "Nothing much to discuss."

"I beg to differ. You could have been injured—or, worse, arrested. A minor Mongolian crown wasn't worth the risk."

He gestured to a case, and I frowned at him. "What?"

"I assume that's what you wanted to find?"

I followed the direction of his long, elegant finger. And all other thoughts flew out of my head. "You've got to be kidding me." I groaned. "They put these things in Cracker Jack boxes or something?"

"So that *wasn't* what you sought?" Amusement laced his words.

I stalked over to the case. On the third shelf, gleaming with polished stones and burnished bronze inlays, sat a near replica of the Mongolian helmet I'd wrenched off some hapless not-quite-a-corpse's head before plunging into the iciest waters this side of Hell. "Does this do the same thing—the long-life business?" I quirked a glance back at him. "Do *not* tell me that's what's kept you kicking around for so long."

Armaeus lifted a contemptuous brow. He could do that better than anyone I knew. "I do not keep the crown for personal use. I have it here for study." His golden eyes tracked me, cataloging my every move. "Who was your client?"

"Some guy with a lot of money jonesing to dig up his family tree." I shrugged. "No one you need to care about."

"It isn't that difficult to learn what I wish to know."

"So why bother asking?"

The rustle of silks was my only warning, then a fresh wave of panic seized me as the High Priestess spoke from another of the room's four entrances.

"Oh, good. The prodigal daughter returns."

Terror blanked my thoughts for the barest moment, but it was apparently long enough for the High Priestess to see my expression. She smiled with satisfaction, and her wide, intelligent eyes mocked me. Today Eshe was rocking the whole Greco-Roman goddess motif, from the tips of her dangle earrings to the toes of her gilded sandals. Her hair fell long and lustrous around her shoulders, framing her perfectly proportioned olive-toned face, and her body practically shimmered in a deep purple robe. "Don't worry, Sara," she cooed. "This won't hurt much. And it's for such a good cause."

I glared at Armaeus. "You didn't tell me she was going to be here."

"You didn't ask." The Magician's voice had also hardened another notch or six, and I fought to keep my stance easy, my shoulders square. I had to play this carefully. A pissed-off Armaeus was a good day's work. A furious Armaeus was dangerous. "If I cannot see your thoughts, I cannot gauge your pain."

"My *pain*?" An unexpected surge of outrage welled up, bolstering and fierce. I stalked forward, jabbing my finger at Armaeus to punctuate my words. "You don't get the *right* to discuss my pain. I've already played that game with you, remember? That *was* you, wasn't it? In my hotel room two weeks ago? Telling me that it 'didn't have to be like this'? Or am I getting my Council members confused?"

"Tsk, tsk, Sara, so much anger." Eshe was enjoying this. Then again, she probably enjoyed pulling the wings off dragonflies too. "It was your choice to protect the twins from Kavala. They are the natural oracles, not you. Serving me is what they were born to do."

"No, they were born to be *gifted,* Eshe. No obligation required."

"Yet you feel obligated to them?"

My own anger flared hotter, treating my brain vultures to a barbeque. "Gee, I don't know. Fifteen years old, kidnapped, and sold to that scum-sucking Jerry Fitz, who pumped their lungs full of gas so they could see visions more clearly? Forgive me if I thought I should cut them a break."

A break. I guess you could call it that. Because after I'd freed the girls from Fitz's hellhole, after I'd also been exposed to his freak show Pythene gas, I'd pledged myself to the High Priestess in place of the girls. Her abilities were specific and needed a prism. She could interpret and even direct present and future events, but she needed someone to *see* those events first. For the moment, that someone was me.

So now, whenever Eshe called, I reported for duty, ready to exercise my gas-enhanced skills of astral travel. Wherever she directed, I went. Whatever she needed to see, I saw. Saw and reported…then slunk off with my handy metaphysical barf bag, a parting gift for flying the not so friendly skies.

Just thinking about it made me wobble a little on my feet.

"Sit down, Miss Wilde."

Armaeus's voice seemed to be coming from too far away, but I couldn't deny that his idea was a good one. I shambled toward the nearest chair, which had somehow gotten…nearer to me than it had been.

I scowled down, testing it with my foot. One thing about the Arcanans, you never could tell what was real with them and what was simply powerful illusion.

Still, the chair felt real enough. Throwing caution to the wind, I sank down into it. The plush leather gave easily beneath my weight, surrounding me with comfort.

To his credit, Armaeus let my relaxation last for another full thirty seconds before ruining it with his voice again. "She's ready."

I stiffened. "No, I'm—"

I didn't have time to complete my sentence. Eshe spoke the ancient words and the thrall of her control held me fast. By the time she stood beside me, I was already fading from this plane, could barely feel her touch on my forehead.

"SANCTUS," she murmured.

I shot out eastward, muscle and sinew shattering apart so that my mind might stretch before me, the visual effect like a hundred satellites all orienting on the same stretch of geography, offering up a multifaceted view. But at least this was a search I wanted to make. SANCTUS was a big reason all the money was so necessary for Father Jerome. A quasi-religious, quasi-military society dedicated to destroying all things magic, SANCTUS had erupted like a napalm strafe across the Connected community...and they were targeting the children first. Children had always been at risk from dark practitioners. Now they were an endangered species. Under the careful direction of Cardinal Rene Ventre, bestie of the pope and closeted zealot against all things magical, SANCTUS had become Connected Enemy Number One, and Ventre the embodiment of everything wrong in the world.

With Eshe's request, I expected to head straight to Vatican City, Rome, to find the group. Instead, my searching mind angled farther east, to Istanbul, where the enormous spires of the Hagia Sophia beckoned me to enter its hallowed dome.

Without consideration for stone or glass or steel, I hurtled into the building, each barrier an unnerving shock to my system. Crashing through physical structures didn't immediately hurt though, not really. The pain always came later.

Down, down, down, I went. Until I finally found my quarry, holed up in a room deep within the bowels of the onetime Church of Holy Wisdom.

Nothing holy was going on here now.

A young woman barely more than a child lay stretched out on a metal table, surrounded by monitors all registering electrical activity that was completely off the charts. I stared, horrified, as men and women in surgical gowns moved industriously around the girl. Finally, through a break in the gowns, I could see more: the young woman's blank eyes, her slack expression.

She was dead. But death offered no repose for her.

Chatter erupted in the room as energy readings jumped and jangled, the Connected's brain waves still responding to God only knew what stimulants they'd pumped into her. The words of the doctors were Italian, Greek, Arabic—a flood of excited babble, while monitors glittered and fingers pounded on keyboards.

Through all of it, I knew I was speaking, reporting what I saw to Eshe and Armaeus, every detail, every nuance. But my attention could not stay focused on the machines, the doctors. Not with a child in the room. A perfect, precious Connected child, who had done nothing to deserve this treatment other than to be born special. Unique.

Gifted.

I heard new voices, arguing voices, but I could not spare them my focus. I drifted closer, down toward the dead girl. No breath would ever pass her lips again; no smile would light her face. No impossible fancy would ever make her hug herself with delight and possibility.

She was gone. I was too late.

Always too little, too late.

I reached out, and another explosion of activity on the monitors penetrated my consciousness. On the table, a ripple shuddered across the girl's face, and I heard—felt —*knew* her last moments: the screams, the cries, the prick of the needle in her neck, and the long spiraling crash toward—

"No!"

I jolted awake, sprawled out on Armaeus's chair. Scrabbling like a crab, I crouched back into the cushions, my gaze swinging around. "What?" I said, too loudly. "What happened! Why am I here? Why did you—"

"I brought you out of the session early."

Armaeus's voice was a rock in the middle of a stormy sea, and I floundered toward it, shaking my head, trying to see. Gradually, too gradually, my eyes cleared and the vertigo edged down long enough for me to breathe.

"Where… what…"

"Eshe has departed. She received the information she needed. You did well, as you always do." He studied me with his inscrutable gaze, and every one of my nerve endings flared with warning. "Perhaps too well."

"I—oh. Good." I realized I was clutching a pillow, and I forced myself to unlock my hands from it, ordered myself to breathe. Carefully, deliberately, I set the pillow on the chair's armrest. Patted it. "We're good, then." I drew in a long, stabilizing breath, and willed myself to pull it together. "We're good."

"You didn't need to flee the city to avoid Eshe."

Irritation crackled through my system, healing me faster than any positive affirmations ever could. I flicked my gaze to Armaeus, glad to note that my eyes were focusing again. "I didn't 'flee.' I got bored."

"Bored." Armaeus twisted his lips around the word. "How intriguing that your ennui coincided with the call Father Jerome placed to you, advising you of the new flood of Connected children on his doorstep. Children who, through his intercession, had barely avoided getting kidnapped, killed, and dismembered for the use of their body parts, whether by dark practitioners, SANCTUS, or both."

I winced, seeing their faces. So many kids, their expressions tight with confusion, their eyes hollow with fear. How many had Jerome already hidden away? How many more would he need to hide as the war on Connecteds continued to heat up?

And why hadn't we known about the pale, fragile

blonde, dead on some table in Istanbul because we hadn't reached her in time?

Armaeus continued, oblivious to my distress. "I presume you are far less bored now, given that Father Jerome's bank accounts have been increased by more than a hundred thousand dollars?"

I scowled. "Nothing in my contract says I can't take on additional work."

"If you needed additional work, I could have supplied it. My assignments will always take precedence over Eshe's, as does my protection. Had I known you were avoiding her, I would already have intervened."

I closed my eyes to avoid having to respond to that one. Armaeus's "assignments" came at the price of me being around Armaeus. And that had its own set of challenges. He wasn't merely sex on a stick. He was dangerous at a primal level, gigging my lizard brain even when I wasn't in the throes of a viselike headache.

Man, my head hurt.

"Miss Wilde."

"Just resting my eyes. Carry on."

He sighed with irritation. "Your instability is becoming a problem."

Oh? I opened up my right eye, the one that hurt less. "Not to me."

Armaeus scowled at me in monovision. "You're on retainer to the Council."

"Not true." I opened the other eye, then squinted. "You talk a good game, but right now, Eshe is the only one of you guys paying me. Trust me. I keep track of that stuff."

"And I would suggest that to take advantage of

additional work opportunities, you must actually be *here*."

Finally we were getting somewhere. I scooted upward on the chair, which was so soft it threatened to swallow me whole. "If you have an actual job for me, why didn't you tell Nikki? She's my people."

"Nikki Dawes is not your 'people.' She's barely her own people." He scowled at me. "I'm not sure you're sufficiently prepared for this new assignment."

"Does it pay?"

"Of course. Further, it involves a direct response to SANCTUS. "

I sat up abruptly, Cardinal Rene Ventre's image giving a face to my pain, all spectacles, squinty eyes and tight lipped grimace. "Then consider me prepared." I worked out a kink in my neck. "What's the gig?"

Armaeus regarded me a long moment more. He did that, sometimes when he thought I wouldn't notice, sometimes blatantly, like now. Eyeing me as if I was some sort of bug in a specimen jar, batting against the lid to escape.

Despite my bravado, I knew what the Magician was seeing: I looked like crap. Skin white and pasty, enough coffee in my system that I practically vibrated, my eyes hung with fatigue, my hands twitchy. I was cold too. Constantly, ridiculously cold, the ache of some deep chill starting in my gut and rising up to put a choke hold on my lungs, my throat.

And then there was this blasted headache.

"I can help you with that."

I riveted my gaze on him. "Help me with what? I didn't say anything."

He sent me a withering glance. "Please. I don't

need to read your mind to know you're in pain. I didn't realize it was so extreme, however." He paused. "Perhaps it's time we employed another Finder."

Hold the phone. "What are you talking about?"

"Nigel Friedman, I believe, was interested in working with us. You remember him, don't you? He proved quite resourceful in Rio de Janeiero, what, fifteen months ago?" Armaeus flashed his teeth in a predatory smile. "I suspect he could have use for a quarter million dollars for one week's work."

"A *quarter million*? You're about to pay out that kind of scratch and you didn't tell me earlier?" I stared at him, struggling further upright. "I had to fight off a *corpse* three days ago, Armaeus, for way less money. You could have said something."

"I had no idea you were planning to leave the city."

"Well, I'm back in the city."

"And how long do you plan to stay this time? Or have you already begun preparations to run once again?"

I tiptoed right around that shard of broken glass, though I could sense the trap of his machinations closing around me. "C'mon. I've done everything you've asked me to. Everything. You can't say I haven't."

"And you've been compensated handsomely for your work. But this job is different. The rules are different."

I narrowed my eyes. "Different in what way?"

"We will be going after SANCTUS directly."

"I like that kind of difference."

"Perhaps, but a rogue employee has limited charm in this scenario. If you want this next assignment for the Council, there is no room for improvisation. I need you to be strong, and I need you to follow orders."

"Check and check."

His smile was grim, almost sad. "And I need you to cease your panicked resistance long enough for me to touch your mind, should I need to do so. As I need to now.

CHAPTER THREE

I stared back at Armaeus, willing the completely unreasonable dread his words caused to compartmentalize itself.

I couldn't let him crawl inside my brain. I couldn't. From his very first attempt to Vulcan mind-meld me to the time I'd tried to get extremely up close and personal with him in bed—an attempt I'd made exactly once—an insurmountable wall of noise and fear had practically leveled me. It was as if the touch of his mind on my inner thoughts triggered an all-out war.

"Or maybe I simply don't get into a situation that would require you to touch my mind. How 'bout that? You tell me what to do, I do it. Easy peasy." I punched down my fear, ordering myself to chill out. If he wanted to crawl around in my thoughts, why shouldn't I let him? Especially if it meant I could snare *two hundred and fifty thousand dollars* for a week's worth of work? I could toe a whole lot of line for that kind of green.

And yet…

The faintest smile creased Armaeus's lips, as if he knew exactly the kind of battle I was waging internally. But I knew he didn't. He couldn't. He was used to getting an all-brain access pass to everyone he met. No way had he ever experienced giving up that kind of control himself.

"Your fear is quite unfounded," he said, almost conversationally. "I've never sought to harm you. I seek to help you reach your fullest potential."

"Yeah, well, right now you're sounding way too creepy overlord. Trust me, I'm good for anything that shuts down SANCTUS. In case you missed the important part of Jerome's call, the refugee situation is out of control over there. He's out of room, and more children are coming in by the day. I know that money won't solve that problem, not for long. But gutting SANCTUS will. So let's talk."

Finally, the Magician nodded. "Very well. One of the most important events of the season is starting this week in the city. There's something we need from it, something you are well positioned to get us."

"Mr. Olympia?" I frowned at him, deliberately misunderstanding. "I didn't think you guys were in the market for pumped-up boy toys. Then again, I haven't met everyone on the Council."

Armaeus's lips tightened. "Not Mr. Olympia. The Rarity."

"Ahhh, the Rarity." Out of sheer perversion, I clamped down on my thoughts, reveling in the spurt of power it gave me. It was childish, but so was I. The upshot, however, was that even as I claimed not to have heard anything about the most celebrated ancient gold and rare jewels show in the western hemisphere, Armaeus didn't know if I was joking...or if I was just that ignorant.

Another beat, and he decided he couldn't take the risk. "The Rarity typically draws investors, collectors, and arcane artifact marketers for four days of trading, selling, and alliance building. This year, it will also do something more. Something most of the attendees won't notice. Something the Council will need to manage carefully, restricting its knowledge to a highly select group of people within the city. And no—spare me your quip."

I grinned. "But it's a really good one."

"I have no doubt. You do know what I'm talking about, I assume?"

His exasperation was a balm to my shattered nerves. "Yeah, I've been to the Rarity before. Never in Vegas, though. They held it in Dubai last year. Really cut down on the riffraff."

In truth, the old gold show wasn't typically super useful to me in my line of work. The sellers were usually there for networking and publicity, not trying to sell stuff so much as form the kind of connections that would pay off down the line. So everyone tended to be on their best behavior. On the buyer side of the house, the collectors ranged from the curious to the shrewd, most of them loaded to the gills with money to spend—but in the market for artifacts with unassailable provenance. Not really my cup of tea. "I'm sure you got a catalog," I said, shrugging one shoulder. "Why don't you simply order what you want?"

"This year, the action will be much more dynamic. Several new vendors have recently joined the convention, with booths in the public sector and VIP suites off the floor."

"Vendors like who?"

"The Mercaults. The Fourniers. The Kuznof Family." He rattled off a laundry list of Who's Who in the arcane black market, and I straightened—as much as anyone could straighten while sitting in a cream puff.

"Those people are *legitimately* trying to buy and sell stuff at the Rarity this year? Why? That's totally not their crowd."

"They would not have been invited to attend otherwise. They are also interested in the same collection we are, a set of unique artifacts which purport to give their bearers highly specialized abilities."

"News flash, Armaeus. That's every magical artifact ever created."

He continued as if I hadn't spoken. He did that. "I need you to acquire these particular artifacts—quietly—and bring them to me for study. If they're judged to be of no merit, you'll then return them to the Rarity, with no one the wiser."

"And if they're judged otherwise?"

"Then the Council will utilize them to help address the power of SANCTUS."

"'Address' as in blowing SANCTUS up, I hope." I didn't wait for him to respond. "*This* is the job you thought Nigel could do in my place? Don't think I haven't forgotten that."

"Mr. Friedman has shown a remarkable ability to follow instructions."

"He's shown a remarkable lack of creativity, you mean." I lifted my brows. "So who else is after these toys? Maybe I could get a bidding war going, if you really are set on someone else being your Finder."

Armaeus's eyes turned a shade cooler. "I would advise against it."

"Just thinking out loud, you know, examining the

angles."

"The job, as I said, *can* be yours. However, utmost discretion is required on this assignment. We want nothing traced to the Council, especially given our proximity to the convention site."

"Why not?"

"If we are to take action against SANCTUS, any action, it must be with the utmost secrecy. The goal of the Council is balance."

"I'm sorry, did you miss the part where SANCTUS is *hunting down and killing the Connected*—especially kids?"

"We don't know if they're behind this newest surge of attacks. Heretofore, those crimes have been laid at the feet of the dark practitioners."

"Practitioners who have been funded by SANCTUS, which my little trips around the world for Eshe have proven to anyone with eyeballs to see. They're stamping out magic faster than we can get people out of their way, Armaeus. Worse, they think they're on a mission from God. That's not something you need to *balance*, that's something you need to end."

A smile flickered over his lips. "As I believe I mentioned, the ultimate goal of this assignment is to enable us to confront SANCTUS. Using the artifacts you will help us obtain."

"What am I missing here? Why the whole business with this show?" I waved around his palatial office. "You've gotten your hands on every trinket worth coveting for the past nine hundred years. And you wouldn't sell any of it to save your own mother. None of you collector types would. So who exactly are the people pawning off these goodies, and why don't you deal with them directly?"

"The owners of these items have long held themselves out of the fray of arcane commerce. But word of SANCTUS's campaign against the Connected has begun to draw notice among the upper level of practitioners, both dark and light. Demand is higher than it has ever been. Those with items of interest sense the unique economic climate and are finally ready to entertain bids."

"Finally?" I narrowed my eyes. "Exactly how long have you been after these—what are they, actually?"

"Egyptian scroll cases. Anywhere from four to eight inches long, two inches in diameter, wrought of gold. This particular set has been missing since the Napoleonic era." Armaeus gave me this information with deceptive nonchalance. I'd been around enough artifact junkies to know the signs when they thought they were onto a big score. Armaeus's eyes were overbright, his hands doing that reflexive twitching thing. Somewhere in South America, an entire colony of butterflies was spontaneously combusting. But over scroll cases?

"Lot of scroll cases in the world," I said evenly. "What's so special about these?"

Armaeus didn't hesitate. "The person who reads the words contained within these cases will, temporarily, wield the language of gods."

"Sure they will." I rubbed my jaw. "What gods are we talking about, specifically? Because that's a pretty wide swath."

"All of them." His lifted hand forestalled my next question. "In a sense, for the time that the language's essence consumes you, you become a god. In the hands of the knowledgeable practitioner, every thought would become reality, every Connected would be swayed by his or her words, and every demigod, demon, angel, or spirit could be called up and bent to the will of the summoner."

I thought about that. "I could see how that would be handy. I can also see why I wouldn't be selling such items at a public auction."

"It would appear the seller, Jarvis Fuggeren, wishes the pieces to be sold in the open. With witnesses. No private showings, no backroom deals."

Jarvis Fuggeren? That was a name I didn't know. And I would have remembered it if I'd run across it. "Okay, but how could any amount of cash counterbalance the voice of God? Seems kind of shortsighted."

"If it is a voice you cannot use yourself…"

My eyes widened. No wonder I hadn't heard of the guy. "He's not Connected? But still—that's kind of a heavy responsibility, isn't it? Keeping that kind of trinketry out of the hands of the dark practitioners can't be a fun job."

"Even in the hands of the light, they are a danger. While locked in a private collection, they were no concern. Now, however…"

I blew out a breath. "Everyone and their brother is going to want those cases, if they really do what you say. When does this circus come to town? I want to check out the convention center. Or wherever the event will be held."

Armaeus tilted his head, considering me. "The Rarity will be hosted at the MGM Grand, in its conference facilities."

"That's not one of your casinos."

"Not at present."

"But that's where I'm going?"

His lips twitched. "Not at present. I would prefer you to acquire the scroll cases at their current location."

I liked the sound of that. "Which is?"

"A warehouse at McCarran International Airport. Today, if you would. I will send—"

"I can go alone, Armaeus. I don't need a babysitter."

He paused just long enough for me to realize my error, and I beamed at him, full-frontal toady. "I mean, of course, Mr. Bertrand. Send along whoever you would like, Mr. Bertrand. I'll follow your orders to the letter. And I can start right away." I turned toward the door. Something bright and blue caught my eye—and I finally remembered what I'd wanted to find here.

"But first..." I moved back to the wall, scanning quickly. Gleaming artifacts from every corner of the world greeted me, along with piles of rich fabrics and chunks of misshapen rock whose very insignificance probably meant they held the power of the universe within their knobby forms. I paused on a bit of gold fabric stitched with red silken threads, clearly some cutaway from a flag or standard.

None of Armaeus's treasures featured little placards. He should fix that.

"That piece is Scots, Miss Wilde. The Fairy Flag." I bristled, but he continued with a thread of impatience. "I don't need to read your mind for something so simple. Was that what you were seeking when you came here today? Since it wasn't the Mongolian crown?"

"No." I gave up, pivoting back to him. "I, ah...I thought for sure you had some dragon kind of thing here."

"A dragon?" His voice was cool, mildly amused. "Really?"

"Like this." I fished in my jacket pocket, pulling out a crumpled piece of paper. Not trusting my tossing skills, I stalked back over to Armaeus's desk, then leaned over to smooth out the small sheet. It was a receipt from a bar at Charles de Gaulle airport, but it'd been the one scrap of paper I'd had when the image had flooded through my memory, crisp and sure. "This part's in red," I said, jabbing a finger. "The dragon—that's a dragon, by the way—is blue. I saw a symbol like that on the plane you sent for Kreios and me in Rome. And I'm pretty sure I've seen it *here*, before. What is it?"

The Magician frowned down at the paper. "A winged dragon on a red background." He paused, clearly sifting through his mental Googlewoo results. "You saw this on the Council's jet?"

The way he asked the question had me doubting my own memory. I narrowed my eyes. "Don't screw with me, Armaeus." I jabbed at the image. "I definitely saw it in the freaking Baikal Mountains, on the robe of the guy wearing the Mongolian crown. You've headed up the Arcana Council for eight centuries, so don't tell me you haven't seen this symbol before. What is it? *Who* is it?"

For some reason, I didn't feel comfortable telling the Magician about the first time I'd seen the dragon. I'd only been a kid then. A kid who'd just had everything go up in a burst of fire and death.

"It's no one for you to concern yourself with." The dismissal in Armaeus's voice was clear and decisive, and it rang through me so forcefully, my head came up. I took a step back.

"Whoa, whoa, whoa. Was that vocal projection? You know I hate that."

He shook his head. "That wasn't my intention." His words were smooth, apologetic, and even though they didn't resonate with me on a Connected level, every nerve in my body pinged in warning. Something was…off here. "I simply know what I keep in my private collection, and a dragon of the kind you're describing isn't one of the pieces I have. It's also not a design currently used on our aircraft. If you saw it, that's…very interesting." He glanced back to the drawing, and I did too.

Embarrassment flooded through me. Had I seriously been seeing dragon symbols where they weren't really there? What was wrong with me? I picked up the scrap of paper quickly, shoving it back in my pocket. I was so unbelievably tired. And my headache was pounding, stronger than ever.

"Right. So anyway, let's get rolling." As I stretched out my neck, I sensed Armaeus's eyes on me once again. The usual rush of conflicted emotions stirred, which at least put me back into comfortable territory.

I didn't know exactly what to think about Armaeus Bertrand. I recognized his power, sure. And I recognized his ability to heal—even if massive sexual overload was an unfortunate side effect of that healing. His magic operated at the basest level, stimulating the body from the core outward, and the more jacked up I got, the faster it worked. So Armaeus played the sensual card early and often, if it helped him get what he wanted. It was how he was built.

However, I also recognized that I was the most curious butterfly in the collection to him at the moment, nothing more. Any actual emotional attachment he had for me was illusion...my illusion. I knew that.

That should have been enough to keep things between us all business. Any normal girl would run the other way and not constantly subject herself to the seductive pull of the Magician's presence, the sharpness of his mind, the mesmerizing lure of his golden eyes.

I wasn't normal, apparently. I couldn't deny my body's reaction to him. My body's or my brain's. The constant push-pull to flee—or to give myself over completely, no matter the fear, no matter the pain, no matter the outcome.

No wonder my cerebral cortex shut down every time the guy got close.

"Miss Wilde." The Magician's words flowed around me, pushing at all the places that needed pushed, caressing everything that needed caressed. "You know I can help you feel better."

"Yeah, that never works out so well for me."

"This time it will."

I glanced up, startled, and sucked in a sharp breath. The Magician stood beside me now. Too close. Close enough to—

"Touch me," he murmured.

CHAPTER FOUR

"Armaeus." My voice sounded like gravel, but I couldn't deny the draw of his body, his energy, surrounding me in a halo of light and comfort. I stood there, wobbling in my own convictions, and Armaeus lifted a hand to my face. Not touching me, not forcing.

"You're not wearing your Tyet," he said.

"I..." I swallowed. I'd thought about putting it on, I really had. When I'd stumbled off the airplane this morning, late for this appointment, I'd realized I could have gone back to my hotel for the twisted knot of silver, with its highly specific properties of sexual protection. But I hadn't. I hadn't wanted to. As damaged as I'd been these past few weeks from serving Eshe, part of me had secretly wanted Armaeus to stand this close to me, ready to touch me, ready to heal. Part of me had craved it more than breath.

And part of me knew that the Magician operated by his own Byzantine (literally: *Byzantine*) code of honor...even though that was a slippery slope. "You won't do anything I don't want you to do."

"I will not." There was no denying the increase in Armaeus's intensity, though. He edged nearer to me. "Touch me, Miss Wilde. It is the simplest of connections. But one that you must make. You know that." His eyes darkened. "I want that connection very much. I want to help you."

My resolve began to fray, my brain and body warring with each other. It wasn't simply my mind that was broken and hurting, however, despite the thundering headache. I flinched against the renewed pain. "Why do you do this to me?" I whispered.

Armaeus's lips twitched, but his golden gaze didn't waver. "You are a mystery that should not exist. Your body, your reactions, your strengths, your weaknesses, are something I must understand. Everything I do, all that I do, is to reach that understanding."

Without warning, an entirely different ache welled up inside at his words. It wasn't entirely physical; it wasn't entirely psychic. I didn't know what it was, but it hurt enough to take my breath away.

Grow up, I implored myself. Stop making this personal. I shouldn't care what Armaeus thought about me. I *didn't* care. He was a businessman. And I happened to be his business right now. Nothing more nor less.

"Touch me," he urged again quietly, apparently oblivious to my internal smackdown. "You don't have to be in the pain you endure, Miss Wilde. It makes you weaker, not stronger. It slows your mind and your reflexes. For your assignment to be a success, I need them both to be operating at peak abilities. I need you to be stretching to your potential, not hiding behind your fears."

"I'm not afraid of you," I muttered, stung to the quick. Before I could consider his request more rationally, I shifted my body slightly and touched my cheek to his palm.

Energy jolted through me, so electric that both my hands lifted reflexively, settling against the fine silk of Armaeus's shirt. I could feel the heat radiating from his body, so strong I nearly passed out. My blood vessels somehow *expanded,* suffusing my body with heat, oxygen, and a healing wash of energy powerful enough to permeate every inch of my body—my face, my skin, my heart, my...

Uh oh.

"Armaeus," I gasped, but the word sounded like an entreaty, and he took it as one, lifting my hand from his chest and pressing his lips to my palm. The resulting shock to my core nearly melted everything south of my solar plexus, and I sagged against him. Armaeus's mouth moved against my hand. If he spoke actual words, I'd long stopped listening. But when his lips drifted up my fingers, I shuddered again, my bones disconnecting at the joints.

"So much of your energy is in your fingers."

I didn't know if he said those words or if I sensed them, but when his mouth closed around my fingertips, I could no longer tell what was real and what was pure fantasy.

At that moment, my mind shuddered with a touch that was unbearably sensual, perfect—and impossible. I couldn't lose myself to Armaeus Bertrand. I couldn't. I'd been running for so long from my past, I wasn't even sure of who I was anymore, not really. And I'd never learn that if I was swept up in the Magician's thrall. I'd simply become whatever he wanted—needed—craved—

"Stop." I stepped back sharply, breaking the connection between us. "Stop. Party's over. I'm good. We're done here. Stop."

"As you wish." Just as abruptly Armaeus stood back, his gaze sweeping over me with smug satisfaction. "As I am at your service whenever you wish. You feel better."

I straightened. I did feel better, damn the man. Demigod. Whatever he was. "That's not the point. I could have grabbed a doughnut and triple latte and accomplished the same thing."

"Of course." His golden gaze lifted, focusing on my forehead. His lips pursed into a frown. "Your headache has not abated, though."

I couldn't help it, I swayed toward him. I couldn't say whether my body subconsciously needed the help he so willingly and blatantly was offering me, or if I was truly becoming addicted to his touch, or if the three-day migraine was finally wearing me down. Some pain is so intense that it takes up residence in your body like an unwanted guest, intruding into every corner of your being. And the Magician could take that pain away with a caress, a whisper. A kiss…

This time, Armaeus didn't give me the opportunity to reject his offer. He caught me when I fell into him, my body jerking rigid in his grasp as another flood of electricity scorched through me. His head bent, and his lips brushed against my forehead, my knees inexplicably buckling in response.

The Magician's chuckle was hard, almost triumphant. But I didn't care. Soothing coolness flooded my brain, starting at the front of my skull and arcing backward, turning fire to snow. The pounding in my head ceased, lulled to a thump, then a pulse, then nothing at all. Armaeus's mouth moved down my forehead, his lips brushing first the closed lid of my right eye, then my left.

Instantly, tears welled up, washing away the grit and ache from everything I'd seen in service to Eshe these past few weeks. The death, the torture. The bound and the weak. The Magician's hands firmed on my shoulders, gathering me close, and he lifted his mouth back to the center of my forehead, his lips warm and sensual. When he reached the center point above and between my brows, he said something in a language I'd never heard before.

A new sensation whirred in my brain, another wash of awareness sluicing away the fatigue and pain that were my constant companions. I wanted to cling to Armaeus, to bury my head in his chest and turn all my thoughts into tapioca pudding, but instead I drew in a long, shaky breath and pulled back from his mouth. I didn't realize I was staring at that mouth, though, until it twitched into a smile.

Then the sight within my sight fluttered open, and I jerked back, the moment shattered. "What the...?" I blinked, suddenly dizzy. "Whoa, whoa, whoa. What did you *do*?"

"Nothing you couldn't have done yourself, were you but open to it." Armaeus let me stumble away from him, his beautiful long-fingered hands dropping back by his sides, his manner loose, attentive. Back to the scientist staring at his prized bug. When I tried to glare at him though, I didn't know where to look. I was seeing everything double.

"Um, I think I'm broken."

"Oh?" His words were too casual, and I tried to refocus on him. The weird shimmery light receded around his body, until finally I could see only one of him. One Magician was definitely enough.

"What was that, exactly?"

"How do you feel?"

"Off-balance." It wasn't untrue. I put my hands out to the side, testing my equilibrium. Everything was brighter, sharper, clearer. The palatial suite, Armaeus's incredibly beautiful face, his damnably curious eyes.

"What was that?" I asked again, reaching up to rub the center of my forehead. It was dry and warm, too warm. But nothing hurt anymore. Not exactly. "My headache is gone, but I feel weird." My brain belatedly caught up to where my fingers were, and sudden awareness galvanized me. I refocused on Armaeus, squinting into the glow that surrounded him. "You mucked around with my third eye, didn't you?"

"It was woefully untapped. I merely reminded it that it could help you see."

Once again, his words were too mild. "What *else* did you do, Armaeus? There were lights, but the colors were muted, indistinct. It wasn't your aura, I'm pretty sure. There wasn't enough asshat in it."

His lips quirked into a smile. "Not my aura. Rather, it's a case of relative energy fields. The more power a Connected item or individual has, the more it radiates energy. You could liken it to a heat signature picked up by military surveillance tools."

I thought about Zee's heat sensor, his reassurances that had proven totally false about the Ninja Death Mask Squad. "Those aren't super reliable."

"It depends on the kind of heat you're measuring." Armaeus shrugged. "In this case, you're not looking for vital signs, but ability. You already had some of that sensitivity. Now you've opened to it further."

"Great, so every time I see a Connected, I'll be staring into the sun?"

He lifted a brow. "Is that how I appear to you?"

"Close enough." I passed my hands over my eyes. "At least I don't feel like dying anymore. That's always a good start to the day."

"Take these." Armaeus turned and picked up a small package on the desk. He tossed it to me. "I understand they are helpful for your headaches, and yours might well come back."

I caught the bag of cinnamon candies in one hand, even as my mind raced through a hundred questions. Cinnamon candies? I hadn't used cinnamon candies as a headache cure-all since I'd been a kid. And how in the—I mean, who—

The answer rocketed through me a split second later. My hand spasmed on the bag, crushing it.

"You didn't."

Armaeus watched me without expression. "It's much more useful for my research into your unique characteristics when I can find someone who knew you. Someone who was there to witness your history. So helpful."

Someone like Brody Rooks. The one man I'd left standing back in Memphis all those years ago. The one man who didn't need to be a victim of my crazy once again.

"Look ." I jerked toward Armaeus so quickly, any normal guy would have flinched. The Magician, of course, was nowhere near normal. I jabbed my finger into his face anyway. "What you do to get your kicks is your own business. You want to crawl around in some broken-down cop's mind to steal answers you can't get from me, knock yourself out. But you more than anyone should know how flawed memory is. Brody's a basket case. His answers aren't going to help you."

"Detective Brody Rooks, Las Vegas Metro Police.

Formerly Officer Brody Rooks of the Memphis Police Department, who worked with a very bright, very skilled young Connected named Sariah Pelter."

"I'm not that girl anymore, and it's ancient history. Ancient and irrelevant."

"You're protecting him. Why?"

I snorted. "Brody doesn't need my protection. *You* do. Whatever he says or thinks he remembers, don't bet on it being accurate. He was a good cop, a cop who tried hard to find missing kids, and I let him down big. The fact that he got tangled up in my mess in the first place was his own bad luck."

"He has feelings for you. Feelings that extend beyond nostalgia."

I ignored the strange pang those words caused. "He thought I was *dead,* Armaeus. And he's seen a lot more death than anyone should. So yeah, me showing up in Vegas ten years later caught him off guard. You may have forgotten what it was like to be human, but not everyone has."

The moment the words were out of my mouth, I knew they were the wrong thing to say. So I held on to them with both hands and pummeled forward, using them like a battering ram. I squeezed shut my newly opened third eye and glared at Armaeus with my normal ones. "You don't get to play around with people just because you're bored. Get out of Brody's head and stay out unless you're there to *help him.* Which we both know you're not. I want your word on that. He's not a toy."

"You have feelings for him too."

"Oh, give me a break. I'd have feelings for Tickle Me Elmo if he were hot enough. Are we done here? Or when does my babysitter arrive? And please don't tell me you assigned me to the Devil. Because my 'feelings' for him would put you in traction."

That arrow seemed to hit its mark. Armaeus's face shuttered again, his tone perfectly even. "Kreios will, in fact, accompany you to the cocktail party hosted by the Rarity tomorrow evening. Given his interest in art, he has several secular dealings with the collecting community's richest families, and he possesses a collection that is renowned the world over. His attendance won't draw attention."

"Clearly you guys don't club together much."

Armaeus continued, his words even more clipped. "He'll brief you on the details later today, I suspect, and give you additional information regarding your assignment at McCarron. He will not be accompanying you for that."

"Fine." A mission brief had never felt more like straight-out warfare. "So whatcha got on these scroll cases. Is there a file?"

"Of course." He pulled a flash drive out of his jacket pocket and tossed it to me. "Everything you need to know about the Rarity job. As I mentioned, the current owner of the scroll cases is Jarvis Fuggeren. He will be easily recognizable and will doubtless be generous, attentive, and gregarious, but do not be disarmed. He is, most of all, very dangerous."

I waved the drive. "Got it. Rich too, I expect?"

"Quite."

"So, he doesn't *actually* need the money, no matter how hot the market is."

Armaeus inclined his head. "He does not."

"And you say he's not Connected?"

"Technically, that is unknown. His abilities may be cloaked by his possession of the artifacts. Or, he truly could be a collector of curiosities seeking to make the most viable sale possible for items of no intrinsic value to him, other than what they can fetch in a highly specific marketplace."

"Fair enough. Does he know I'm coming to the party?"

"Merely as one guest among many."

"And who else are you sending to play chaperone? Don't say you either."

His gaze shifted back to me. "It would disturb you to have me there?"

"Not at all. You, me, and Kreios? Total psycho sandwich."

"An interesting experiment." Still, Armaeus was cool as a cucumber mojito. "I'm sending you with the Fool."

"Oh no. No, no, no. The last time that guy came within ten feet of me, I ended up bald-assed drunk in some dive cantina, convinced he was named Luscious and I was Miss Chiquita Banana. That wouldn't be a good start to this little mission."

Something flickered in Armaeus's expression. Annoyance, irritation, defensiveness, I didn't know. Didn't much care either.

"Simon will accompany you to the airport site and get you in, ensuring that you breach all technology barriers," he said. "It's a simple enough request, Miss Wilde."

The not so subtle reminder of who was the boss in this working arrangement shut me up. Sort of. "Fair enough. Have him fetch me whenever he's ready." I tucked the drive into my pocket. "Meanwhile, what do we have on SANCTUS? You really think they're coming to Vegas?"

"All indications would say yes." He held up a hand. "But we do not expect any sort of attack until solstice, later this week. Your work may well be done by then, which might significantly change the nature of a SANCTUS intervention."

"Change it how?"

"That depends entirely on what you discover with the scroll cases."

"And if they're the real deal, we use them to implode SANCTUS." I frowned. "What are we going to do, throw the things at them?"

"I think it would be better for you to focus on the task at hand first."

"Trust me, I've got enough bandwidth for both now *and* later."

"I have no doubt. But it's not the future I am most curious about. Or the present, actually." The Magician shifted toward me, and I blinked, refocusing on him. "To ensure the success of your work with the Council, there are things I wish to know about you, Miss Wilde. Things I must and will know."

Careful, careful, careful. The sweat pooled between my shoulder blades, then traced a shivery trail down my back. "What kind of things?" I asked, though I was pretty sure I knew the incident he wanted to "explore" further. He'd been fascinated, not repulsed, by my blackout the night we'd planned to spend together. It had never happened to him before, and for someone pushing nine hundred, that was saying something. "Maybe I can tell you the answers and save you the trouble."

As usual, however, Armaeus was not merely one step ahead of me, he was through the door and around the corner.

"I wish to see the day you left Memphis as a seventeen-year-old girl. Your memories, Miss Wilde. Not Detective Rooks's. Your feelings. Your mind. If you would give me access—"

"What?" I gaped at him. I'd spent most of the past ten years trying to bury those memories. Seeing Brody here in Vegas had stirred up too many emotions, too many regrets. Letting Armaeus kick through that sandbox was not going to help anyone. "Why? Why would you possibly care?"

Derision dripped icily off the Magician's words. "It is not a question of caring. The job of the Council—my job—is to ensure the *balance* of all magic. That means understanding the capabilities of the Connected, whether those stray to the dark or the light. I do *not* yet understand you. There is something about you I cannot place, a puzzle I have yet to solve. Until I do solve it, you remain a risk to magic as a whole."

Irritation flared anew. "A risk? Me. I'm the one trying to help the Connected, in case you missed that detail. I'm hardly a risk."

"Exactly my point. Your work is admirable, almost a crusade. I suspect the events of your last day in Memphis might shed some light on the reasons and motivations behind that crusade. That, in turn, will help me understand how you came to be, and how you fit into the larger picture."

I blinked at him, overwhelmed with a rush of emotions that were neither welcome nor particularly impressive. Betrayal. Hurt. Incredible, unreasonable loneliness. I scowled, stuffing down my useless feelings. "I tell you what," I said. "You break your rules, I'll break mine. If I screw up, or if I need you to forego your precious balance in order to protect

Connecteds from SANCTUS, and you do it, then you have the right to muck around in my head, fix what needs fixing, see what you need to see. Because nothing matters more to me than making sure the Connected don't get wiped out by those freaks. Nothing." He watched me impassively, and I willed my heart to stop thudding so hard. "But if that happens, you'll get one shot. And one shot alone."

"That's all I will need—"

"I'm not finished yet. After this job closes, my brain and all its contents are off the table." I jabbed my finger at him. "I mean *off the table*. Never again do you ask, never again do you try. I want your word."

Armaeus regarded me with his cool golden eyes, always assessing, always weighing. The true Tarot Magician, with every element in play, all the possibilities in the universe, and no single future yet chosen.

He nodded.

"You have my word as bond, Miss Wilde."

CHAPTER FIVE

The cab ride back to my temporary digs at the Palazzo Hotel had done little to soothe my nerves. Neither had the cheery waves of the front desk clerks, despite their apparent obliviousness to my train-wreck appearance. No doubt, they'd seen far worse.

Ah, Vegas. City of No Judgment.

But while Armaeus's flash drive had supplied the basics of the assignment, I needed to understand more. The Rarity was coming here. To Vegas. For the first time in forever. And apparently on the docket were magical artifacts that hadn't seen daylight since Anthony and Cleopatra had checked out each other's asps. Surely that was causing a ripple in the Connected community.

There was one surefire way to find out. I peered at my laptop as the cab turned off the Strip, angling us toward Dixie Quinn's Chapel of Everlasting Love in the Stars. I'd first set foot in the chapel a few weeks ago, but it had already become sort of a command base for me, second only to the Magician's trans-dimensional ultra-highrise. From deep within her white stucco and kitsch shrine to star-blessed love, Vegas's number one romance astrologer played mother hen to all the Connecteds in Vegas, whether they be wide-eyed newbs or shifty-souled veterans. She'd know if there was anyone talking about the Rarity, or anyone poking around I should watch out for.

On the laptop screen in front of me, Jarvis Fuggeren smiled winningly for the camera.

Thirty-something, patrician, richer than God.

Check, check, and check.

"Why are you selling the scroll cases, Jarvis?" I muttered. "Who has you spooked?" Studying his smug face, it was hard to imagine anyone or anything making the Austrian financier nervous. Then again, his family had been wheeling and dealing with kings, emperors, and popes since the Middle Ages. That was a lot of time to cultivate enemies.

The cab bounced into a large parking lot, and I glanced up, then froze. "Um—go on past the chapel and idle in a space next to the tattoo shop, okay? Keep the meter running, I'll pay."

"Whatever you say."

Ah, Vegas, City of Chill Cabbies.

I hunkered down in my seat, glad for the tinted windows, and took in the perfect Sin City chapel view: tortured topiaries, sun-blasted concrete, and a cheerful line of white plaster geese, all dressed up in wedding finery. Standing in front of those geese was the real show.

Today Dixie Quinn was dressed in another white cowgirl outfit, this one accented with a pink scarf and a bright pink cowboy hat that set off her tumble of perfect blonde curls. She was a tiny thing, barely taller than five feet even in her thigh-high boots, but the top of her hat almost came up to the chin of the man whose chest she was leaning against. She smiled up at him coyly, beseechingly, as if completely unaware that she was perched in the middle of a parking lot, being watched by God, the world, and a row of geese with marriage on their minds. From my angle, it kind of looked like marriage was on Dixie's mind too.

The athletically built man with her was dressed in nondescript browns, his jacket open to reveal creased pants and a scuffed belt beneath his white button-down shirt. His hair was a little too long, his body a little too tense, his expression impossible to read at this distance. There was no denying that he wasn't pushing Dixie away, though.

And she, maybe suddenly thinking the same thing, edged ever so much closer toward Detective Brody Rooks.

Great.

My phone chose that second to vibrate, and I stuck my hand in my hoodie pocket, fishing around while I kept my eyes glued on the Dynamic Duo. One person in the world had my private number, and I spoke his name as I fit the phone to my ear. "Father Jerome. You're safe? Everything's okay?"

"I should be the one asking that question, no?" As usual, Father Jerome's rich voice filled a hole inside me I didn't realize stayed empty most of the time. I'd known the old priest more than five years, and he was an immovable object in the dark maelstrom that howled ever louder through the Connected community with each passing month. "What is this second payment to my account, Sara? You only returned to the U.S. this morning."

I smiled, warmed by the musical inflection of the old priest's accent. "What can I say, I'm a lucky girl."

"We would be so lucky to have you back in Paris,

to stay longer this time than a morning, yes? It would be good for you to be here with us."

"Why?" I frowned, focusing. What's wrong?"

"Not wrong, Sara. Never wrong. It all is as it must be, good and bad." Jerome's words soothed my momentary panic, and I returned my gaze to the intent conversation of Dixie and Brody. I didn't have anything against Dixie, I liked the woman. Really. And if she liked Brody, well, that was perfectly fine. I had no claims on the man.

Then Jerome's words penetrated my brain. "We are getting reports of increased trafficking activity out of the Ukraine. The community is stirring with worry and fear, and there's a sense of them being driven underground, of being hunted, that is becoming a part of the conversation no matter who is doing the talking. The house in Bencançon might not be enough. It might be the wrong idea altogether. The children may need several homes, in secret, where they can stay hidden."

I frowned. "Hidden from what? SANCTUS or trophy hunters?"

"Both. There is a great agitation here, it worries me." Jerome paused. "I did receive a visit from a young man who said he was a friend of yours. Max Bertrand?"

For the first time in days, something approaching happiness swelled inside me. "Max! Yes. Do you like him? Do you think he has promise?"

"I think he has great promise." Jerome chuckled. "As to do I like him, it is difficult to say—he speaks almost nonstop. He has taken a job as a taxi driver in Paris to burn off his energy, he says. He seems very nervous about the prospect of having his abilities tested."

"He'll get over it." I said the words lightly, but I wasn't so sure. I'd encountered Max in Rome. He'd been the hired driver of my limo from the airport on my most recent assignment for the Council. That limo had been commissioned by Armaeus...whose last name, not coincidentally, was also Bertrand. I was still trying to wrap my head around the idea that Armaeus had a family of any kind, let alone one that had spawned new generations with Connected abilities. "Start him out with something easy, and go slow. He will come to his abilities in a rush, I suspect, but his mind may take some convincing."

Jerome chuckled. "Sounds like someone else I know."

"Oh, please. I've been throwing cards for a long time now. I know I'm good at it."

The moment stretched between us, heavy with unsaid words.

"Jerome?" The old priest was a master at drawing out the abilities of the Connected children he safeguarded, nurturing and protecting those skills by equal turns. But I'd come to him already formed, so to speak. There was nothing new to discover.

My third eye began blinking rapidly. I swatted at it.

"Your gifts *are* a blessing," Jerome finally said, as if he'd never paused. "I feel Max's will be too. He's eager to help with the children, to ensure their safety. But more of them arrive every day, Sara. It isn't merely the refugees from the war that everyone can see that swell our cities and strike fear into our citizenry. It is the refugees from a war that no one knows is being waged."

I nodded, though the old priest couldn't see me. "You think you'll be caught out?"

"Perhaps. We're preparing to move. I'll take a sabbatical from Saint-Germaine-des-Prés, and my absence from the city will help to reduce the attention."

"A sabbatical? You can do that?"

"I'm expected to take one every five years." Jerome's laugh was wry. "The last I took one was in nineteen eighty-two, however, so I am a bit overdue. I'll have to leave my belongings here, of course. I can't have it appear that I'm doing anything but going on a short holiday." He paused. "I pray a short trip is all it is."

"And you'll take your phone."

"Of course. It's the property of the church."

"I don't like it, Jerome. Where will you go?"

"Be at peace. Max will travel with me. As to where we are going, I am worried about this latest influx of children. Each new set is more terrorized, less able to communicate. Something is affecting them beyond my understanding. They are all passing through Poland, so that's where we will start."

"You and Max."

"I've traveled before, Sara. I'm not some feeble old man."

"No, no, you're not the one I'm worried about." A total lie, but Jerome let it pass. "Be careful, okay?" I glanced outside again. Dixie and Brody had moved into the lee of the building, in search of shade. Which put them out of sight.

My cue to ditch the car. Finally.

"I will, Sara," Jerome said into my ear. "You'll call within the next few days?"

"Sure, of course. Or soon, anyway." I shut and stowed my laptop in my bag then fumbled for money, handing it forward to the cabbie, who grinned at me as if he knew I'd been avoiding Dixie and Brody. Well, he wasn't wrong. Jerome and I said our good-byes, and I hauled myself out of the car.

It was hotter than the surface of the sun outside. Squinting to make sure the Wonder Twins weren't in sight, I stabbed the phone into my pocket—missed, tried again. The second time it made it, but something scraped against my fingers. As I pulled my hand out, a business card fluttered to the asphalt. I reached down and picked it up, barely avoiding the departing cab.

Grimm's Antiques, it read in finely scrolled text. A small address in block lettering was beneath it.

Grimm's Antiques? That hadn't been on Armaeus's thumb drive.

Still, I hadn't been working with the Council this long not to recognize its games. If the Magician wanted me to go to Grimm's, I'd go to Grimm's.

Pocketing the card, I pushed into the foyer of the Chapel of Everlasting Love in the Stars. No one was there to greet me, but I figured out why quickly enough.

"Up on your toes, sweet cakes." The sharp bark of Nikki Dawes's voice rang out from the main wedding suite. "Stilettos aren't for sissies, and this is the biggest day of your life. Unless you're planning to dump the guy after Christmas, in which case you'll definitely need those pumps again. So up on your toes."

I entered the chapel and slid into a back pew, embracing the cool darkness.

At the front of the room, Nikki was holding court with three brides-to-be. Despite the drive-thru nature of this chapel, plenty of brides came through these doors without being under the influence of anything more than an excess of optimism. Nikki helped out at the chapel whenever Dixie had an astrology reading or a wedding planning session or, say, an impromptu meeting with a local detective.

As in all things, Nikki took her role of bridal guide seriously.

Today she'd paired her severe high-heeled black patent-leather boots with a tan minidress, red neck scarf, and black beret, the very picture of a retro Hollywood director. She'd found a bullhorn somewhere, and it sat mercifully silent by her canvas-backed high folding chair. The girls, who I guessed were the brides, given their pink tiaras that sprouted glitter-dusted tulle, watched Nikki with rapt attention. Nikki, for her part, sauntered up the center aisle with definite swagger, demonstrating how to properly work a set of platform bridal stilettos with enough hip swing to knock the moon out of its orbit.

"That's right, hon, own the floor. Nothing's hotter than confidence in a corset." She turned to a second bride, and I hunkered down in my pew, glad enough for a few minutes more of rest.

The pew creaked, and Nikki glanced back with sharp focus, then waved at me with a wide smile. "Great timing, doll. We're finishing up." A few minutes later she ushered the brides on their way, then she strode back to me, her beret jaunty on her head.

"You looking for me or Dixie? Because Dix—"

"Is talking to Brody, I know."

She leaned on the pew railing and eyeballed me, her painstakingly feathered brows arched high on her forehead. "I told you he wasn't interested in her."

"It's fine." Something was definitely wrong with my throat. "It doesn't matter."

"Don't ever try that line in public, okay, sugar?

Because you seriously suck at it." Nikki tilted her head. "And unless you want Dixie to know you and Brody were a thing—"

"We weren't a 'thing.' He was ten years older than me, and I had a crush on him. That's not a 'thing.' I was a stupid kid."

"Uh-huh. Well, unless you want Dixie to know that you're still a stupid kid, time to turn that frown upside down." She grinned. "Welcome back to Vegas, by the way. What brings you down to the chapel?"

"Information." I blew out a breath. "I need to know what the Connecteds are talking about, if there's any chatter."

"There's always chatter." She shrugged. "Nothing specific that I know of, though. You want to get Dixie?"

I winced. That's why I'd come here, but now that the moment was upon me, I didn't really feel like interrupting the flashy, big-eyed astrologer, not if she was on the make for one of Las Vegas's finest. I thought of the business card in my pocket. *Grimm's Antiques.* "There are some other angles we could run down, first, I guess," I said, happy for the reprieve. "You have the Council's car in the lot?"

Nikki's grin widened. "I got something better. C'mon."

CHAPTER SIX

We exited the chapel onto the driveway beneath an enormous archway festooned with giant plaster roses. On either side of the exit to the street sat large topiaries carved into the shape of champagne flutes. Between them sat a whale of a white limo. On its side was emblazoned a pink-and-white banner proclaiming The Chapel of Everlasting Love in the Stars.

"Tell me you're joking."

"Dix likes me to tool around in this every so often to remind new visitors in town that if love is on their mind, we've got the chapel for them. There are giveaway cards offering a sample horoscope reading too. You should try one. They're fun." She waved her keys, and the doors popped their locks. I reluctantly got inside.

"This isn't exactly incognito."

"We going to take down a mob boss today?"

"Well, no."

"Then relax. In Vegas, driving around in a gaudy limo is pretty much going undercover. It's part of the scenery. Buckle in, or the damned thing will start playing the Wedding March. Ain't nobody in this car wants to hear that." She eased the car off the driveway and slipped into traffic. "Where are we headed?"

I thought about the notes I'd jotted down at the hotel, after plundering the Magician's thumb drive. Then I thought about the business card I'd found in my pocket. When in doubt, always pick go with the crazy first.

"You familiar with Grimm's Antiques?"

She tilted her head. "Off Flamingo? Sure. Haven't been in there in years, though. Why?"

"I need to talk to someone in Vegas who's known for collecting artifacts—not the big and obvious ones, but more your back-alley art gallery kind of thing. The sort of place that seems legit but really is barely more than a pawn shop. Someone who might maybe be into the arcane black market too."

She tapped her fingers on the steering wheel. "Grimm's is run by an old guy, or it was. Like I said, it's been years. He might be dead. Or they might have stuffed him and put him on display too."

"How long has he been working there?" I had my phone out, fingers poised. Anything to avoid the neat pile of marketing flyers that sat on the console between Nikki and me. I wasn't going to be handing out cards like we were trolling for an escort service.

Nikki snorted. "Don't even try finding him on the Internet. Grimm's Antiques is about as wired as a ball of lint. I'd be shocked if he had a Yellow Pages ad, let alone a website. Better for us to just go."

We idled at a light, and Nikki poked a red lacquered nail at the stack of flyers. "Earn your keep, dollface. Give out a few of those." She leaned over, me focusing on a knot of college girls waiting for the light to change. "Hey, ladies!" Nikki elbowed me in the kidney, hard, and I grabbed a half-dozen brochures, shoving them through the window. "You keep us in mind if you find the man of your dreams tonight, 'kay?"

The girls laughed and leaned against each other, clearly delighted by our enormous white limo with its pink-trimmed seats. I passed out a fistful of flyers before the light mercifully changed.

"You seriously have to do this for Dixie?"

"I don't have to do anything for anyone but myself, sweetheart. Those days are long gone. I do this because I get a kick out of it. And you never know when cupid's arrow will strike next. Dixie's a real believer in true love."

"Her wedding chapel has a drive-thru option."

"She's also a believer in efficiency."

We hit three more red lights before we turned off the main strip at Flamingo Road, and I scanned up past the real building to take in the soaring shadow casino of Scandal, which the Devil called home.

Nikki gave a low whistle. "That was one fine hunk of demigodliness, I have to agree," she said, though I hadn't said anything. "You see him since that night? He's not been mingling among the rank and file."

"They do that a lot? Mingle?" I angled in my seat to eye her as we motored up the street. Given the length of the limo, parking was going to be a bit of a challenge.

"Often enough. Their homes may not show up to un-Connecteds, but the Council isn't invisible, if that's what you mean. I've seen the High Priestess and Armaeus out, definitely. And the Fool. He favors the tech shows, mostly, but I'll see him on the street. As to the Devil—hell, he may have made an appearance in the past week, but not that I recall, and believe me, I would have recalled." She gave a small grunt of satisfaction. "Here we go. We'll pull in here and lock down tight. No one will bother us."

She parked in a space in front of a Vegas-themed gift shop and tugged the beret and scarf from her head. "Just another girl getting her shopping on." She fluffed her hair in the mirror. I'd never once seen Nikki adjust her makeup in all the times we'd driven through Vegas. It was like she applied it with a death threat, and it stayed put until she told it to move.

We headed down the street, the storefronts remarkably nondescript for being this close to the Strip, but they were clean, well cared for. And there was some foot traffic, just not the typical Vegas tourist crowd. No frat boys or sorority specials, no middle-aged Midwesterners clutching plastic cups they hoped to fill with tokens. It felt almost like small-town America… In a small town whose main street hawked wigs and burlesque wear, anyway.

"Where has this been all my life?" Nikki sighed as we slowed in front of the wig shop. "I really have to get out more often."

"Go ahead. Grimm's is right there." I gestured to a faded shop sign. "It might be better for me to tool around on my own at first."

"True." Nikki eyed me. "We really do need to work on your style, though. You can't keep looking like a homeless person who raided a Hot Topic."

I gave her a push. "Go. Come get me in ten minutes if I'm not already out of the store."

Nikki opened the door of the wig shop amid a clanging peal of bells, and I moved up the sidewalk. I caught sight of my reflection in the mirror—lightweight hoodie, black tank, black tights, boots.

Okay, so, clothes weren't really my thing, but Hot Topic? Seriously?

I frowned, thinking about Dixie with her soft blonde curls and pink cowboy hat, her perfectly curved cupid's lips smiling at Brody. Was she his type? Did he have a type?

Focus. Brody was a cop, and that was all that mattered. Cops weren't something I needed in my line of work. Yet another reason to get the hell out of the city after I wrapped this job. My work with Eshe had an expiration date of the oracle twins leaving Vegas. That was going to happen any day, which meant I was almost home free.

The storefront of Grimm's Antiques had the veneer of elegance even as it stood almost invisible between a used bookstore and a bondsman. The windows were framed in actual polished wood, and the front door boasted a small gold placard that stated no solicitors were allowed. On the shelves within the windows, several items of jewelry were nestled lovingly in black velvet—rings, cuffs, a torque that looked impressively old. Some of the items seemed expensive, but most didn't. The perfect lure for the amateur collector.

I pushed inside the door.

Unlike Nikki's wig shop, there was no happy peal of bells. There was no one inside the shop, period; though I suspected somewhere there was a camera recording my entrance. It smelled of dust and old books, and I glanced to the walls. Sure enough, Grimm's Antiques also featured leather-bound tomes that gleamed with age. I suspected most of those books hadn't been moved since the turn of the century. I drifted toward them, then got waylaid by low cases filled with shimmering gold coins. They appeared

Roman, but something about them niggled at me, poking at a memory deep in my brain. like they weren't exactly right. Copies? Fakes? Or simply a variation on the usual selection. It'd been a while since I'd studied coinage. Typically, the artifacts I was charged to find weren't used in normal commerce.

I leaned forward for a closer look when a shuffling noise drew my attention. "May I help you find something specific?"

The man who spoke was small and hunched, thin as a whisper and just as bold. His skin was pale but curiously smooth. His eyes were nearly black. He wore a threadbare suit that hung on his slender frame, but I got the sense that it wasn't due to poverty or illness that he dressed so shabbily. His sheet-metal-gray hair gleamed with a light oil that caught in the soft yellow lights, and his manner was watchful.

I knew better than to ask his name. Nothing made you sound creepier than asking someone to identify themselves. Instead, I went for near honesty. Easier that way.

I beamed at the man. "Hi. I'm in town for the collectibles convention later this week, and I know next to nothing about this stuff." I gave an embarrassed hand flutter. "I would love to walk in with at least a passing understanding of what'll be there."

"Ah, the Rarity." It was impossible to tell if Mr. Thin was judging me or the event, but I caught the faint whiff of a sneer in his tone. "Not the best show for a novice."

"Probably true," I sighed, willing myself not to punch the man in the throat. Really, we'd just met. I needed to learn restraint. "But I got this freelance job for a travel blog, and it sounds really cool. I think it'll make a great story." I glanced around brightly. "Is this your store? Like, are you the manager here?"

"I own Grimm's, yes." The man straightened a little, puffing out his chest. "It's been in our family since we came to Las Vegas."

"Oh my God, really?" I widened my eyes appreciatively. "How long ago was that, then?"

"How long has the store been here? Ah." He seemed surprised by the question. "Since nineteen forty-five. A good year."

"And you've made a living selling antiques? All this time?"

The disbelief in my voice was leavened by enough wonder that Mr. Thin hopefully didn't take offense. "For the discerning seller, there is always a market." He nodded. "And there are always new discoveries to be made, and new entrants to the field." His gracious smile intimated that I might be one of those new entrants, and I had to hand it to the dude, he was sucking me in. I wanted to be a part of this discerning group of discerners, all of whom were discerningly rich enough to buy gold.

"So will you be at the Rarity too? Or is that not really your thing?"

His smile didn't waver. "It's not, but the show is rarely in Las Vegas. That it is this year is somewhat of a surprise."

"Yeah? I'd think Vegas would be perfect for that kind of convention."

"Las Vegas is a bastion of new money, not old. Shops like mine"—he waved to include the gleaming cases and the empty spaces in between—"are the true rarity. For a show to bring old gold to Vegas is a very special event."

"What prompted it, do you know?" I stopped shy of clasping my hands together under my chin in unabashed wonder, but it was a near thing.

"I do." He smiled, and every one of my nerve endings pricked up. There was something almost…familiar about that smile. Then he went on, completely not answering my question. "What sort of artifacts are you interested in?"

"Oh gosh, I don't know." I gave my best aw-shucks shrug and pointed at the case beside me. "I've done some studying up on coins, but I think I'll have to do more. These look sort of Roman, but I've never seen them before."

He stepped forward, the huckster in him unwilling to stay hidden. "They are…quite unique. That case is fortified with special glass because I simply could not keep such a treasure hidden from public view. Everyone who enters my shop is drawn to them." He was drawn to them too, clearly. He walked all the way up to the case, then dropped a light hand on its edge. He leaned forward, and I did too. The mirrored bottom of the case reflected upward around the coins, and I frowned, distracted as I noticed something else odd in the case.

Grimm's voice drew me back. "What I was told when I acquired these coins were that they were from Atlantis."

I blinked at him, this time completely without artifice. "No way."

"Indeed." He drew his odd hands along the surface of the case. "I found that ridiculous of course, but I could not find an exact match to the coins. After a while, I stopped looking. It became too romantic to believe that they might have been part of a lost civilization."

"How much do those kind of coins go for?" Armaeus wouldn't be stealing these, not from a dealer so open with his display. But he could outright buy them if he wanted them. And given his penchant for Atlantean trinkets, most of which I was sure were fake, he'd definitely be wanting these.

"Oh, they're not for sale. They're part of my personal collection." Mr. Thin smiled and took his hand away from the case.

"But if you would sell them, what would they go for? Like, say they were your typical Roman coin of that era."

He shrugged. "Depending on the condition of the coin, anywhere from a thousand dollars to perhaps twenty thousand. It's a very accessible market."

Accessible to trust funders maybe. Still, trust funders were my kind of people. Maybe I should broaden my area of expertise. "Well, these are really cool. Think I might find some more this weekend?"

"You'll not find anything like them at the Rarity, I'm afraid. Or if so, I have not been made aware of them. And I assure you, my information is quite good."

"Fair enough." Another winning smile. "What will be there, then?" I pointed at the case. "Atlantis is a myth, yet here are these coins. Will I find that kind of thing—pieces based on mythology or legends?"

He regarded me with the first thread of suspicion. "Is that what you will put in your article?"

"Well, it would be cool—if they had such a thing. But straight-up gold is cool too."

"Straight-up gold is the province of the Rarity. Any mythology attributed to their pieces is, I assure you, strictly a fool's tale to get you to buy something for more money."

"Good to know. So, again, will you be going?"

Mr. Thin blinked at my sudden change of tack. "I will make an appearance. I have many colleagues who will be in attendance, from all points in the world."

"That's so great. I'll be going to the opening-night-gala thing. Who'll be there who's awesome? Like, who's the biggest wig of all?"

"I suspect you will determine that easily enough on your own."

"Oh, c'mon." I decided to play on my hunch. I leaned forward toward the man, never mind that he was at least forty years my senior, and gave him a slow-eyed stare. "I haven't found anyone in the city able to give me the information I need. It's all I really want, and I want it from you."

To his credit, Mr. Thin didn't flinch. Instead, his smile widened, and I could feel him lean closer to me, too, a con warming to his kill. "And what would you be interested in trading for this information?"

"I suspect you have something in mind." I lifted a hand and turned it, my fingers skimming down the side of his—

The image flickered just enough.

"Got you," I smiled.

CHAPTER SEVEN

Mr. Grimm's hand closed around mine, pinning my hand to his cheek. The shock of the electric pulse lifted me off my toes for a half second as I watched his face shift to one of such heartbreaking beauty, if I hadn't already seen it, I would probably have fainted dead away.

"When did you know?" Aleksander Kreios asked me.

The Devil's outfit was largely unchanged from Mr. Grimm's attire, but in much better repair. His suit jacket hung open, the white silk of his shirt gleaming and his bronze skin peeking through his open collar. His hair was blond, but instead of the casually windblown style it'd rocked the last time we worked together, the Devil had slicked his hair into submission with the aplomb of a New York model. The refined overlay of an expensive timepiece was the perfect addition.

He squeezed my hand, recalling me to his question. "Your smile was the first thing," I said. "It slipped and became pure avarice. Which fit the old man but seemed too young, too hungry." I pulled my hand away to avoid electrocuting myself. "But the real tip-off was your fingers."

Kreios displayed his hands for me, long slender fingers tipped with nails I would swear had been manicured. The mere thought of that hand being polished, pummeled, kneaded—

"My hands?" he prompted.

I blinked at him. "Not hands." I shook my head. "Fingertips. No prints."

"Ah, yes." He turned his hands over and regarded the perfectly smooth finger pads. "Fingerprints are generally not a necessary affectation, and they take a surprising amount of focus. Most would not notice. Most who did would assume Mr. Grimm had spent some of his untrammeled youth in lines of work for which fingerprints were an unnecessary hazard."

"I thought about that." I shrugged. "Then again, your card magically appeared in my pocket earlier today. I'd assumed it was Armaeus, but that little trick is a thing with everyone on the Council, I guess."

"It passes the time."

"Dollface, you'll not believe it… Hel*lo*!" Nikki burst into the door with a whirl of brightly colored bags, then stopped fully as her gaze took in Kreios in all his glory. "Sweet Baby Jesus on a tricycle, you should post a warning sign. Give a girl a heart attack, why don't you?"

"Nikki Dawes. It is always my pleasure to see you." Kreios leaned back on the glass counter, and I shifted away too, glad to put more distance between me and the Devil. "How may I help you?"

"In every possible way." Nikki winked, then took in the room. "This place has cleaned up a lot since the last time I was in here. I'm thinking my credit isn't going to be up to snuff."

Kreios's smile teased at his lips. "Most of the items on the display are less than a thousand dollars. If there is something in particular you crave, I'm sure we could work it out."

As Nikki attempted a strangled response, Kreios shifted his gaze to me. "I'll have a car sent to the Palazzo tomorrow evening for you." His gaze flicked over my outfit. "And clothes."

"Hey—"

"Good." Nikki had recovered herself. "Clothes for what?"

Apparently, discretion wasn't in Kreios's job description. Then again, he was also a big believer in honesty in all things. He favored Nikki with another appreciative glance. "Sara is going to accompany me to the Rarity gala, unless she manages to steal the items we need first."

"Steal?" Nikki's brows went up. "From the Rarity? Their security is Techzilla, Inc. Totally top-shelf."

"Borrow," I interjected. "Armaeus told me he wants to review at the items and assess their value. If he decides to acquire them after all, I'm sure he'd be willing to pay for them."

"Willing, yes. Except the Council requires anonymity. An anonymity that Jarvis Fuggeren might not want to grant." He shifted his gaze to me. "Which brings me to your purpose here. I would like to outfit you in suitable jewelry for the event, but I need to see how your body will react to the various base metals."

"Be still my heart." Nikki was back to sounding strangled. "I'll be over here. Watching."

"Not at all." Kreios waved his hand, and a tall, heavily-muscled man appeared in the doorway behind the counter. "There is an extensive collection in the back that you might find interesting, if you will allow Stefan to guide you."

Nikki's throat worked as she took in the bald body builder in a sleek black tee shirt and jeans that were slung low on his hips. Even at this distance, I could see her pupils dilate. "That's for me?" she whimpered.

Kreios waved the man forward, and he stepped up to Nikki, taking her hand like she might break. Nikki dropped her shopping bags to the floor, then blinked at me. "I don't—"

"Please, take your time," Kreios said. "Stefan has a habit of tying guests up for a while. We'll wait."

Nikki's eyes might have rolled back ever so slightly into her head, but she went.

"That's you, isn't it?" I asked Kreios when they had cleared the doorway. "You're doing that Dr. Manhattan thing again, like when I'd first met you. Except..." I glanced over to the doorway. "I didn't realize you could change your appearance multiple times when you manifested a new incarnation. That's sort of cheating."

Kreios laughed. "If you prefer to think that, it's your choice. I consider it more an opportunity to multitask."

"Yeah, well, how many illusions can you keep going at once?"

"When I am strong? I have maintained five simultaneously."

"Five." I shook my head. "That gives a whole new meaning to being a team player."

"That number of incarnations becomes more of an effort." He shrugged. "When it ceases to be pleasurable, I no longer see the value. As you might suspect, simply winking out of existence tends to be a bit alarming for people."

"I can only imagine." I considered the shop cases again. "So, jewelry? Really?"

Kreios smiled. "A harmless subterfuge. Nikki would not have allowed herself to become distracted otherwise, and I need to discuss the particulars of this afternoon's assignment." He flexed his fingers. "It's good that the Council is getting in the game again."

Oh? "You haven't been for a while?"

"Armaeus has held activity to a minimum for decades—rightfully so, I suspect. But he can no longer keep us completely apart from the affairs of man. The affairs of man have a way of prevailing in the end."

"What made him stop in the first place?"

"Let's just say that the experimentation of the sixties had a stronger impact on the Council than it should have. We'd been based in Las Vegas for about thirty years by then, and the city was a whirl of graft and booze and money and drugs. Some of that was bound to find its way to the Council, as there are always seats to fill. But twisted up with psychic abilities of an altered level…"

This history lesson on the Arcana Council was already way more interesting than the high school Western Civ class I'd never finished. "What kind of drugs, and what kind of impact?" I tried to imagine Armaeus hopped up on coke or LSD. Failed. "You guys all seem pretty capable of holding your liquor."

"Some of us better than others. But that wasn't precisely the experiment that turned the Council inward. Armaeus is a bit of a slave to his concept of balance, and he allowed himself to be swayed by the dark side. Quite literally."

"What do you mean, dark?" I frowned. "I didn't

think you guys worked with the dark practitioners, not directly. Same way you don't work with the light."

Kreios shrugged. "Any may ascend to the Council if the conditions are right. Light, dark, neutral. One must simply be selected by an existing Council member in full standing." His lips twisted. "And there must be an empty position. It was Armaeus's error that he didn't recognize the danger of both conditions being present in a world where the line between real and apparent abilities had effectively blurred."

I was still trying to wrap my head around the idea of dark practitioners on the Council. "But I've met—Sweet Christmas, you mean Eshe?"

Kreios laughed. "Despite her challenging nature, Eshe is neutral. Her abilities to interpret the future would be compromised otherwise. But the Council is now comprised of nine seated positions. How many have you met? Not even half."

The bells of the front door pealed again, and Kreios glanced up, his smile wide and welcoming toward the young man who pushed into the store. "Simon, well-timed as always."

"It's what I do." The Fool grinned at me, appearing to be every inch the twenty-four-year-old hacker he presented himself as, and I tried not to stare. No way could he be on the dark side. No matter how many times he hacked the Pentagon.

"Hey." He nodded to me. "Found a new Reposado we need to try once we knock over the Rarity. Seriously smooth." He waggled his brows. "I promise not to leave you hanging this time."

"Not going to happen, Simon." That was the name I knew him by, anyway, but in the short time I'd known him, I'd also heard the Fool referred to as

Raven, Gwydion, Kutkh, Hermes, and every other trickster god from the mythologies of the world that happened to catch his attention. He refused Loki, of course, since that was overdone, but there was no denying he could pass as a younger, distinctly crazier version of Tom Hiddleston. Which was a good look on him, if slightly unsettling. Especially combined with the double T-shirt, worn jeans, and camo Chucks he was sporting, his wavy hair constrained under a Deadpool skullcap.

How old Simon actually was, I wasn't quite sure. He'd never told me when he'd been incarnated onto the Council, but I got the impression he was new enough to at least *understand* the tech revolution, even if he'd been kicking around before the birth of it. Then again, he did tend to favor steampunk anime, so there really was no telling.

Now he fairly bounced on his toes. "So, the airport? Really? Kind of slumming it a bit." He lifted the leather case I never saw him without, a beat-up messenger bag bristling with electronics. "I bet we can go straight into the show and get what we want."

"Not worth the risk." Kreios shook his head. "The Rarity has exceptional security."

"Yeah, yeah, Techy-zee." Simon shoved his hands in his pockets and rocked up on his toes. "The black box we recovered from the Binion's explosion last month was a complete bust, but their hands were all over that place." He grimaced. "We've been trying to track down Techzilla's power base, but we keep running into minions. Who keep ending up dead."

"Well, the guy in charge of Binion's was in bed with SANCTUS, I can tell you that much," I said. "If you've found Techzilla gadgets in the wreckage beyond standard security measures, then the odds are really high that SANCTUS and Techzilla have more in common than a burned-out building."

"Now that would be something worth exploring." Simon's eyes were sharp, almost feral with intensity. He turned to Kreios. "You coming, K? Because if Tech-Z is running security at the hangar, this could be fun." He shrugged. "And if they aren't, there's a great hot-dog stand out that way, and I'm starving."

"I'm otherwise engaged," Kreios demurred.

"Your loss." Simon shifted back to me. "You ready?"

I glanced over to the doorway through which Nikki had disappeared. "And what about her? Eventually she's going to notice that I'm gone."

Kreios lifted his elegantly arched brows. "Not for a very long time."

"Right." I turned toward Simon as another thought struck me. "Hey—while I've got you here, I wanted to show you..." I reached into my hoodie for the crumpled-up drawing of the dragon, but nothing greeted my fingers. The other pocket also came up empty. "That's...weird."

I could feel Kreios's gaze on me. "What's weird?"

"Oh—nothing." I scowled and tried again, but the scrap of paper was nowhere to be found. Instead my gaze snagged on the gleaming case of "Atlantean" coins Kreios had featured in the center of the...

Those were gone too. In their place was a set of ornamental jewelry, artfully displayed to catch the light. I lifted my startled glance to Kreios, who watched me with amusement. "I'm happy to answer all your questions, Sara Wilde, when you see fit to ask them. But for the moment, let's see what magic the

Fuggeren family has hidden away from the Council lo these long centuries."

Simon's laugh was derisive. "Trinkets, you ask me. A lot of smoke, no fire."

"Perhaps." I could tell from Kreios's expression, though, he didn't think so.

No—it wasn't solely his expression. Expressions could be altered, faked. The Devil's very energy burned differently today. It was eager. Excited. Or was I the different one, with the third eye whammy Armaeus had put on me? I tried to remember my reactions to others—but nothing stood out. I hadn't noticed any change in Nikki either.

Nikki. I hadn't heard her voice since she'd disappeared with Kreios's better half. Or better fifth, whatever. "Go easy on her, okay?" I asked, turning back to him. "She's frail."

Kreios smiled. "I assure you she will be in good hands," he said. "Several of them."

CHAPTER EIGHT

McCarran International Airport was a short five mile drive from the city and seemed smaller than it should be, given how many passengers flowed through its gates. Still, that made for an easy recon mission. We headed toward a cargo building behind Terminal 3, and I surveyed the place critically as we pulled up in our bright white utility van, emblazoned with a FedEx logo.

C'mon, c'mon, c'mon. Too slow, too slow, too slow. I ached to jump out of the van and hit the building on foot, my skin too tight over my bones. Instead, I ran the plan through my head again, locking it down. Get to the goods, assess the goods, and, if the stars aligned, make off with the goods. My favorite kind of job: simple, clean, easy.

Except for all the workers, buildings, and tech standing in my way.

"A lot of bodies for a cargo center. I thought these places were automated."

"On the inside, sure. Otherwise our job would be a lot harder. Out here, it's simply a wall of people we have to get through."

Simon's voice was tight, amped, but the

detachment of his words made me glance at him. "Wall of people? You sound like Armaeus."

He flashed me a smile. "I *am* like Armaeus in some ways. Except for the tan, of course. And the big fancy house on the Strip. Not for lack of him trying, though."

"Oh, yeah?" That was news. "He's pushing for you to build on the Strip?"

"Well, 'build' is more a matter of thinking really hard for a few minutes, but yeah. He wants every active Council member to have a presence on the Strip. Adds to the power base."

"Even the ones who aren't actually here?"

"Even those." His smile turned into more of a grin. "Roxie, at least, is close. She just would rather keep her distance from Armaeus. Sort of like a country club, you know? She shows up to a few meetings, eats a little chicken, and she's good."

"Um… Roxie?"

"Dude, the Empress." He shifted the truck into neutral, letting it idle in the queue. "Maybe stick around the city for a minute and a half, meet the neighbors." He narrowed his eyes. "Whoops, here we go. This should all be straightforward. Just gotta get you inside."

The first checkpoint was easy enough. Simon waved his FedEx credentials at the gate as I crouched amid the maze of boxes in the back of the van. We made it all the way to the intake bays before we both saw the problem.

"Is that normal?"

"Not according to my intel." He adjusted his side mirror. "But it shows me that we are definitely in the right place."

A tight knot of Las Vegas Metro cops was clustered

around a makeshift security checkpoint at the loading dock, talking with someone in a suit. We pulled into the queue to wait for our turn, and Simon lifted a hand to his mouth, chewing on a fingernail as he watched. "Too many questions, too many answers," he muttered. "I might need to play this remotely, send you in solo."

"Remotely? How?" I had one hand on the door handle already, my gaze sweeping the crowded swath of asphalt. Another truck moved forward, and the cycle of questions started again.

"I've already been out here once this week." He tapped his credentials against the steering wheel. "Modeling the security and creating a blocker tied to your key cards wasn't hard. One use only on the cards by the way, but getting out won't be as much of a problem as getting in. You want to be in a truck or cart if you can manage it—nobody moves around here on foot for any distance. Any one will do. You'll drive up to a terminal at a cargo check-in point and can talk your way from there. You're in uniform. People don't notice people in uniforms."

"Unless they're also in uniforms." My fingers twitched toward the Tarot cards tucked inside my shirt, but I forestalled the impulse. There were too many variables for a clear reading, too many questions of equal importance that needed answering. Without a firm question in my head, the cards' usefulness tanked dramatically.

Simon's voice interrupted my thoughts. "Whoops, cavalry arrived. Maybe our commando cop team is about to be redeployed."

I refocused on the check-in station, and my hand tightened on the door. *Crap.* "Um, I know that guy. No way should he be here."

"Yeah?" Simon turned to me. Whatever he read in my gaze had him reaching for his messenger bag. "Know him how? As in he knows you?"

"You might say that." I took in Brody's rumpled brown suit, his tight, no-nonsense stance. Was his suit any more disheveled than when I saw him last, maybe with a smear of bright pink lipstick on the collar? Was his hair any more tousled?

I shoved that line of thinking down. He could dishevel himself with whomever he wanted. Not my circus, not my monkeys. "Trust me when I tell you we don't want him to know I'm here."

"Roger that." Simon was keying in data on a small black device with one hand, his chin up, his expression open and relaxed. "First door is easy. Your key card will get you in. Then in about—" his glance jerked to the dashboard clock—"two minutes, all interior doors will be unlocked for approximately fifteen seconds. By then you'll be at the second door. It will happen again thirty-seven seconds after that, which is the amount of time it should take you to get to the third door, higher security. From there, ditch your outer suit. FedEx doesn't go that deep, but airport security does." He nodded, more to himself than me. "After that, you're on your own. If I can be there with you, I will, but if not, use this."

He worked off a watch from his left wrist by stretching the band, then handed it over.

"I'm feeling a little like James Bond right now."

"I aim to please. Baseline operation is a psychic field neutralizer, in case there are any wards on the place. After that, it's straight-up safecracker. There are two settings: laser and bomb. Depends on how much of a blunt instrument you need to be. I suspect Armaeus would be a fan of the laser approach."

I slid the watch on. "If I go bomb, what's the blast distance?"

"You'll have sixty seconds to get clear. Had to make it strong enough to obliterate trace evidence, even from Connected eyes."

Through the windshield, I watched Brody turn and survey the long line of trucks, and I hunkered down, though there was no way he could see me. "It's not going to be fun getting past that."

"Not so hard, actually." Simon pulled out another device from the bag and set it on the dashboard, then pointed to my feet. "Take that clipboard and walk like you're pissed off. That usually keeps people out of your way."

I pulled the clipboard up from the floor, grabbed a pen from the center console, and marked up the topmost form. "Okay. Two minutes after I get inside?" I tugged on my black ball cap.

"You'll see the door. Just keep on moving." He depressed his thumb on the jammer device. "Go."

He wasn't even finished with the word before I'd popped the door and hopped down. I strode quickly across the open space toward the entry Simon had designated, jerking to a momentary stop along with everyone else when a loud crash reverberated from the far end of the loading bay. The cops all headed in that direction, and I didn't hang around to see if Brody was with them. I set my face into an irritated scowl, and almost bowled over a kid in a bright yellow shirt with red letters. He scuttled out of my way with impressive speed. Excellent. The uniform was doing its job.

I pulled my entry key and scanned the door,

breathing a tight sigh of relief as I slipped inside. The second door was easy to spot. Checking my watch, I walked down a corridor flanked with storage shelves that contained tagged boxes and oddly shaped bags. Above, a disinterested-looking camera was trained on me, and I kept my pacing steady, my attention deliberate. I was making good time—too good. I still had thirty seconds to kill. I stopped three feet short of the door and pulled down the nearest box, comparing it to the information I'd scribbled on my clipboard. Just when I was starting to feel the panic skitter along my nerves, I heard a tiny click.

I moved forward, waving my keycard in front of the reader as if that was needed, then opened the door and stepped inside.

This room was a lot bigger, with rows and rows of shelves, each stacked with bins tagged with electronic routing numbers. Snaking between the rows and lifting high above the floor was a track, currently silent in this location though I could hear the grinding gears indicating other moving sections deeper in the room.

Thirty-seven seconds. I had thirty-seven seconds, according to Simon, to find the third door, which should be obvious, since it had to be within a thirty-second radius. I moved swiftly down the corridor, but all I could see were shelves. Reaching a break, I spun into a cross corridor, looking left, then right.

Two doors. Great.

Heading to the right, I moved down the corridor while reaching into the pocket of my shirt. I pulled a card and glanced down. *Well, that helps.*

Hanged Man. Time for a change in perspective.

I turned back and almost fled the other way, moving fast. I approached the second door, and, sure enough, heard the click when I was still a few steps away. Abandoning all pretense of caution, I vaulted forward, yanking the door open before the second click sounded. I stepped inside the next chamber and sucked in a deep, shuddering breath.

"Fine, fine," I muttered, straightening. I stared around in the gloom of this new room, trying to get my bearings. Unlike the tidiness of the other areas, this one seemed almost haphazard—emphasis on the hazard. Bags with warning stickers lay in rough piles to my right and left, up on pallets, all of them marked "non-biological" so I supposed that was good. A quick scan overtop didn't indicate any cameras, at least not in this section. I moved forward, transferring my deck of cards to my pants pocket, then stripping off my FedEx top and cap and shoving them under a bag. I smoothed down my blue button-down shirt that screamed "generic airport security." I even had an ID badge clipped to the breast pocket, which was a nice touch.

But where to next? I walked deeper into the maze of boxes and rows, and eventually realized this wasn't a single big room at all but an outer room with a box in the middle. A box with yet more doors. At least a half dozen I could see on this side. I felt like a rat in a maze, but as I reached for another card, something shifted in front of me, like my cable reception had shorted out, then come back.

I blinked. The six doors remained, but the second one in from the left seemed different. Glowing, almost.

Whatever was behind that door was arcane. I stepped forward, unable to square my own reactions. I should be happy that my psychic sensitivity had been amped up, but I wasn't, not really. This wasn't me. This was something Armaeus had done to me.

Whether he'd woken up an innate ability or simply screwed with my brain, I wasn't sure, but it felt ...awkward.

I stepped forward checked the door. It was locked, and so was the key card unit. To get to it, I needed a key. Should I use the watch? Blast a hole?

A sound at the far end of the room froze me for a second—a door opening, sharply striding feet. A lot of them. And a voice that I swore at this point would follow me down into the pits of hell.

"Check it and secure it for transport. We don't have all day." Brody Rooks seemed more than a little annoyed now. I could relate. I backpedaled several steps, then crouched low, wiggling myself into a space about the size of a hamster cage just before several tan pants legs came into view, along with one no-nonsense pair of pumps.

"I assure you, Detective Rooks, we've taken good care of the package." The woman sounded middle-aged and efficient, though an edge of irritation frosted her voice. "We're happy to release it to your custody, but if there is any fallout about this from—"

"Fuggeren knows. He sent me."

That did send my brows up. Brody was working with the owner of the scroll cases? Why? What had tipped him off?

"But I received no notice—"

"Open the door now, ma'am. If you would."

The woman gave a disgusted sigh and stepped forward. I could hear the jangle of keys as she opened the card-reader case, then the soft electronic beep of the room's door. Instead of opening conventionally, it slid back like an elevator, making the whole thing yet more surreal. Then she and Brody trooped in.

Every joint in my body was protesting my cramped position, but I couldn't fall out into the center of a bunch of cops. Instead, I strained forward, trying to see into the open room. It appeared empty other than a small table in the center, where Brody and the security manager stood. A box no bigger than a suitcase was between them, but their bodies shielded everything but the edges.

Then Brody reached out and opened the thing.

The force of the pulse was so strong I was shoved back three feet, shooting out the other side of the shelf and sprawling onto the floor like a flipped lizard. Alarmed cries rang out and I spun into a sprint-crawl, barely making it onto another pallet between two piles of bags as the cops came around the corner. Brody's voice cracked through the stillness. "Report!"

"Sounds, sir, something falling. Could have been a shifting bag."

I tried to breathe without making a sound, but the energy racking my body made it feel like my bones were coming apart. There'd been no light, no flash of any sort emanating from the box holding the scroll cases. There'd been no sound. But as soon as Brody had lifted that lid, it was if a hand had reached out and punched me in the sternum.

What was in those scroll cases?

I managed to quell my gasps, closing my eyes to stop the clanging in my head. Meanwhile Brody returned to his inspection with the cargo supervisor. I'd stuffed my hands beneath me to quiet their trembling, but it wasn't until the inner room had been closed off and the electronic wards reset that I could begin to breathe more normally.

Brody, the security woman and the last of the cops

finally left. Carefully, gingerly, I crawled out of my hiding place, oozing onto the floor. I pulled myself up to my feet, then felt a new touch on the very doorstep of my mind. *"You do not have to go further, Miss Wilde."*

"Those are definitely the real deal, Armaeus," I murmured. He wasn't here, and I could just as easily think the words to him as speak them, but muttering into thin air somehow seemed less crazy right now than talking in my head. I felt the pressure mount and narrowed my eyes. "Rules, Armaeus. Talk but don't touch."

The Magician obligingly quit pushing on my brain and I moved forward, my legs post-bender wobbly, and braced myself on the nearest ledge. "Almost there."

"Stand down, Miss Wilde." Armaeus's voice was rich with satisfaction. *"You've accomplished what you needed, without laying a hand on the scroll cases. Which you couldn't do anyway, now that I've seen their strength."*

I frowned. "I'll be careful."

"Your reaction is all that was required. Fuggeren will have to present these artifacts in such a way that the Connecteds attending the Rarity are not compromised. Or, alternatively, that they are, depending on his goals. Either way, we will be prepared."

I passed a hand over my forehead. "So, what do you want me to do?"

"Exit quietly. If you are waylaid, it's important that you leave nothing behind to trace you to the Council."

"Pack in, pack out. Got it."

Armaeus said nothing further, and I turned away from the artifact's holding cell, a little too grateful to show it my back. Then I turned toward it again, despite the Magician's orders. The glow around the closed door remained, but something else was there, too. Something that called to me. I moved toward the room and stood in front of the door for a long minute. The glow seemed to envelop me—teasing. Taunting. Hovering just out of—

The hand around my mouth jerked me backward into a sturdy chest, the voice at my ear achingly familiar.

"Why did I somehow know I'd find you here?" Brody Rooks murmured.

CHAPTER NINE

Going against my natural instincts to drive my elbow into Brody's gut or my heel into his instep, I held perfectly still until he dropped his hand from my face to lock it onto my left shoulder. "This is completely not what you think."

"Yeah?" The detective wasn't moving, and he wasn't letting go. I was pretty sure that wasn't exact police protocol, but I tried to keep my cool.

I'm super professional like that.

"I was following someone, Brody," I said. This was, technically... Okay, this wasn't even remotely true. But it was close enough to true to work. Brody pushed me away and let me turn around.

His gaze raked my face. "Who?"

I took a gamble, throwing more sand to distract him by using the one name I knew would get a rise out of him. "A contact of Dixie's, some guy who let drop his interest in the Rarity, that he was going to break in early, do a smash-and-grab. She got nervous about a Connected committing a crime on your turf right after you'd come over to talk with her, and asked me to check him out. One thing led to another and...I ended up here."

"Dixie," Brody repeated. "She put you up to this." I could see him considering that, working the angles, trying to figure out if he needed to upgrade the astrologer from a gorgeous handful of Southern Comfort to the status of "useful contact."

Oh well. Couldn't be helped.

"Didn't matter, though." I shrugged. "I thought the guy came in here—then I lost him. Then you showed up, opened up Door Number Two, and I…slipped and fell." Close enough.

"That *was* you." He smiled smugly. "Who's the guy you were following?"

"Nigel Friedman," I said, without hesitation. "British operative, blond, medium build. Seriously bad news. You need me to spell that for you?"

"I don't." Brody pursed his lips, thinking. I almost felt bad leading him on this way—almost. "You lost him in here?"

"I followed him pretty close, figuring whatever tech he was using to get in would remain active for a narrow window after he passed through, jamming the security system. I was right on his heels to get through the door using his key card, but he was already running when I hit the inner sanctum. After I picked myself up off the floor, he was long gone." I blinked up at him brightly. "But if the cameras are back online, you'll be able to find him, right? They are, aren't they?"

He scowled. "They are, at least in the outer rooms. This chamber is still on the fritz."

Thank you, Simon. I rocked back on my heels, suddenly very aware of the highly unusual watch I was toting on my wrist. If Brody took me downtown for questioning, which he would simply to piss me off I suspected, the watch would need to go.

Brody took a step back and swung around, surveying the interior. "Something's going on here. There's way too many people in the city this week. Too many for the gold show."

"Isn't Mr. Olympia in town too?"

His glance back to me was startled, then his expression soured. "If you know what's going on, Sara, don't hold out on me. I don't have time for bullshit."

"No idea." I faced him directly. As always, his flinty blue-gray eyes seemed almost stark in his hard-planed face. "And it's not like there's a flood of tourists in here. Just me—and you—and, well, Nigel. What were you checking up on, anyway?"

"That's official police business."

"Yeah, 'cause I heard Nigel was after some Egyptian scroll cases, super expensive too. So spill." I grinned at him. "Were they cool? Did they glow when you touched them?"

"They did not." He frowned. "Dixie's contact thinks they have magical properties?"

"Nigel. Nigel Friedman. And maybe yes, maybe no." I shrugged.

"Well, at least that would make sense." Brody's face took on a mutinous cast. "This flood of tourists—they're all Connecteds. There's a mess of them in the lower-level casinos and bargain hotels. And I get that solstice is coming up, but I'm not buying that's the reason they're here."

I wrinkled a brow. "Um, not to put too fine a point on it, but if they're not making any trouble, what do you care? I'm willing to concede that the LVMPD might engage in profiling of bad guys, but keeping a sheet on fortune-tellers and hypnotists? Doesn't really seem like low-hanging fruit on the tree of evil."

"It's not profiling." Brody glared at me. "It's a convention of crazy descending on my city, not two days before this rare gold show. Except these Connecteds seem to have pretty much zero point zero interest in the damned thing, unless these cases are their focus. So, if the Rarity didn't bring them to Vegas, what did?"

"Great TV ads?"

His gaze snapped up to mine so abruptly I almost took a step back. "You know, I'm not sure when we ended up on opposite sides, but I would suggest you knock it off."

I couldn't move for a second. In Brody's glare, there was more than irritation, more than confusion. There was hurt. I'd gone ten years without gazing into those eyes, hearing his voice on a regular basis, yet now I couldn't help but relive The Sariah and Brody Files every time I saw the man. I'd dreamt up a decade of possibilities, a lifetime of future plans, with impossibly hot, impossibly sweet, impossibly unattainable Officer Brody Rooks, and he didn't know any of it.

He *wouldn't* know any of it either.

He'd been the sole person I'd left unscathed back in Memphis, the sole person whose life I hadn't irrevocably damaged. I wasn't going to ruin that now.

I strolled over to Brody, close enough to make him tense. God, he even smelled like the cop I remembered, a heady mixture of cheap shampoo and warm skin. "I'm not trying to get on your bad side, Brody. I'm not trying to get on your good side." I shoved my hands into my back pockets, shielding them from his view as I worked the watch off my left wrist. "I'm just trying to get by, like anyone else is."

"Get by?" He was clearly fighting an inner battle with himself, and I didn't know which way it was going. Arrest Sara or let her go? Take her in for questioning or walk away from her? Pull her into his arms and kiss the daylights out of her or—

"Miss Wilde."

Absolutely worst. Freaking. Timing. Ever.

I focused on Brody, who kept talking. "I don't like the idea of you having to get by, Sara. That's no way to live, and I get the feeling you've been living that way for a hell of a long time."

I blinked at him, the sudden startled emotion his words caused drowning out the Magician's mind touch. Whether Armaeus had something important to share or he was just cop-blocking me, he could wait. "You don't need to worry about me, Brody. I'm not your job anymore."

"You're not, but that doesn't mean I don't care about you." His mouth tightened the moment he said the words, obviously regretting them.

My chest squished inward a little, the stab of pain on a totally different level from the psychic and physical jabs of the last week. So, naturally, I went on the defensive. "Hey, whoa. I don't need your pity. I'm doing fine."

"Sariah—"

"It's *Sara.* Sara *Wilde.*" I didn't know who I was trying to convince more, but my little walk down memory lane with Officer Brody Rooks was over. "Will you stop with the Sariah crap?"

"Jesus." He scowled, glanced away. Taking advantage of his distraction, I edged to the side of the open space and dropped Simon's watch into a crease in the packages there. Hopefully they weren't flammable.

I guess we'd see. "Sorry, you're right." Brody muttered, looking back at me. "Sara."

"It's okay." I crossed my arms, hugging myself. Time to go. "You gotta search the place or something? I don't think he's here—"

"No…no." Brody remained flustered, but when he finally turned, I fell into step with him. *Fifty-two, fifty-one, fifty…*

We covered the distance between across the floor to the main doorway quickly enough. Then he hesitated again. "Sara—"

Not a good time for hesitating. Fortunately, I didn't have to reach too deeply to channel my inner mad. Brody was a good man, a decent man, and I was absolutely about to screw him over. Again.

Because if he didn't key open the damned door like now, my little diversion was completely not going to work. *Twenty-seven, twenty-six…*

I forced myself to sigh impatiently. "Something else we should probably get straight." My own hurt twisted my words into an ugly snap. "I'm sure you've pulled my file, okay? The misdemeanors, the drunk tanks. The fights. And probably a whole lot more since the last time I checked. But unless and until I commit a crime you can actually pin on me, Detective, we've got nothing to say to each other. So back. The hell. Off."

That finally did it. *Thank God.* Brody's face shut down, and he straightened. Swiping his key card angrily in front of the monitor to our right, he planted a hand on the door and pushed.

"Fair enough. We'll just need a statement from you at the station, then, Miss—"

The explosion behind us drowned out the rest of his words.

CHAPTER TEN

Brody turned back, cop-reflexively, and I surged forward. I beat it into the maze of shelving as a half-dozen officers pounded toward us, then I climbed up a set of shelves. Scrambling along the top of it, I hauled ass until I got to the main doors, dropping down to exit the cargo building at a full run.

"Bomb! Get the fire trucks! Bomb!"

I didn't have time to decide if that was too much shouting or too little, because two other explosions went off in different areas of the building, resounding with percussive booms that lifted everyone half off their feet. *Nice touch, Simon.*

Pandemonium ensued.

As sirens wailed, I followed the least capable, most frantic delivery lugs as they bolted for their electric carts. The second-to-last one looked like he was one Ho-Ho short of a heart attack, so I cracked him on the head, catching him as he collapsed onto my body. Barely able to shove him into the cart without cracking a rib, I swung into the driver's seat and fired up the cart, joining the surge of refugees from the cargo building. I didn't bother keeping an eye out for Brody. He'd have his hands full for a while.

Dumping the cart and the passed-out delivery guy at the base of Terminal One, I was in the building and up the stairs sixty seconds later, stopping behind a potted fern to pull off my airport-sanctioned top. The gray tank underneath wasn't inspired, but it wasn't supposed to be. I stuffed the uniform shirt into the first food-court trash bin I could find, then ratcheted my stride down to a stroll as I triangulated myself toward the airport's main entrance. That done, I pulled out my phone, to all appearances texting my brains out while I negotiated one moving sidewalk after the next.

Like Nikki's limo in downtown Vegas, walk-texting in an airport was pretty much the equivalent of donning the cloak of invisibility.

I emerged from the front doors of McCarran International with my heart clawing its way up my throat, but at least I was moving in a more or less straight line. I wasn't sure whether or not Brody was going to have me followed once he'd sorted out the mess I'd caused, but I suspected he'd be up in my business again soon enough.

If he thought I was part of the Rarity event, that could go badly for all of us.

I didn't have time to ponder it further. No sooner had the doors closed behind me than I saw Nikki standing at the edge of the taxi stand with a placard titled "Angelina Jolie." She'd changed clothes into a gingham-plaid microdress, white tights, and Wizard of Oz ruby-red stilettos.

"Kreios said you'd need a lift." She opened the door to the limo when she saw me, tossing the sign inside. "Doll, you're my new favorite friend. And I wouldn't say that to just anyone. I mean it."

I slid onto the pink leather seat, trying to process

her statement. Then it hit me. When I'd seen her last, she was about to get between the Devil and the deep blue sea. "The tour of Grimm's back rooms went well?"

"If I could only Yelp it, I'd break the Internet. So how'd the gig go?" She met my startled gaze. "Kreios filled me in. He's pretty much a fan of information sharing, I gotta say."

"The mission—didn't go," I said, hunkering down in my seat. "I got close enough to touch the damned things, then Brody showed up with a whole SWAT team and rousted me out of there before we could get the goods."

"He saw you?"

"Oh yeah."

She went from blissed-out to serious with whiplash speed. "Was he looking for you specifically? Is that why he was there?"

"I don't think so. He's tangled up in the Rarity job, but I don't know how. Or why. Last I checked, no crime's been committed there. There's nothing for him to detect."

"Could be something simple." Nikki drummed her fingers on the steering wheel. "He's got the pretty face, so he's been pulled into political glad-handing duties before that the police don't want to deal with on their own. He could simply have been asked to pregame the Rarity, and running into you along the way is a happy coincidence, but I don't like that idea so much."

I didn't either, but I suspected our reasons were different. "Why not?"

She shrugged. "Technically, Detective Delish is part of the Homeland Security Division. The gold show is bringing a lot of folks with questionable friends into

Las Vegas. That could be all it is. But this particular gold show has Connected stink all over it, and now you're back in town too. If he's done his homework and knows what you do for a living, he could be excused for thinking you might be targeting the Rarity." She blew out a breath. "Then again, he was over at the chapel today asking for Dixie, not you. And once he found her, he chatted her up for a good long while." I winced, but Nikki kept going. As Nikki did. "He definitely wants something from her. Question is what."

"He's Homeland Security, though. What kind of terrorist threat lies in the Connected community in Vegas?"

Nikki snorted. "Not much, fair point. He may just want to get in touch with his Connected roots. You know, throw back a beer, talk about the good old days in Memphis."

I slid her a glance. "You're not going to let this drop, are you?"

She chortled. "I sure as shit Googled Sariah Pelter, if that's what you mean. And girl! You were about the cutest little thing that ever lived. What happened to you?"

"Back on track, Nikki. Like you said, Brody didn't seem to be sniffing around for me this morning. I couldn't have been the reason why he went to see Dixie."

"Which is my point. If he was playing her soft side, and believe me, she is more than willing to be played, he might know something she doesn't. And that would mean..."

"Don't say it."

"Yep. He's not just whistling Dixie."

Nikki's laugh turned into a full-on cackle as we bounced down Las Vegas Boulevard, and she was in such a good mood that she didn't make me hand out any more of her flyers. When we took the turn into Dixie's chapel, though, she sat up a little straighter.

"Yokely-dokely. This is strange."

"What." I scanned the parking lot, but other than a distinctive lack of parking, nothing seemed out of place. Dixie's looked quiet, or as quiet as a stark-white wedding chapel festooned with hot-pink flowers could, and the shops across the lot were open, but no one was lingering outside.

"This place is *never* this busy, not at this hour of the day. And Dixie, for all her many talents, doesn't play things close to the vest. If she was throwing a party, she would have told me."

Despite her light tone, something in Nikki's voice caught my attention. She sounded like she had her feelings hurt. I didn't know the six-foot-four force of nature that well, but the idea that she might cry was more upsetting than I would have expected.

We parked beneath the overhang of the drive-thru portal, and piled out of the car. "You want me to stay out here?" I said. "She might be more forthcoming if I'm not there."

Nikki slanted her gaze at me. "What are you going to do? Catch some rays?"

I shrugged, glancing around the parking lot at the tattoo parlor and liquor store. "I can go shopping or something."

"Nah, you guys need to kiss and make up. I can't have my besties giving each other the stink eye. It's too damned exhausting. And besides, if she did diss me for some reason, I could use some human armor."

She sauntered into the chapel with me in her wake, a scrubby buoy bouncing after a glitter yacht. Most of the action appeared to be centered on the main wedding chapel, but we'd no sooner reached those doors than Dixie came striding down the corridor from another direction, tugging a girl with her. Her tagalong couldn't have been more than sixteen, her eyes luminous in her small face.

"Shields up," Nikki muttered, and I sensed it too, the same kind of insistent poke that I experienced when Armaeus was nattering about in my mind, though at a far lower level. "Aura reader."

I lifted my brows. What I knew about Nikki's abilities was minimal, since it wasn't something she talked about much. She'd said she was a seer, and I knew she could communicate with a bit of telepathy. But how far did her Sight really go?

This wasn't the time to ask, so I plastered on a smile and pumped up my aura with happy thoughts as Dixie breezed up to us. "Lord, I thought I'd never see you again, Nikki. You disappeared without a trace! And Sara." She turned to me, all smiles that for the life of me seemed genuine. "You won't believe your eyes when you see Jos and Prayim again. They're recovering so fast! And they talk about you day and night."

"Oh?" I hadn't thought about that. Having oracle girls in your fan club might not be the coolest thing.

"Nothing but accolades, don't worry." Dixie dimpled. She turned to her sidekick. "This is Naeve. She reads auras and is new to Vegas. She's not here long, though, isn't that right?"

"I'm not." Naeve ducked her head, apparently embarrassed by the direct question. "This week alone.

For the solstice celebration. But you've been…very kind." She regarded Dixie with a sense of wonder. I couldn't blame her. Dixie had traded in her white cowgirl ensemble for a Jackie-O supreme, complete with a pink, exquisitely cut wide-collared sleeveless dress, tied in a bow at the waist, pearls, and a glorified pink hat that resembled a barely restrained meringue. Dixie squeezed Naeve's arm and turned her toward the chapel.

Nikki peered inside. "You hosting a revival in there?"

"They heard from local Connecteds that this was where to go for information, but they're not looking to stay in the city beyond solstice, like Naeve here," Dixie said. For someone who appeared placidly perfect, her voice carried an unmistakable edge. "Thank you, sweetheart. Tell the others I'll be right in."

The white-blonde waif wandered off, her movements almost ethereal. Dixie watched her until she disappeared inside the chapel doors, then glanced back to us. "First Detective Rooks shows up this morning asking me about the influx of newcomers, about which I knew *nothing*, I'm telling you, and boom, they're on my doorstep asking for hotel recommendations. They're coming out of the woodwork!"

"What's changed?" Nikki frowned. "Are they here for the Rarity?"

"Not that they've said, and why would they be? It's a gold show, not a Connected circus of the stars." She turned her gaze to me. "Do you have any idea? You find artifacts, right? That's your gift? Is there any reason why Connecteds are gravitating here? And don't tell me it's because of solstice, the detective already asked. I've lived through far too many Vegas solstices to count, and this is not normal."

I chewed on my lower lip, still rocked from my own close encounter with the artifacts at McCarran Airport. Was that what was drawing the Connecteds to Vegas? Couldn't be. They'd only just shown up. I hadn't felt any pull to the city in recent days, other than the call of money, so that didn't make sense either. Did Brody know something he wasn't sharing?

Don't think about him. I had an aura to keep chilled.

I focused on Dixie's question. "The artifacts for the Rarity could be doing it, especially since the show hasn't been hosted here in recent memory. But it seems kind of a stretch. Most of these people won't even go to the public viewing, right? And besides that, from what I understand, the majority of the artifacts on display won't have magical properties.

The tenor of the crowd inside the chapel leapt a notch, and Dixie pursed her lips. "What am I going to tell them?"

"You're not," Nikki said, her voice surprisingly calm and resolute. Whether she was relieved that Dixie hadn't planned a party without her or simply relieved to be in charge, I wasn't sure, but she wore her confidence like a blinged feather boa. "You're going to ask, and you're going to listen. This part I'm good at. Let's go."

She moved into the main chapel, Dixie right on her heels. I let them get ahead of me, then slipped into the farthest-back row I could find, surveying the room.

It was a...surprisingly tame bunch. Men and women dressed both in street clothes and business attire, some looking like Midwestern tourists, others like rejects from a Marilyn Manson concert, and still others like slightly harried research librarians. As I'd suspected, they *didn't* look like they had the kind of money to be shopping the Rarity. They definitely were jumpy, though. A few of them maybe scared. I settled back in a pew for the second time that day, and tried to open my third eye...

Nothing. Not even a twitch.

Nikki reached the stage, then turned around and surveyed the crowd. She seemed suddenly in her element. Like she was giving a press conference.

"A lot of you have come into the city on short notice and are getting your bearings. That's what we're here for," she said, her voice clipped and sure. "What brings you to Vegas?"

Silence. The room shifted and squirmed under her gaze, but she held her ground. Finally, one of them said, "Well, starting last week, the visions said to come here, and here we are. Everything said, 'Go to Vegas.' This chapel wasn't part of it—but it sure is nice."

"Visions," Nikki confirmed. I shot a startled glance toward Dixie, but she merely smiled with a desperate *I have no idea what they're talking about* grin plastered on her face.

"I don't know about visions. I got a notice from my New Age shop—an e-mail alerting us to the solstice celebration." This from a man sitting two rows away from the first woman. "Then we got here, and there's no information anywhere."

"Well, of course we're having a celebration, sugar," Dixie interjected. "We simply weren't expecting out-of-town guests is all."

"So who sent the flyers, then?" asked a girl in the back. "Or made the website? They said if we were believers, to come. And I talked to my friends, and they got the same thing. The store has a policy that they post anything that's related to the metaphysical, and they checked the website, same as us. We didn't think to call first. Vegas isn't that far."

I pulled out my cell phone to the sound of agreeing voices all around. "What's the website?" Nikki asked.

"Don't bother, it's not there anymore." A twenty-something goth from the third row held up his phone. "It crashed this morning, no explanation. You ask me, it makes being here even cooler. I mean, no one's asked us for money or anything, right? So it can't be some kind of scam. It's like a rave, but one filled with the power of solstice."

"And we're happy to help you make the most of your solstice experience," Dixie said warmly, immediately easing the tension in the room. I focused again, and my third eye finally blinked open, casting everyone in shades of pinks and yellows and greens and blues. But none of them were anywhere close to the Magician's level of brightness. Nikki and Dixie shone more vividly, but as to the rest... These were normal people. The kind of people who read their horoscopes online for fun or visited psychics to work out their love lives.

Nikki seemed to be thinking the same thing. "How many of you work in the psychic trade? Even if you merely dabble in it?" About a third of the room responded with a show of hands. "And the rest of you?"

"My sister lives in Dallas—she asked me to come. Said she couldn't come up but wanted me to bring back any info that sounded cool."

"I bought some books at the store, but I haven't started yet. Still, I live close and figured...what the heck."

Something about their naïveté sparked warning bells, but Nikki and Dixie had what they needed.

"Well, since you're here, let's get things organized," Nikki said. "What'll help us is if we know how to reach you once we get some of our last-minute plans in place. I'm going to send around a sheet for you to give us your contact information if you want—or at least your e-mail. Meanwhile, Dixie, why don't you let them know about the special astrological configuration this week?"

Dixie blinked at her. "The what?" Then she recalled herself, sliding smoothly into a patter about the unique significance of solstice *this* year, of all years, a significance that was undoubtedly being felt the world over, given their presence here.

Nikki gestured to a girl with a notebook in the front of the room. The book went around the room for signatures, and I rocked back into my seat, my sense of dread building. These people weren't high-level psychics. They weren't even working practitioners. They were cannon fodder. They were rats flooding in before an oncoming storm. A storm that was scheduled to hit…on solstice.

Exactly when SANCTUS was scheduled to come to town.

Just that fast, the pain hit me right between the eyeballs, fast and hard, closing around my brain like a vise.

I knew that pain, and I knew where it led.

The High Priestess demanded her due.

CHAPTER ELEVEN

I stumbled out of the chapel amid the general bustle of information gathering, and barely made it to the sidewalk. A limo was there, of course. Not Armaeus's personal town car, but a long, sleek model that screamed Arcana Council all the way.

Eshe had learned quickly that if she trusted me to get to her on my own once she started playing "twist the nerve endings," she'd just as likely find me in a gutter as in the Luxor lobby. She was getting better at playing fetch.

And what was her deal, anyway, freeloading at Council headquarters instead of having her own digs? I mean, the Fool didn't really have a home either, and I'd never met the Emperor or Empress, so I had no idea if they actually lived in their castles in the air. But presumably they'd lived there at some point instead of couch-surfing it, Arcana style. Not Eshe.

The pain jabbed me again, blinding my third eye with white-hot agony, and I curled into a ball in the back of the limo. "I'm coming, I'm coming."

As usual, there was no response. The High Priestess didn't go in much for mind chatter. Beyond being able to interpret oracular visions, she was skilled at afflicting the nerves and emotions of others, to bring about the futures she most wanted to see happen, and to forestall the futures that didn't fit with her shopping schedule. With me, she used that skill like an invisible leash. If I was anywhere within a hundred-mile radius, she could bring me to my knees.

Once the oracle twins were out of the city, I'd technically no longer be beholden to her. But that didn't mean she wouldn't keep trying. Because my newfound skills at astral travel should have faded already—and they hadn't.

I struggled to an upright position, my head against the cool glass of the window, and considered my options. Maybe if Eshe *thought* I was weakening in my skills, my vision dimmer, cloudier, she would leave me alone. It'd only been a few weeks, but I couldn't seem to remember a time when the itch of the gas hadn't squirmed through my skull. Or when I hadn't been on the edge of falling down into an abyss of darkness and vertigo.

This needed to stop. And it wouldn't stop unless I made it.

Maybe…

Another blast of pain exploded against my eyeballs, and darkness swept over me.

I awoke in a familiar setting: a conference room table fronted by large, comfortable chairs, lights gleaming from fixtures in the table's surface. Surrounding the enormous, sleek table, shadows encroached from all directions. I was alone today, the other chairs empty, which was not how this normally went. Usually, either the Magician or the Devil was on hand to witness my attempt at oracular gymnastics. Either to record my responses or to scrape me off the floor when I was done, I was never sure. But given that I was currently collapsed on the Arcana Council's conference table, my head in my hands, my mouth dry with panic, their absence seemed…notable. And ominous. Slowly, I lifted my gaze, blinking into the shadows.

"Are you prepared?" Eshe's disembodied voice floated over me as I sank back in my chair. I felt like three-day-old sushi, so it wasn't too hard to look sullen. I didn't favor her with a response, just a quick, brusque nod.

"Do you swear to see all—"

I waved her off. "Give it a rest, Eshe. We've done this often enough to skip the theatrics."

Her disapproval radiated through my fog of pain, which made me feel better. Something shifted at the side of the table, and I realized Kreios *had* joined our little séance. Armaeus remained absent, probably shining his astrolabe. "Hey," I managed.

Kreios inclined his head politely enough, but his gaze drifted over my face with sensual intensity, his blatant carnal interest apparently undimmed by my appearance. Then again, this was Kreios. He had resting sex face.

"Focus." Eshe's command pulled at me, a primal calling. I fell back into the chair, my face tilted up, my own breath gagging in my throat. Instantly, a spill of images assaulted me, one after the other, as they always did.

In a burst of pure energy, I moved out of Armaeus's conference room, out of Vegas. Eshe burbled and muttered in my ear, sneered and poked, and I angled down toward a familiar location with its soaring domes and cathedrals, its crowds of people in the street. I plunged once more into Vatican City, a broken falling star.

And found…nothing.

The last time I'd been here, the rooms beneath the Vatican had held men hunched over a table, blinking schematics flush against the wall, carts bristling with tech. This was SANCTUS's main stronghold, the cadre of men and presumably women who were dedicated to erasing magic and its wielders from the face of the Earth. They'd already made quite a dent in the Connected population, particularly in parts of Eastern Europe. Everywhere they went, they left behind scattered remnants of the community, mourning their dead.

Now the place was empty. Not merely of robed figures leaning over screens, but of all their tech too. The room could have been any subbasement stone chamber, its walls craggy, its floor swept clean but already showing signs of encroaching dust.

I must have spoken, because I was pulled out of the Vatican and thrust farther east, a rag doll shoved into other rooms of a dollhouse, looking for someone to play with. But I saw no one in the places I was sent—not the fancy homes of Roman officials, not the outlying abbeys dotting the countryside. Not farther south or east. Had SANCTUS disbanded? That seemed…unlikely.

Armaeus's voice sounded near me, his words sharp. Apparently, he'd decided to show up.

"They know we've been spying on them."

"Impossible," Eshe hissed. "They are not that strong."

"They could have moved operations to ensure their safety." This was the Devil, but no concern marred his voice. Simply speculation. Curiosity. "The Vatican has come under fire."

Their voices faded. Another pressure urged me forward then, farther to the west. The hills of Tuscany gave way to the Alps of the French borderlands, and then the sprawling beauty of château country. I thought I'd rush by, but something drew me down into the bosom of the French countryside. I'd been here before. Some of the most entrenched of my clients lived here. I hovered, an oracle without anything to see as the Council argued around me. While I hung in the odd embrace of space and time, my third eye fluttered open.

Instantly, the world changed beneath me, becoming a kaleidoscope of color. And I saw everything more clearly, more sharply.

I knew this place.

Able to move without being pushed, I angled down.

The château of the Mercault family was as ostentatious within as it was outwardly classy, a huge stone monument to generations of wealth and privilege. That privilege had not merely survived the French Revolution, it had thrived during it, staying far away from the barricades of Paris and keeping its own ruthless vigil on the family's private holdings. Monsieur Mercault preferred to operate his business from afar, never wanting to see the help, but he'd asked me to deliver an artifact directly to him once: a jewel-encrusted drinking glass. It was small, fragile, and impossibly old. I'd found the thing in a bazaar in Mumbai, though not exactly on the shelves of some open-air market stall. It had taken a bit to secure it for Mercault, but he'd been very generous in his thanks.

Now as I approached his home like a ravening wraith, the place seemed…strangely still. The usual swarm of gardeners wasn't bustling over the grounds and when I entered the walls, the psychic pain that jolted me had nothing to do with my own molecules being rearranged.

"Death," I whispered.

If the Council took note, they didn't stop me. The bodies started in the foyer—a dozen of them piled on the floor. The servants and grounds people. They had been killed recently—the air hung with the cloying sweetness of drying blood. More bodies were in the kitchens and the bedrooms. Mercault's wife had been struck down before she could exit their bed. At least one set of adults, Mercault's children or guests, had also been killed. The murders weren't clean, but they didn't appear to have been motivated by torture, either.

I wasn't happy that I couldn't find Mercault, though. He was more than the brains behind his operation; he was its *only* brain. His minions were legion, but he'd trusted none of them with the information on his empire. It was how he managed to hold on to it.

Something shifted deep in the bowels of the building, and I turned, flowing forth.

I found Mercault in his office. He wasn't alone.

He wasn't dead yet either.

With the benefit of my third eye, he also appeared different to me. I'd never touched the man, so I would have had no way of knowing this before but…Mercault was a Connected. A weak one, untrained, but there was no doubting the shimmer of power in his spirit.

Now his eyes were glazed with pain. He was

bloody, the right side of his face gashed, his mouth agape. His clothes were half-rent from his body, the dishevelment giving him a wild, unstable look. The men who faced him were the exact opposite. They weren't gowned as priests, but they had that feel. Serviceable suits, quiet faces, soft hands. Hands that were now busy at Mercault's computer.

I scanned what they were doing, reporting it, and the arguing Council members around me grew quiet, allowing me to focus. Mercault's screen was up, but I didn't understand the complex codes running across it. I did understand the racks of flat cases the intruders had lined up on the table, however, along with the long, sleek syringes that were lying next to them. My gaze swung back to Mercault, and in his eyes I saw something that unnerved me far more than his ragged body ever could.

I saw recognition.

Crap. I shifted back, rewarded when the big ox shook his head, his voice garbled as he attempted to answer a question of one of the men. French wasn't my strong suit, but it seemed pretty clear that he was being asked if he'd seen anything. Whether he was desperate enough or drugged enough, he shook his head, spitting blood. But I knew better.

"Miss Wilde." The Magician's voice was in my ear again in the conference room, almost as if he knew what I was thinking.

Either way, I didn't care. Mercault was no prince, but he'd never cheated me. And he'd never stolen children, nor trafficked Connected. Because he was one himself?

It didn't matter. I knew what I had to do.

I had appeared before, wraithlike, to people while

I'd served as an oracle to Eshe. But my body had always been incorporeal. I'd moved through buildings, enduring the drag of stone and walls while willing myself further toward vapor to escape some of the pain. How hard would it be to will myself the other way? And maybe really scare someone?

"Miss Wilde. No. We have agents on the way. Watch and report. Nothing more."

But Mercault wouldn't stop staring at me, at the place he was convinced I'd been. There were only the three men—impressive, really, that they'd bearded the lion in his den with so few people. They must have had something to help them. I scanned their bodies, noting the heavy gunmetal gray wrist cuffs, etched with symbols. Jerry Fitz had worn a sheath similar to that, though it'd been blown to bits when his underground lair had exploded. Was there a connection?

I faded back into a different room, this one mercifully free of dead bodies. But not of a living one.

I blinked. "Simon?"

The Fool glanced up at me from behind a newspaper, his legs crossed. "Hullo, Sara."

"Who—how?" I struggled to understand. "Are you...you're not traveling, not the way I am. You're here. You're corporeal."

"All true," he nodded. "Armaeus asked me to come to you, so come to you I have. Sadly, my ability is limited. I can't leave the structure into which I've teleported. And, incidentally, I can't wear clothing." He grinned as my gaze dropped to the newspaper. "I'm sure I'll scrounge up something. More importantly, though, I've been instructed to tell you to wait, but that seems like no fun at all. So instead, I can let you know that I'll keep an eye on Mercault's tech while you take out the assholes who rearranged his face."

"Take them out?" I frowned at him. "I'm a ghost."

"You *were* a ghost," he corrected. "You're becoming charmingly corporeal during this little jaunt, much to Eshe's surprise and Armaeus's fascination, I'm warning you. And you have clothes." I frowned down at my body, but he was right. I remained dressed in the same outfit I'd been wearing when I'd dragged myself into the Arcana Council chambers. "Armaeus does have a team on its way. We'd prefer to take at least one of them alive. And Mercault, of course."

"And what, you won't help me keep him alive?"

He placed a hand on his chest, his eyes aghast. "My dear Sara, I am a member of the Council. We do not involve ourselves in the affairs of mankind. We merely watch."

"I think you need to revisit your charter."

"You're running out of time." Simon tilted his head, as if he could see through walls. "They've figured out Mercault is holding out on them."

"Right. And if there are more guards roaming the hallways? Are you going to be safe?"

Simon returned to his newspaper. "I'll be more than safe, trust me. Run along."

I tried to will myself back into incorporeal status, but there was nothing doing. It appeared I'd have to do this the hard way, by actually using doors. I exited the room, which opened onto a hallway.

Getting my bearings became a lot easier when Mercault screamed.

CHAPTER TWELVE

I knew enough about Mercault's toys to know what I had to do. The Frenchman was one of the foremost leaders of the technoceutical market, a nasty bit of business that combined pharmacological pills and injectables with high-tech, magic-infused ingredients, predominately to help users achieve an altered state of consciousness—or unconsciousness—with some additional side effects of physical alterations. Heavy users had permanently dilated eyes, and their pain receptors dimmed enough for them to become a threat to themselves. Simultaneously, their pleasure receptors were stimulated, so their kink was…pretty intense. Not a good crowd to get on the wrong side of at a party.

I was pretty sure that the three ninja soldiers of SANCTUS didn't have a lot of experience dealing with a technoceutical high. Assuming I could rush in, grab a syringe, hurl it like a javelin of death at the Kevlar-armored men, and have it magically strike home, I should be set.

Piece of cake.

As I slowed, however, a nagging voice in my head brought me up short. It wasn't Armaeus—it wasn't Eshe. It was, however, speaking English. With a heavy

French accent.

"Clock…bench. *Gun!*"

I winced as Mercault screamed in my head, but turned up the hallway. At the far end, an imperious grandfather clock loomed over a delicate upholstered bench, the kind of bench no one ever sat on. I ran for it, crouching down when I reached it, and swiped my hand beneath. The gun I found was oddly weighted in my hand, a semiautomatic but with an unnatural heft. As if Mercault had filled it with the kind of bullets you'd need to take down a Transformer. Worked for me.

Keeping time with his anguished howls, I crab-walked along the floor. When I reached the door to his office, Mercault sagged forward in his restraints, either passed out or faking it nicely.

"Knock, knock."

The man ministering to Mercault turned and shouted, and I squeezed off my first round, aiming for his neck.

The gun exploded in my hand with the force of a bazooka, and I fell back even as my target spun around. Then the other two men sprang into action. One of them had apparently read from the same bad-guy playbook I had and grabbed a syringe from the table, hurling it at me with impressive force.

I ducked in time, but guy number two was more nimble. His shot clipped my shin. Pain exploded in a fiery bolt, and I fell back on my ass, bringing the gun around and blasting it toward his face. He jerked sideways with the blast, and I skidded back against the wall with the force of the report again, waving the gun to clear the smoke. Mercault hung more heavily in his bonds, pretty close to dead, but his eyes were fixed on me with a fierce, unwavering stare. I couldn't quite read that stare, whether it was happy or sad, but I was struck again with the conviction that this had been an inside job. There were too many bodies for it not to be.

Which meant Mercault needed to pick his friends a little more wisely going forward. If the Council really did have men on the way, his life wasn't about to get any easier.

The momentary distraction was a bad choice on my part, however. A sound at the front of the room caught my attention too late, and suddenly there was another sharpie zinging toward me. The gun went off in my hand, but my aim was nowhere near on target, and a bolt of fire seared through me as the needle struck home. I wrenched it out of my arm and fired again, then a third time, praying I wasn't hitting Mercault in the process but not really caring so much. Dizziness swamped me, and I dissolved just that quickly, back to incorporeal state. Had I ever really been truly animate in this place? Would I ever be again?

I had no recollection of moving back through the walls of Mercault's castle, but soon I was drifting through the woods like smoke, noting the long, sleek limo barreling along the private lane. I felt …detached. So detached. A ghost, a wraith, a flitting shadow dissolving into ever-thinner wisps. Pain enveloped me, but not in any specific place—I'd been hit in the shin and the arm, but in this state, I had no legs, I had no arms. In this state, I was naught and nothing and—

The hard crack of a palm against my face woke me with a gasp.

"Kreios!" Armaeus's sharp voice brought me the rest of the way. I jerked back reflexively, twisting out of the Devil's grasp. His smile was harder, fiercer than

I remembered it, and I brought my fingers to my abused cheek.

"Ouch."

"My apologies," he said, looking distinctly unapologetic. "You were going into shock."

"Remind me not to recommend your bedside manner."

"I wasn't finished with her!" Eshe's petulant whine drew my attention. Her getup today was inspired—colorful toga, darkly outlined eyes and painted lips, long dark hair, golden armbands: Katy Perry in full-on Cleopatra mode. "She went entirely different places than we wanted her to go. What use is she—"

"None. No use." I dragged myself up in my chair and scowled around the room. "Someone saw me. Actually saw me. Multiple someones." I turned to Armaeus. "Thanks for the Fool. He didn't do jack shit."

"He did what he was told, at least."

Worry riddled through me at the low warning in his voice, and I blinked, trying to bring myself back to focus. There was something…important about his choice of words. Something critical.

Eshe sniffed. "You couldn't have been seen. You weren't physically there."

That distracted me from the panic fluttering in my gut. "Yeah? Ask Mercault, if there's anything left of him. Ask the boys in black that I interrupted in his office." I scowled at Armaeus. "So, really, the Fool can teleport? You think someone might have told me?"

He just gazed back at me, like Darwin studying a barnacle. "Simon's abilities are not yet fully tapped. He has not been long with the Council."

"Well, that skill is kind of a big one." I pulled myself up gingerly in my chair, then frowned down at my shin. It appeared unharmed. I wiggled it. It wiggled back appropriately. "I really was vapor that whole time. Like some sort of hologram." I frowned. "Why did I feel pain?"

"Even without your Connected abilities, the mind of a mortal is extremely suggestible." Kreios was regarding me with the same undisguised curiosity as Armaeus. I lifted my right hand to my left arm, palpating the skin. It felt ...tender. Apparently, my mind was going to keep up that part of the illusion for a little while longer.

"You got what you needed, then?"

Eshe's whine reached DEFCON 2. "I did *not*—"

"Yes. And your role of oracle is reaching the end of its usefulness, I'm afraid." Armaeus's words drowned out Eshe's. "Simon has already begun removing the technology from Mercault's home. The man himself has been secured."

"And the bad guys?"

He flicked me a glance. "The intruders were no longer on the premises when our team arrived. Two of Mercault's technoceutical cases were gone as well."

That did catch me up short. "I was there. I shot them."

He nodded. "And they shot you."

"Except I shot a gun—not my gun. One I picked up."

"Our agents found it. Under the bench by the grandfather clock, correct?"

I blinked at him, my brain going into a serious cramp. "I *saw* them."

"I'm not disputing that an altercation occurred, that shots were fired and men were hit. I'm disputing the events that transpired immediately *after* you left the scene. The illusion lifted. The men realized they were restored but compromised."

"Why didn't they kill Mercault then? They should have. I would have." Realization dawned. "Simon was there. Really there, not…whatever I was. And he let them go."

"Simon can be very alarming if he chooses to be. When he provided the men with an opportunity to flee, they took it. They will have time later to consider the ramifications of their decisions."

I blew out a breath. "Why do I get the feeling that I'm missing some extremely important information here?"

"You need to rest."

"No." Eshe's fists crashed down on the table. "Her abilities are clearly cresting."

"Yo, these aren't my abilities. This is that blasted gas."

"It is *not* the Pythene," Eshe snapped. "That hasn't been in your system for three days."

I blinked at her, but she was already turning to Armaeus. "If you mean to take her from me, I get one last session out of her before she goes. You are not doing all that you should to bring the Council together. The Empress remains uncalled. The Emperor. Even the Her—"

"That's enough, Eshe," Armaeus snapped. "We do not need the full Council here to meet this challenge. Those that are on assignment elsewhere must be left to finish their tasks."

She stared at him, disbelieving. "Assignment! I assure you Roxie Meadows is not 'on assignment' in between rounds of booze and boy toys."

This had to be the same Roxie that Simon had

mentioned. I mean…that name. Either way, she sounded like my people.

"Is she staying, um, above the Bellagio?" I offered. "I'd be happy to go fetch her."

Armaeus's voice was quelling. "Roxie Meadows should never have been accepted to the Council. Her abilities were artificially enhanced with technoceuticals at the time of her accession."

"It *was* the sixties," Kreios put in lazily. "Everyone's abilities were."

"And she adds to our overall strength," Eshe insisted. "You know that we need her to present a united front. Light and dark, Armaeus, yin and yang. For the Council to be at full capacity, we cannot have the powers of the neutral and light alone. Not if Llyr is returning. We must recall everyone pledged to the Council."

Llyr? I felt like I was swimming in a deep, rolling sea. Of Jell-O.

"Who's Llyr?" The name rang in my ears, chasing along my nerves, familiar yet utterly foreign to me. No one paid attention to me. Armaeus looked more pissed than I'd ever seen him, the conflict on his face plain.

Whoa. Eshe was going to win the battle of the sexes with Armaeus, and get Roxie recalled to the Council. Whatever that meant. I was all for girl power, though, until Eshe spoke again.

"You've put out your call for the Council to be returned," the High Priestess said, turning toward me. "But you have not reached all who must be reached. Now it's my turn."

She lifted her hand gracefully—and I tipped back in my chair.

CHAPTER THIRTEEN

I woke up at the table, sprawled facedown on the smooth, cool surface. I wasn't alone.

"You're close—very close." The voice was soft, almost soothing. If only it didn't belong to the Wicked Witch of the Strip.

"Shut up, Eshe." I slung myself back in the chair, staring blearily around the room. "Where's the rest of them?"

"I said you would need privacy to recover."

"And that doesn't count you?"

Her smile was automatic, and it didn't reach her eyes. She was watching me with that same curiosity I'd now witnessed on every Council member's face, like I was the most fascinating thing to hit them in a millennia. These people clearly needed to get out more.

I lifted a weary hand, scrubbed my eyes. So far as I could tell, all of my skin still hung on my body, which was a bonus. Except… "What happened to me, that last time? I don't remember any of it."

"The deeper you go, the more immersed you are in the field, the less you can retain when you return. It will take time and practice to improve."

"Yeah. No." I scowled at her. "There won't be any

more 'practice' after the twins leave."

"You have abilities beyond your understanding that you refuse to explore."

"It's the blasted gas—"

"We both know that's not true." She turned and removed the lid from a bowl at her side that I hadn't noticed. Steam wafted up, and she shoved the thing toward me, pressing a spoon into my fingers. "Eat."

"I'm not hungry," I grumbled over my squalling stomach. I tried not to look at the swill directly, but obligingly dipped my spoon in it and took an experimental taste. "Fine." The soup was made up of cream and chunks of meat and…something sketchy that wasn't quite a vegetable. But it tasted better than anything I'd eaten in the last six months, so I wasn't going to argue.

Eshe watched me eat for a few moments, then spoke again. "You cannot merely serve, Sara, to achieve your goals. You must also lead."

I eyed her, too tired to do more than sneer. "Is this the self-help portion of the meal?"

"Armaeus will take you apart muscle by bone by sinew until he understands how you have the powers you do. He should not be more interested in exploring your true capabilities than you are."

I focused on my soup again. "I've been busy."

"You've been afraid." She pulled back in full regal disdain. "But you can't afford that fear if you would truly protect your community. Because Armaeus *won't*, Sara. Nor will he protect you. You need to remember that."

"Oh, like you will?" I scowled, not waiting for a response. "How old are you, anyway? You're new to the Council, right? Or new-ish?"

Eshe's smile could have frosted over Hell. "I am the oldest sitting Council member. Older even than Armaeus by a thousand years."

I stared at her. "Whoa."

She lifted a heavily lined brow. "You're surprised?"

"I guess I would have thought age would've made you less of a bitch somehow."

"And I would have thought youth would've done the same for you." She leaned forward. "You must take responsibility for the care of the Connected yourself, Sara. And for the care of your own abilities."

But fatigue was dragging me down again, drowning out the last of her words. I waved my spoon at her, but refused to respond. Not when she asked me more questions, not when she told me more lies. I eventually pushed the soup away and put my head back on the table.

At some point, she left.

At some point long after that, after night had fallen and morning came…so did I.

Now I held my hand to my eyes for meager shade as I moved through the crowd at the SLS Casino pool, the closest anyone was ever going to get to the once-grand Sahara. The Sahara Casino had been a bastion of Vegas Connected magic from the time it had opened in 1952 until its closing in 2011. Despite the implosion of the building and the subsequent construction of the SLS (or maybe because of it), the site remained one of the most magical places in Vegas. After all, there had to be *some* kind of magic involved to get a casino built in Vegas in the current real estate market. And by every indication, the SLS seemed to be doing well. It was ten a.m., and the bar was already going strong.

Resolutely moving forward, I kept my eyes pinned

on Nikki. As usual, she was easy to spot. Today she sported a hot pink golf ensemble that had likely never seen an actual golf course, more was the pity. She lifted her drink and waved it at me, but her expression changed markedly the closer I got to her, until finally she simply gaped, openmouthed. She pushed her drink my way as I sank down onto the open stool beside her, and signaled the bartender for another.

"Girl, you look like death in a dog bowl."

I shrugged off my hoodie and tied it around my waist. "Give it a rest, Nikki."

"I'm just saying, I've seen armadillos less in need of a spa day. Consider it." She squinted into the bright sun that bathed the bar area beyond our shadowy oasis. "We've gotten in another fifty Connected overnight. High rollers this time, keeping to themselves. Not this crew." She shook her head. "Dixie can handle the lookie-loos, keep them corralled and safe. They trust her. This new group, however, they're going to be trouble."

I sipped my drink, wincing at the sting. "Trouble how? I thought this was some kind of big solstice meet-up. Is this new group focused on the Rarity?"

"Not so's you'd notice. Instead, the visions motif keeps presenting itself, in both the higher-level crowd and some of the scrubs. And now that we've got people talking, the visions are starting to match up in one critical way: a storm from the east. Apparently, the apocalypse is coming to Vegas."

I slanted her a glance. "Have you, um, *seen* anything?"

She shrugged. "I don't really see the future so much. I see the present that others can't see, or aren't willing to talk about."

"That's handy."

"It has its moments. Proving what I see can still be a bitch, however." She slid her gaze toward me. "I will tell you what, though. Your present is no picnic."

I stiffened. It hurt. "What do you mean?"

"I mean the fact that you look worse every time I see you. Paler, sicker, closer to dead. At first I figured you were just unhappy with being in Vegas, but it's more than that. The Council is sucking you dry. They may be hotties on speed, but they're not good for you, dollface."

I shrugged. "They pay."

"Not enough." She rested her elbows on the bar. "I can't see what you *see*, you know. I can't hear what you're saying. I can only see *you*. The you that you don't tell people about, the you that you maybe don't know either. The closer I get to you, the more time we spend together, the more I can see of your location, your circumstances, your physical self."

"And you saw…"

"You passed out in a chair, mostly, your mouth moving a mile a minute, clearly in distress, in pain. Sweat pouring off you, but Armaeus, Kreios, Eshe—none of them touch you. They don't really get near, other than Eshe. She holds out her hands over you like you're some kind of fire she's warming herself by. Kind of creepy. Otherwise, they argue a lot. They don't make a move toward you until you start to convulse. Then they pull you out of your trance, some times more gently than others."

She scowled, and I remembered the last time. "Kreios slapped me."

"Not at first he didn't. He shook you, he lifted you, he did everything but make out with you… Though he honestly should have tried that, because, my God, girl. That mouth." She sighed, then soldiered on. "His slap came after you started to scream."

I halted my glass mid-lift. "Scream?"

"That's what it looked like without the sound turned up." She regarded me stonily. "You need to tell me what's going on, sugar bun. I'm not going to be able to help you if I don't know what you're doing."

"I don't think I fully know. I thought I did. But now…"

Nikki grimaced, scanning the pool show. "Oh, freaking fantastic. No wonder Dixie wore that suit."

I peered into the sunlight. I was rocking the same tank, hoodie and leggings I'd had on the day before. Dixie Quinn, however, was making full use of the pool's dress code. Standing in waist-high water, she bounced up and down energetically, her barely there hot-pink swimsuit gamely trying to hang on. She waved at a man standing at the edge of the pool, a man who looked impossibly out of place in his rumpled brown suit.

I closed my eyes. "I don't have time for him today."

"Doesn't seem like he's after you." Nikki's voice betrayed her curiosity. "He really is focused on Dix, but not for the reason I bet she thinks."

As we watched, Dixie clambered out of the pool, daintily accepting a towel that she used to blot dry…her face. The rest of her shimmered in water-soaked perfection as she beamed up at Brody. He pointed our way, the only strip of shade in sight, and I groaned.

"Suck it up, Buttercup. It might be good to hear what he wants. Dixie has been after him to take an interest in the Connected community for the past couple of years. Maybe he finally has."

"He doesn't look happy about it."

And he didn't. In fact, as Dixie and Brody approached, he looked distinctly pissed off. He recognized Nikki first; then his gaze slid to me. If he shared Nikki's concern for my appearance, he didn't betray it. "Ladies," he said gruffly. I kept my face neutral, and Dixie's watchful expression eased into a sunny smile.

"We'll just be a jiff, won't we, Detective Rooks?" she asked, rubbing his biceps with her long, manicured fingers.

He grunted again, and they moved down to the end of the bar. Nikki's eyes were back on me, and I'd had about enough of that.

"How long were you a cop?"

She blinked, then smiled wryly. "Don't think interrogating me about the bad old days is going to get you off the hook. That was a long time ago." She flapped a hand in front of her defiant D-cups. "Before the change."

"Did they know?"

"They knew enough to get me kicked off the force." She shrugged at my wince. "I was lucky, though. Back then, I got lumped into a slightly different class than today's more enlightened naming conventions, but it was still sexual harassment, and it was still Chicago. And I was still a loudmouth. The lawsuit paid for the work I wanted done, and the rest sort of played out the way it needed to."

"And now? You ever go back there?"

"To Chicago? Nah." She took another swig of her drink. "You ever head back to Memphis?"

I snorted. "That would be no."

"I was serious when I said I'd Googled you, you know. That Psychic Teen Sariah stuff was pretty cool. You were good at it."

"Not good enough, often enough. And not good at all, in the end."

"Yeah, well." She rolled her glass in her hand but didn't wait long for the follow-up. "You ever figure out who killed your mom?"

The question was an honest one, a basic one, but it hit me unexpectedly hard. My throat closed up, and I shook my head, forcing the surge of emotion down. "Not yet. Didn't look for a long time, and then, once I could—didn't seem too smart."

"And now?"

"Jobs keep me busy. My work has problems enough without seeking out trouble." Her silence went on a little too long, and I glanced at her. "What?"

"Nothing, maybe." She shrugged, her eyes fixed on Brody and Dixie. "Seems to me if you've got the big bad Council on your ass twenty four-seven, you might as well get some benefit out of it. Surely they can find shit out about your mom that you couldn't. I mean, come on. You said the Fool was some sort of hackster genius. Couldn't he break into the police records?"

"What would be the point?" I took a long slug of my drink, trying to understand the panic flaring through me. My mother's death had been a long time ago. Ancient history. "Brody said he never found anything."

"And I'm sure Brody, being a good cop, has never ever lied in the course of duty in his life." Nikki waved off my scowl. "All I'm saying is it's a possibility. Something to check out in between errands you're running for the Council or whoever else you have on the line right now. You could always ask Simon, see if it's something he'd be interested in."

I thought of the Fool and his eyes alight with wonder at the prospect of breaking into Mercault's tech. "He'd probably do it just to see if he could."

"Exactly."

Dixie's laugh brought our attention around to the far end of the bar. She was leaning over a printed list of names, the angle allowing her impressive assets to spill out over the document. Brody's scowl had gotten deeper, and I almost felt sorry for the man. Almost. "You find out anything about Brody's involvement with the Rarity?"

"His role, I think, is done," Nikki said. "Like I told you, glad-handing and the face man. From here on out, I don't think you'll have to worry about him until you want to."

The second she said the words, I knew that was too much to ask.

"Sara? You have a minute?"

Brody's voice sounded a little too crisp as he waved at me from the edge of the bar. as if we hadn't already been at each other's throats already once this week. "What the hell?" I muttered.

Nikki also pitched her voice low. "Dix doesn't like you coming into her chitchat either. Tread lightly, Kemosabe. I've got your back."

"Right." I moved off the barstool and trudged to the end of the bar. Shoving my hands in my pockets, I rocked back on my heels. "Can I help you?"

Dixie kept quiet, her face perfectly sweet-tea, but her sharp eyes missed nothing. I dug deep and straightened under Brody's narrow-eyed gaze.

"You look like hell," he said.

"Noted. Anything else?"

"Who do you know on this list?"

He pointed at the list of names that Dixie had been hovering over. She, thankfully, had scooted back enough for me to see it without getting an eyeful of cleavage, and Brody moved the paper toward me to emphasize the separation between Dixie's view of the situation and mine. Very cute, very cop. I sometimes forgot about how much I remembered about this man.

Shaking off that thought, I scanned the list and tried to keep my voice neutral. "I've heard of some of them, but I can't say I really know any of them."

"None of them?"

"I mean, not really." I leaned forward, committing the list to memory. It read like a who's who of Connected. "I know a few of the names from, you know, gossip."

"They're all Connected. You're a Connected." He swiveled his gaze back to Dixie. "You both are."

I rolled my eyes. "It's not like we all have the same 401(k), Brody. The community doesn't work that way."

"She's right, it doesn't." Dixie's voice was a touch harder-edged too. Still sweet, but with enough steel to drive her point home. And at least she wasn't directing her irritation at me. "Which you'd know if you'd ever shown an interest before now."

"Consider me officially interested. Who are these people, and, more to the point, why are they in my city?" He shifted his glance to me. "The people on this list aren't here for solstice. And *all* of them can't be interested in the Rarity, no way."

I shrugged. "Come on, you don't think Connected folk like to gawk at pretty trinkets? We're still human. Most of us."

If I'd wanted to unnerve him, I didn't succeed. At least not outwardly. Instead, he got that long-suffering look on his face, like he'd somehow drawn the short end of the stick, but by God, he was going to make the best of it.

"Thank you for your time," he gritted out. He swiveled his gaze to Dixie. "Always a pleasure, Dixie."

"Always will be." She smiled with enough force behind her interest that Brody blinked, a faint rush of color flaring along his cheekbones. Dixie opened her mouth to keep going, and I wheeled around, heading toward Nikki. Dixie Quinn had more game in her little finger than I had in my whole body, and I suddenly didn't feel so good. I made it back to Nikki in time for her to grab my arm in an iron fist, her hand all that was keeping me upright.

"What did he say to you? You look even worse than before, and I didn't think that was possible."

"It's nothing—nothing." I didn't shake off her hand, though. "What do you know about Roxie Meadows?"

"Grifter Queen of the Seventies?" Nikki chortled. "She's practically Dixie's inspiration—knew everyone who was anyone in Vegas, back in her day, literally had the who's who of the Connected community in her little black book. Hit it big with a card-reading act that apparently sucked in everyone from the mob to the pope. Cashed in with a series of rich-as-Croesus hubbies and bought a huge mansion west of the Strip. She hasn't been out and about much, but what would she be—seventy now? More?"

I thought I'd test out my new-found information on her, see what stuck. "Is she the Empress?"

"Oh, hell no—" Nikki's eyes widened as she stared

at me. "I mean—there's that fairyland-castle place. That's the Empress's crib. Roxie's home is way off Strip."

"So you do know her?"

"Well, I don't know-know her. I know *of* her."

"You've been here how long and have never met the woman herself?"

"Well—I wasn't really—" Nikki shook her head. "Look, doll, when I first got here, I was totally rookie grade. I couldn't see any of the Council's digs until Dixie pointed them out to me. Once I knew how to see, I was fine. Before..." Another head shake. "Dixie was the one who showed me Armaeus, Eshe—eventually the Devil. She never mentioned the Empress, not once. And she's talked about Roxie a lot."

"They still friends?"

"Sure they are." Nikki shrugged. "But like I said, Roxie is getting up there."

I grinned at her. "Not if she's on the Council she isn't. What say we check it out? I figure if Dixie *doesn't* know about Roxie's extracurricular club membership, she'll appreciate the heads-up. Especially given everything going on."

"You've got that right." Nikki's gaze swiveled to Dixie, who was now chatting on her bedazzled white cell phone. "This...is gonna be good."

CHAPTER FOURTEEN

"Roxie's not the Empress. She should be, she'd be the perfect Empress, but she's not," Dixie said for about the fiftieth time since we'd left SLS. "She's not the kind of woman to hide her light under a barrel."

"Well, maybe she had a good reason," Nikki said reasonably. "She sure lives rich enough, despite the fact she's off Strip. You said yourself that she looks like a million bucks."

"Probably because she's paid a million bucks to do so." Dixie shook her head, her blond curls catching the sunshine. "And I haven't seen her in—Lord, it's been forever. She's been a recluse for years."

We were tooling north on the Strip in Dixie's white convertible, leaving behind the high-rises and even the low-rises, heading deeper into the city. Nikki was at the wheel, and Dixie rode shotgun. Now Dixie turned around to me.

"Roxie's refused the last four or five times I've asked her to meet. Said she didn't want to be seen when she wasn't at her best. Instead, she has a thriving telepsychic service and website—totally international. She makes more money than God."

"But she's not on the Council."

"No—I mean..." Dixie sighed. "I surely would be surprised." Her gaze swiveled to meet mine. "Not as surprised to learn you were born Sariah Pelter, though."

I was getting really tired of that name coming up. "That was a long time ago, Dixie."

"Vegas has a way of making you face your past." She laughed at my expression. "Don't give me that look. Detective Rooks didn't out you. He clearly knew you from somewhere, and I know he's never been stationed anywhere but Vegas and his hometown. Even back in the dark ages of actual newspapers, stories were archived, you know. It wasn't all that difficult to find Brody Rooks's name in Memphis and cross-reference it with members of the community who showed up more than once. Especially when one of them was a teenage girl whose mother was—"

"I'd be super careful if I were you." My words were mild, but not mild enough. Dixie recoiled. *Down girl.*

"What I'm trying to say is, I understand the energy between you two now," she said. "I couldn't figure it out before, the push-pull of his emotions. He never would let me read his chart, and I get the feeling you don't know exactly when you were born, so that's not incredibly useful. But there was clearly a connection there, and now I know what it is."

Beside Dixie, Nikki's eyes snapped up to the rearview mirror. She didn't have to speak inside my head for me to get the message. *Go with it.*

I uncurled my fists and leaned back against the white leather seats, letting my eyes drift shut. "Yeah, well, like I said. A long time ago." The sun baking down on me felt better than it had any right to. "When's the last time you saw Roxie?"

"Two thousand and…" Dixie's voice held a frown. "You know, I don't know. We were thick as thieves when I first got to Vegas. She introduced me to the community, helped set me up, really. I secretly think she got financing cleared for the chapel, and then the loan was canceled—I owned it free and clear."

I opened one eye, unsurprised to see Nikki staring at me in the rearview mirror. Totally sounded like a Council move.

"She do that sort of thing a lot?"

"I don't know—probably. She was generous to a fault. And her parties! Lord, they were famous, especially in the seventies and eighties. Before my time, of course. But I'm sure she's kept up her connections." She pursed her mouth into a perfect moue. "I wonder if we should have Detective Rooks with us?"

"No." Nikki and I both spoke the word at the same time. Then Nikki angled onto I-15, and Dixie turned forward again, no one bothering to talk once we hit the highway. I was glad of it. Seeing Brody again today had been…unnerving. I still felt beat to shit, psychically and emotionally, and when he'd commented on my appearance, it sounded so much like the younger Brody, it brought back an entirely new, unwelcome flood of memories.

He'd looked so much younger then too. So strong and earnest and all "just want to see if you can help, Miss Pelter. Finding these kids, it's what we have to do." He'd filled my whole world with the belief that if you simply fought hard enough, long enough, you would win. If you kept searching far enough, deep enough, you could find anyone. My skills might have been mine at birth, but I had gotten better at them after

I started working with the Memphis children's crime unit. Just not good enough.

Not ever good enough.

I burrowed farther into the seat, trying to lose myself in the upholstery. It had been good practice, honestly, for what came after. By the time I'd found Father Jerome, learned about the plight of the young Connecteds, I was better at my craft. Quicker. Smarter.

Most importantly, I knew what I could—and couldn't—do.

Some of the kids I'd tracked back in Memphis had been Connected, but not all. I hadn't realized then that there even was a psychic black market. I'd thought I'd been more or less alone, that my abilities made me special, separate. And they had, in the middle of Tennessee. But the world was both a much bigger and a much smaller place now that I was grown up, now that I worked in the community. Now that I'd seen so much more.

We finally slowed, turning off the highway into an area completely different from the scrubby, sun-beaten homes I'd seen close to the Strip.

"You can live here on a fortune-teller's income?" I stared at the houses we were passing, each bigger than the next.

Nikki snorted from the driver's seat. "Roxie wasn't just any fortune-teller. She started out as a carnie queen, yeah, but she had a thing for the rich and famous—men, women, she didn't care. She'd party with any of them, and the more she partied, the more prescient she became."

We turned up into a steep driveway, and I gave an appreciative whistle. "She seems to be doing okay."

Dixie laughed. "This place was her wedding

present from her third husband, and she's remodeled it from top to bottom. It's nice."

We turned onto Orient Express Court, snaking up through palatial homes landscaped within an inch of their lives. A fair amount of that landscape involved green. Never mind that we were in the desert.

When Nikki turned boldly into a gated driveway whose gate was open wide, though, I frowned. "Is she expecting us?"

"Open-door policy." Dixie said. "You've got a question for Madame Roxie, she'll send out a minion to meet you. And that minion will tell you first what your question is, and then what you can pay if you truly want to know the answer."

"Really." I considered that. "That's a pretty neat trick. If I guess the right question and have a reasonable idea about the answer, I've won the lottery."

Dixie grinned. "It's what got her the third husband."

We pulled up to the front door of the mansion. A valet trotted out from a small, air-conditioned guardhouse, all fresh-scrubbed youth and earnestness. Every one of my bones creaked in response. "Welcome to the Aerie," the kid said cheerfully, taking Nikki's keys. "Madame Roxie is receiving in the front sitting room. She'll be with you herself in a few minutes."

I slanted Dixie a glance. "I thought you said she was a recluse."

She shrugged, clearly surprised. "She must be feeling better."

I reacquainted my feet with the concept of moving, not missing the way Nikki hung back to keep an eye on me while Dixie clicked forward in her stiletto heels.

She'd shimmied out of her neon swimsuit and into a white shift and shoes, but her clutch purse provided the necessary pink—a bubblegum-hued base with large white polka dots. I tried to remember the last time I'd carried a purse that wasn't for any other reason than to hold a gun. Couldn't.

"You're doing great, dollface," Nikki said. "You'll be the bait. Given your beat-to-shit face, ain't no way Roxie won't figure out you're the one with the question."

We entered the house and were transported immediately into a different world. The outside of the mansion looked perfect Vegas chic—the pool, the landscape, the sweeping views of the Strip. Inside, we were treated to an interior designer's nightmare.

"Not exactly relocation beige," I murmured.

"Well," Dixie shrugged delicately, "I'll allow she's a bit nostalgic."

"Really." The foyer was stuffed with memorabilia—sandwich-board signs hawking palm readings, flyers for everything from séances to spectral audiences, black mirrors, pink lanterns, crystal balls, sequined scrapbooks stuffed to the gills, and Aladdin's lamps. The walls were shrouded in ornate purple and red hangings, forcefully setting the scene. "Has it always been like this?"

Dixie gazed around the space, appropriately awed. "I've only visited once, right after we met. Then she was working the whole Arabic Fortune-Teller motif—imagine tents. A lot of tents."

"Got it."

A woman dressed in an old-time movie usher outfit emerged from a back room, her smile radiant under her sleek blonde bob. "How lovely of you to come," she said warmly. "Madame Roxie is delighted to welcome you and heal your pain."

The girl addressed us all, but her gaze drifted to me. Beside me, Nikki stiffened, but with my newly acquired sensitivity, I could feel it all on my own. The girl was definitely Connected.

"Yep," Nikki said quietly as we followed the young woman to the right, through large oak doors into an equally shadowed and draped room, this one set up like a miniature theatre of the strange. "She's got the gift. It's pretty strong too."

"Please, make yourself comfortable."

There was a small stage at the center of the room, with a table, two chairs, and an honest-to-God fainting couch. Surrounding the stage was a semicircle of chairs. I kept glancing around for Penn and Teller, but it appeared we were alone in the room.

"You'll be the focus of Madame Roxie's reading, yes?" Our usher set a glass of ice water in front of me.

That jolted me. "She told you that?"

"She's very eager to see you." She smiled at me, and reached out her hand. It was gloved, so I took it. You simply couldn't be too careful around Connecteds. She drew me up on the stage and offered me the couch. I took a chair. Nikki sprawled in one of the viewer seats.

"Have you worked with, ah, Madame Roxie long?" I asked.

"Oh no," she said. "Madame Roxie allows her assistants to stay a year each, at the most. But it has truly been an honor. She's paying for my graduate studies in psychology."

"My stars! That must be exciting. Where are you going to school?" Dixie drew the woman's attention away, giving Nikki and me the chance to exchange glances. Yearly interns? That was interesting.

A bell sounded deep in the house, and the assistant straightened, her pleasant demeanor taking on an edge of excitement. "You'll see. She's unlike anything you've ever encountered before."

She was wrong, of course.

The woman who swept into the room took Dixie's bombshell status and raised it several notches. The first thing you noticed about Madame Roxie was the bourbon in her hand; the second was the Venetian half mask that covered her upper face, tucked neatly into her flowing golden curls. But there was no denying that beneath that mask flowed the smoothly perfect skin of a young woman. Wrapped in a fire-engine red silk dressing gown that was slit up to her thighs, Roxie strode boldly forward with both hands outstretched to greet us, her red lipstick smile stretched almost to the breakpoint over straight white teeth.

"Darlings! How perfect that you're here." Her voice was bright, sunny and, like everything else about her, way too young for the age we knew her to be.

Dixie gawked, totally losing all sense of decorum. "Madame Roxie? You're...you're the Empress?"

Roxie turned to Dixie, startled for a second, then appeared to take her presence in stride. "Why, Dixie Quinn. I didn't think I'd see you again. Cooped up here in this house as I am, I don't much entertain my old friends." She surveyed Dixie critically. "You've aged. Pity. Still, now that we can all verify that I did at least *try* for discretion regarding the Council, there's no need for this silly thing anymore."

As Dixie stammered a blend of indignation and awe, Roxie set down her drink and pulled off the

Venetian mask. She shook out her hair, and I blinked, momentarily transfixed by her blond, boozy beauty. She was like the original good-time girl, preserved for all eternity.

She tossed the mask to the table. "I don't know why I care so much. One of the Council's tricks grants us the ability to hide in plain sight—or did it never occur to you that no one ever questions that the stunning Eshe never ages, that Kreios looks the same now as he did the day he took his seat on the Council?" She threaded her hand through her curls. "I should have learned about them maybe three years earlier than I did, but still. You have to take your opportunities when they come."

She turned to me, picking up the glass of bourbon and taking a long, appreciative sip while she studied me. I studied her back. She was worth studying.

"Sara Wilde," she said at length. "I've heard so much about you." She gestured to the couch behind me. "You should lie down. You are…so tired."

"I'm good in the chair, thanks."

"As you wish."

Roxie drifted toward her chair and sat, and I could feel the energy swell up and around her, the very air giving way. She regarded me with an almost palpable pleasure, a cat surrounded with bowls of cream.

"Let me guess. The Magician doesn't know you're here. Eshe sent you, and she's keeping it from him. Eshe, I always did like. Kreios too. But then, what's not to enjoy about Kreios?"

"No one sent us." I shifted in my chair. "But while we're on the topic, why aren't you on the Strip? There's that castle—"

"Lovely, isn't it? Makes me happy that it's there, off

in the distance." She leaned back. "And I'm not hiding, sweetie. I remain in the city to spite Armaeus, not to cower from him. I stick in his craw like a piece of gristle he can't spit out, and Lord, if that doesn't make me sleep easier at night." She winked at me. "Still, you can tell him I have no interest in joining his crusade. The Council has proven quite beneficial to me, and I thank them for it. But I'm quite fine with my limited involvement." She waved the glass, grinning at me. "I can tell you what you want to know, though. The newcomers to Vegas. Why they're here. I'm right, aren't I, about your question? I'm always right."

She took a long drink as I nodded. "And your payment?" I asked.

"Oh, we can dispense with that." She leaned forward, her face suddenly intent. "Despite the fools who've flocked to the city, there are some legitimate players of interest here too. Perhaps fifty who are dangerous, but maybe three of real concern. There had been four, but Monsieur Mercault has quite unaccountably gone missing. He will not be in play for the scroll cases Armaeus covets so deeply."

"He's…" I tried not to gape at the flood of information. "Do you know what happened to Mercault?"

She smiled. "That is another question, Sara, with a different price." She lifted her glass in a toast. "For your purposes, you most want to pay attention to Grigori Mantorov, Russian and quite proud of it. Appears to be a gentleman, and of course, there's that divine accent, but make no mistake, he's as dirty as it gets. You want to know who is behind the Connected trafficking, particularly the trafficking of the youngest of souls, you need merely to go to his door."

The youngest of souls? "How do you know him?"

She shrugged. "It's a shared knowledge. I don't have to sit on the Council to know what they know. Another advantage of living in the city. They tend to think very…loudly."

Anger riffled through me. If Roxie knew this guy, that meant the Magician knew him too. Knew him and hadn't told me about him. "Grigori Mantorov."

"Yes, but he's not the only one who will be here. Annika Soo will be too, and she 's not to be ignored. Chinese, also proud of it. Powerful, deadly, and constantly furious. Her, I would watch out for."

"Agreed." I did know Annika Soo. I'd never been hired by her, but I'd narrowly escaped her minions twice. I tried to tamp down my mad to get the information I needed. If Annika Soo was actually here, that was out of character. "She usually prefers to poach artifacts from finders after the fact, instead of hiring out the wetwork herself. Why is she getting involved personally?"

"A strategic move to show she's still very much in the game. It's no secret that the balance of power is shifting in the arcane black market. Her interests are at stake, and her position, and her pride. She won't allow anyone to take what she believes should be hers."

"So Annika, Grigori—are they Connecteds? Or just rich?"

Roxie lifted a silk-clad shoulder. "Power is a matter of nuance. You know that. One man's intuition is another man's psychic gift. One woman's ability to shift is another woman's hallucination brought on by mental illness. It's all in what we can accept into our lives, or what we choose to use."

I stared at her. "Are. They. Connecteds?"

"I think for your purposes, it is best to assume so." Not exactly an answer, but Roxie kept going. "The third party is your primary concern, however. He has money and intelligence and charisma. And, unless I miss my guess, he's a Connected too: Jarvis Fuggeren."

"Wait." I sat back. "I thought Fuggeren was the one *selling* the gold."

Roxie smiled. "Jarvis Fuggeren, as was all his family before him, is a master of playing both ends against the middle. You want to know the real reason why he is conducting this sale at the Rarity and not in the privacy of his own home?"

"Showboating?"

"Information gathering. He knows about SANCTUS but not who is behind them. Who the power players are. And he knows better than to invite them to meet in secrecy. His caution is for naught, though. Wherever he goes, the arcane black market follows. They trail after him like dogs, ready to feast on whatever spoils he leaves behind."

"Yeah, well, what about the low-level psychics who're here in the city? They don't know Fuggeren, or about his gold. They frankly shouldn't know about SANCTUS. What's set them off?"

Roxie lifted her brows. "There are some questions even I don't deign to answer. Not yet. But I will tell you this. SANCTUS is an organization that thrives on its secrecy. They prefer to pick off the Connected community in a death by a thousand cuts."

Yeah, I'd witnessed a good dozen of those "cuts" littering Mercault's estate.

"But the collection of Connected currently assembling in Las Vegas is, if you'll pardon the pun, a *rarity*," Roxie continued. "It will prove to be a temptation that SANCTUS cannot ignore. Here they can kill a community of psychics and believers in significant numbers, without any repercussions. Here, more importantly, they can warn off the next wave of the curious, those low-level Connecteds who aren't yet fully aware they have abilities."

I thought about the people I'd seen in Dixie's chapel. "Those people aren't SANCTUS's targets."

"Of course they are." Her smile was hard, jaded. "Curiosity must be punished as much as action, in a war like the one SANCTUS is fighting."

"But why, specifically, are they here, anyway? Who lured them? There were *flyers*, Roxie. Some of these people had visions. All of them were being instructed to come here, to Vegas, for solstice, and it's all come together in the past several days. There's no way SANCTUS has that kind of infrastructure on American soil."

Her gaze didn't waver from mine, but neither did she speak for a long moment. Long enough for me to play connect the dots with my fried cerebral cortex. "No. No way."

Roxie sighed, then sat down her drink and reached out to touch my hands. I let her do it, too. The flow of her energy was light and full, but it couldn't reach the hard center of me, a core that was quickly turning to ice and stone. "The *Council* drove them here?" I demanded. "All these innocent people? They herded them here like *sheep* to draw the wolves down on them?" Not the Council, I knew. Armaeus. Armaeus had done this.

Roxie's mouth tightened, but her eyes remained steady. "The role of the Council is to assure the balance of magic."

"Are you freaking kidding me?" I yanked my hands away. "These people have no idea they're about to be dropped into the middle of a *war*, Roxie. You and your precious Council *know* that."

"Not mine." She drew herself up as well. "I have not allied myself with the Council for decades."

"Well, maybe it's time you reconsidered that. These people can't stand up to SANCTUS—they're not prepared for it."

"Armaeus believes—"

"Armaeus is *wrong*, Empress." I spit out her honorific like a curse and stood. "You're all wrong. And a whole lot of people are going to die if you freak shows don't get that through your heads."

Dixie's phone buzzed, and she jumped, clearly not expecting it. "I swear I shut it off..." She frowned down at her screen. "Sweet Mother Mary and the angels." She looked up at us, eyes wide. "The Deathwalkers are here."

CHAPTER FIFTEEN

Nikki fled the room first, moving faster than I'd ever seen her rock a pair of stilettos. Dixie was on her heels. I stayed put, staring at Roxie as color flooded her face.

"Deathwalkers?" I asked. Clearly I needed to keep better tabs on my Connecteds, but I'd been *busy*. "What's a Deathwalker?"

"A coven of witches from the Old Country."

"Like, what, Germany?"

She flapped a hand at me. "Chicago. They were prominent during the mob rule in Vegas but lost interest in the seventies and the mob tried to carry on without them. That went well. Since then, the Deathwalkers entered into international finance and trade, went clean, you could say. But if they're here..."

My head was spinning. "You're telling me that Armaeus sent *them* an e-mail too? To sweeten the pot further for SANCTUS?"

"No. That wouldn't have maintained the—"

I turned away, unwilling and unable to hear the word "balance" anytime in the next century. Nikki and Dixie were already screaming at each other when I joined them in the car, and we raced back to the Strip in a blur. The coven had decided we would meet in a diner, and we roared up to the Blue Moon at three p.m.—typically a downtime, according to Nikki, unless a bunch of Deathwalkers had recently shown up. Instead, the parking lot was packed with vehicles.

Inside, however, there was only one table taken, by three people. Whether the diner had been full before and everyone had taken a convenient walk, or the cars in the parking lot were an illusion, I wasn't sure. But a line of servers stood frozen behind the counter, not making a move toward the trio—two women and one man.

I couldn't blame them. The group was preternaturally pretty, in a high-cheekboned, perfectly chiseled sort of way. The woman in the center, clearly their leader, stared at us with stony disapproval. The other two focused their attention on their hands, which they held in a loose cuplike formation on the white paper place mats on the table in front of them. Their lips moved in a silent concert, but I couldn't see any power sparking from them. Nikki was too tense for there not to be something going on, however. And then there were the servers. You didn't work long in Vegas without becoming jaded, but these people were seriously spooked.

Dixie strode ahead, her pink purse clutched in her grasp, pressed against her dress. It was the only sign she was nervous. Nikki, beside me, was up on her toes. I wasn't certain where she'd hidden a gun on her body, but I was pretty sure she had one.

For my part, I simply stared.

The trio regarded us with hollow eyes, tracking Dixie's march across the diner. "It's been a long time, Danae," Dixie finally said.

I did my best not to applaud. *Danae and the*

Deathwalkers? Best. Band name. Ever.

"I'd hoped it would be longer." The woman who stood to greet Dixie was as dark as Dixie was fair, her long ebony hair falling from a sleek part in the center of her head. She wore flawless makeup, and a black tank dress that bared chiseled arms and long, muscular legs in platform stilettos. She nodded regally to Nikki and me, and I managed to rehinge my jaw. "We have foreseen great damage to the city. We have interests to protect."

"Great damage how?" I asked.

The witch's eyes flicked to me, a glance that shifted her from traditionally beautiful into the realm of the seriously eerie. Her eyes were smoke gray, far too light against her dark skin.

"You pledge yourself to turn back the tide of evil, yet you light candles when you could cast the sun," she said, regarding me somberly. "You could wield the sword of justice, yet instead allow harm to befall those you would protect."

Something hard snapped within me. It wasn't that I didn't understand what she was doing. She was a sorceress, and psychic manipulation was a skill. Identify the weakest points of your opponent and magnify them. People were always much more willing to believe the bad about themselves than the good. Hang-up of being human.

Still, I didn't need a Windy City witch judging me. Especially when what she said hit so close to home.

"No one will be harmed," I said. "We'll do whatever it takes to weather the storm that's coming."

"You will fail." She peered at me, her gaze raking over my battered body, my scruffy clothes. "I know you."

"I'm pretty sure I would have remembered someone who goes by the name 'Deathwalker.'"

She creased her lips into a shape that could almost be called a smile. "We haven't had occasion to be known by that name for many years. Even here"—she waved her hand—"we were quite domesticated. The old ways were better suited for the old times. There are many who've fallen away from that path."

"But not you?"

"And not you. Not yet anyway." She turned to the woman beside her, but the woman shook her head.

"The newcomers are not enhanced." The woman pointed at me. "She wears a Tyet, but primarily for—"

"Hey, hey, hey." I held up my hands. "I didn't agree to a strip search."

Danae lifted her own hand to quell my outburst. "Our magic remains pure because of our commitment to holistic practices. Not all of our kind agree. The pull toward enhancement is strong, particularly when we must fight the dark practitioners—which the city reeks of at present. We do not have much time."

I stifled a groan. "Who *isn't* coming to Vegas, exactly? We're kind of a little full up right now."

Danae ignored me. "Who in the city is enhanced?" she asked Dixie. For her part, the Welcome Wagon of Vegas looked distinctly uncomfortable. "Besides you," Danae added dryly.

Wait, what? Dixie's face was a mask of Southern hospitality. The kind shown by rebel housewives right before they gutted carpetbaggers. "We don't judge *enhancements*, merely actions," Dixie said smoothly. "A person shouldn't be judged by anything but that."

"Power, sister," Nikki put in. She had leaned forward ever so slightly, in full mother-bear mode. For once, it wasn't me she was protecting. "You got something you need to say, Danae, go ahead and put it on the table."

The Deathwalker turned to Nikki for a moment, studying her. "We were so named because wherever we passed, naught but death remained. Yet we never took a life, seer. Consider that."

"Very spooky." Nikki's voice was harder now, sharper. "You want to get a little more clear, or are we all wasting our time? Why do you care about 'enhanced' Connecteds? And what do you mean by that, specifically?"

"It is the left-handed path. Once you embark upon it, the way to darkness is but a few steps." Danae's mouth twisted. "Why do you think so many have fallen to the way of the dark practitioners? There was never so much evil in the world, waiting to spring. It has been helped along."

"By whom?" I prompted. If she said the Council, I was totally picking up my Nerf ball and going home.

"The dark practitioners themselves, in part," Danae said, returning her attention to me. "The technoceuticals that have flooded the arcane black market. However, they are not simply ending up in the hands of unConnected patrons and clients to provide a temporary magical high. They're afflicting Connecteds too. Changing them. Poisoning them. That is not balance. That is not purity. That is defilement."

Coming from a group of tree huggers, this wasn't a surprising attitude. But I was mostly glad that I didn't have yet another crime to lay at Armaeus's feet.

Nevertheless, something about this didn't add up. "Technoceuticals aren't addictive."

"Aren't they?" Her glance was withering. "Power

is the most seductive drug of all. You should know that more than anyone. And if you don't, you should learn it. Not everyone you count as friend is worthy of your trust. Not everyone you count as foe deserves the title."

It was her second jab, and I was full up on my quota of being used as a punching bag.

"You trying to get me to call your psychic hotline?" I asked. "Because you're really, *really* good at saying nothing in a very impressive way."

"Then let me say this clearly." She shifted her gaze to Dixie. "The lines of energy have shifted. The old maps no longer hold. You will help us reconfigure them before the storm hits the city."

"There are no ley lines that run through Vegas," I snapped.

"They do when the Council is seated here. As they have throughout time, in city by city, country by country. Wherever the magic is strongest in the world, eventually the very energy of the Earth's core gets drawn up through the crust and bowed out, amplified. That is what is happening here. A great force has stressed the lines too much, compromising the underlying power that binds the world together. But once we map the new configuration, we can manage any new influx of magic."

"But that's—"

"I'll help you." Dixie's voice was resolute. She turned to me. "There are too many Connecteds here, Sara, and more coming every day. You tackle the job from your angle. I'll do it from mine."

"Speaking of which, tick tock." Nikki held up her arm. Her knockoff Rolex was completely at home on her large wrist, and she flashed the brightly polished face of it at me. "You still look like split-pea soup on toast, and you've got a party to crash."

I blinked at her, then remembered. The Rarity pregame gala was tonight. That was not going to happen. "I don't care about—"

"You may not, but that's where the action is, sugar pie. Maybe if you get those thingamajigs for the Magician, whatever's coming down on us will veer off in another direction…or stop in its tracks. C'mon." She started to stand, but I waved her off.

"You stay here. I can make it back to the Palazzo on my own."

Her lips turned down. "This saving-the-world shit requires the hardest of choices. I definitely don't trust you to do your own shopping."

I glanced down at my scrubby clothes. Shrugged. "I'll figure something out."

Of course, I didn't have to.

CHAPTER SIXTEEN

Rich people don't walk anywhere.

The limo that the Arcana Council sent to collect me was their standard sleek town car, but for a change, it wasn't idling at a curb. Instead, I'd been instructed to take an elevator down to a parking level I didn't know the Palazzo had.

The elevator doors swished open, and a young man in a tailored suit stood at the edge of the tiled entryway. "Miss Wilde," he said deferentially.

I peered into the back of the car while he opened the door. No Kreios. I didn't know if that made me feel more or less self-conscious. I half fell, half slid into the car, struggling not to flash the unflappable driver, who said nothing about my lack of coordination and merely shut the door with a decided thunk.

I straightened in the seat, shimmying down my dress. Which, of course, wasn't much on shimmying.

Dragging in an experimental breath, I tried once again to decide whose choice this outfit was. The micro leather sheath that had been waiting for me in my room at the Palazzo was meant for a woman about six sizes smaller than I was, who'd apparently just had surgery to remove all her internal organs. It came down far enough on my thighs to render walking problematic, but not enough for anything remotely approaching propriety. If it had been any shorter, it would have passed as a halter top.

The dress had no back to speak of, and its neckline dropped from a severe choker collar to reveal a slender teardrop of skin from neck to cleavage, though I supposed I should be grateful the slit didn't extend to my navel. Either way, with so little in the way of material, Spanx had been out of the question. Which was too bad, since I hadn't had time to break a rib.

At least the boots made up for the dress. I stretched out my legs in the wide space and admired the knee-high stilettoed wonders, the leather as scrunchy as the dress above it was tight. I'd passed on the leather cuffs that had been helpfully sent along—again, not knowing if it was Kreios or Armaeus with a bondage fantasy, and not super interested in fanning that particular fire. But the secondary option, a string of stones that I hoped were crystals but had the weight and flash of diamonds, now glittered from one wrist. I felt like a star on Oscar night, only with half the clothes.

The driver angled the car through the subterranean garage, lights flashing against the walls, and I checked the palm-sized clutch the Council had sent along, complete with a handy phone. I was fresh out of burners, so it was just as well, but it'd been the other items in the purse that had intrigued me. An ID card issued to my real name, and a slender clip of fifties and twenties. For tips, I assumed.

The ID card bothered me, though it shouldn't. Kreios was using his name, and surely some of the attendees at this little shin of diggery knew he was the

Devil. Then again, until I'd begun working with the Council, I hadn't known the group existed. I also hadn't known that a former Council member was hanging out in the burbs, or that there were more in the wind, holding out on their contracts.

What was it Roxie had said about Armaeus and the cloak of normalcy that he cast over the Council? No one questioned the Arcanans' lack of aging, sure, but maybe it went beyond that. Maybe his skills extended to ensuring people saw nothing more than they expected to see. A fancy hotelier instead of the Magician; an international art collector instead of the Devil. Lord knew that no one ever took note of their real estate ventures on the Strip.

Grudgingly, I had to give Armaeus some props. He might be the most megalomaniac micromanager I'd ever met, but he was covering a lot of bases.

Still, that didn't excuse him from luring Connecteds to Vegas as bait for SANCTUS. If he'd truly done that...

"Miss." We'd moved out into Las Vegas Boulevard traffic, and the driver was watching me through the rearview mirror. "Mr. Kreios will meet you at the door of the Grand. He regrets that he was unable to accompany you—" The man stopped, shook his head a little, then glanced back into the mirror, his eyes shaded subtly darker. "He regrets nothing."

My attention sharpened as the driver's voice dripped with the smooth intonations of Kreios's rich Greek accent. He scanned what he could see of me. "You wore your hair down."

I frowned, lifting my hand to my head. I'd spent way too long in the shower, pounding the ache from my body. But I was clean, which had to count for something. "I wasn't aware there was another option."

The driver's smile was miles different from the deferential expression he'd worn at the door, and his eyes glittered with an otherworldly sheen. "It suits you," he murmured.

Then he blinked, hard, and returned his attention to the street. When he spoke next, his voice was once again blankly professional. "We'll be there in a few minutes, miss. Las Vegas traffic at this hour can be challenging, but at least it's a nice evening."

"That's certainly true."

The limo came equipped with a tinted sky roof, opaque to outside viewers but which afforded me an unrestricted view of the Vegas Strip skyline. With night falling on the city, I couldn't help but look up. Soaring above me was the white tower over Treasure Island. To the right, atop Caesars Palace, was an equally impressive monolith, a gray stone castle keep I'd begun to suspect was the Emperor's domain, for all that it appeared dormant. Opposite Caesars was the Devil's home, Scandal, which glinted and writhed in full neon splendor above the Flamingo. Beyond that, over Paris Casino soared another tower, black as pitch. Opposite Paris was the Bellagio, sprouting its fairy-tale castle.

And finally, near the very tip of the Strip, was the Magician's domain, Prime Luxe. It was an enormous holding, with spires of steel and glass reaching up to the heavens, proclaiming its dominance. How could any of the Connecteds who were here and who possessed any amount of ability not see it? Was Armaeus's power that intense? It simply didn't make sense.

"Once again, you are asking the wrong questions, Miss

Wilde."

"Hey!" I turned in my seat, but Armaeus's touch on my mind slipped away. Instead, the limo slowed.

"Here we are, miss." We turned into the drive of the MGM Grand, which was lit up like a Christmas tree. A crowd milled in front of the entrance, but no one was dressed as painfully as I was.

I frowned. "Are you sure this is the right place? Maybe they want us in the back or something?"

"You'll be escorted directly up. The ownership of the Grand preferred the entry to be public." His smile was reassuring. "You'll find that most people won't notice you."

"I've made a living off it." Still, when we eased to a stop and the door opened beside me, I didn't think too much about the hand that reached in to help haul me and my microdress out of the vehicle. Until I touched it.

The Devil was back again.

Electricity sparked through me, rich and hot. Holding on to Kreios's hand was like catching a live wire, but I gritted my teeth against the sensation that turned my nerves into silly string and used his grip to launch myself out of the car and onto the pavement.

"As I imagined in my wildest fantasies, Sara Wilde," Kreios murmured, lifting my hand to his lips. He looked devastating, as usual, his golden-god hair drifting over the shoulders of his immaculately cut tuxedo, more gold glinting at his neck and wrist that somehow made him appear exotic, not like some seventies-era lothario. I never could figure out how he pulled that off.

Then I focused on what he was doing. His lips connected with my fingertips, soft as a sigh. The double pressure of his mouth and his fingers made my head swim, and I pulled my hand away, smiling brightly.

"And Armaeus has no problem with you squiring me around tonight."

"Fascinating, isn't it?" Kreios tucked my hand into his arm, the thin protection of his suit sleeve doing nothing to shield me from the warmth of his sheer physicality. "Your arrival is well-timed. About half the guests are here, and all the important ones besides Fuggeren. He is an attention seeker of long standing, so I suspect he will be among the last to arrive."

"And the items in question? You've seen them?"

His smooth, rolling chuckle enveloped me. "Everyone has seen them. If I didn't have your report, I would assume they were merely part of the show. They seem quite…muted."

"Muted?" I stared at him. "Kreios, those things practically blew me across a room."

"Then my congratulations are due to the men and women of Techzilla, Inc. Because, though they are kept in clear glass, the cases presently give no indication of their power." He nodded to me. "I'll be interested to see you experience them yourself. An interest I harbor about so many things I would enjoy watching you experience."

When I tried to shift away out of a belated sense of self-preservation, he held me close, his mouth hovering over my hair. "You have nothing to worry about from me, Sara Wilde. Not yet. Once you say yes to all that I might offer you, then your worries will begin."

The doors to the elevator chose that moment to open, and we boarded along with a small selection of other guests, men and women alike dripping designer couture and bling. The women, though, were dressed...differently from me.

"Umm..."

Kreios's hand firmed on my arm, but he didn't speak until the elevators opened again. There was nothing more magical than an elevator for rendering its occupants mute.

The moment we stepped into the showroom, however, he bent to me. "Look around. As I said, your attire is perfection."

I scanned the room and noticed two things immediately. First, most of the women were gowned and tiaraed to the hilt, except for a tiny fraction who looked like they'd taken the wrong turn in a *Resident Evil* screen test and found themselves here. Those women were not hanging on the arms of their dates, but staring around the room, picking out competitors. And not for Miss Congeniality awards. The other female guests faded into the background by comparison. So did most of the men. But not all of them.

"That's Mantorov, isn't it?"

"Yes. Grigori Mantorov was among the first to arrive, and he received a personal walk-through from the organizers. He is rumored to be interested in acquiring the entire collection, without singling out any specific item."

"The entire..." I stared at the treasures under glass. "No one could have that much money."

"His work appears to be uniquely profitable."

I considered that, rage firing in me anew. I hadn't seen the man's face before this moment, but I'd seen the face of what he'd done. "Who else?"

"Annika Soo is watching you, so it's less advisable

for you to observe her at the moment." Instead, Kreios took the opportunity to pull me around to face him, appearing for all the world to be a young man in love. Never mind that he'd been kicking around for nearly a hundred years. Still, there was nothing ancient about the way his gaze raked over me. "Your mind is too active, Sara Wilde. You must learn to cloak your emotions. Particularly those about the Council."

I lifted my brows. "You really want to do this now?" I didn't wait for his nod. The Devil seemed uniquely designed for confrontation. "You—the Council—have been driving people here. To Vegas. This week. Forget these stupid artifacts; that's just icing on the cake for you. You wanted SANCTUS, first and foremost. And you're getting them too, aren't you?"

Kreios shrugged lazily. "There are two low-level lieutenants on the guest list, Vatican priests who are artifact experts. They appear to be here for nothing more than reconnaissance. They do not appear to anticipate any play for the cases tonight."

"Which experts?" I took the opportunity to intercept a passing server's tray full of champagne flutes and scanned the room as I selected a glass. I saw the two men almost instantly, once I started searching for them. The priests' robes were a dead giveaway. "Not exactly subtle."

"They don't need to be. Their official role here is for the Vatican, nothing more. But what they're fixated on is not surprising."

The scroll cases did not command the center case of the room, but a small highlighted case to the side. Lined fully in purple velvet, it featured the cylinders on raised glass stands. I didn't catch the slightest murmur of power from the scroll cases. "Simon has seen these?"

"During the walk-through this morning." Kreios nodded. "The security is top of the line, every item chipped, the glass unbreakable. The wards within are the trickier subject."

"Well, they're definitely doing their job." I frowned, peering at the gold glinting in its case. "It wasn't this heavily protected in the warehouse."

"And now?"

I shrugged. "We're all still upright, and at least half the people in here are Connected. So they're doing something right." I lifted my glass to my lips, aware of another gaze on me. I turned and caught the cold, black stare of a beautiful Asian woman across the room. Like me, she was dressed in a black sheath, though hers was crafted of thickly embroidered silk, and her boots were low. Low and much more serviceable. She surveyed me critically but didn't appear to pass judgment, despite my ridiculous getup. Which made her more dangerous still.

"So what's the—"

"Miss Wilde, what a surprise."

I shifted back, instantly on the defensive, but there was nowhere to go but against Kreios's body. He, predictably, didn't move, absorbing my weight as if born to the task. "Detective Rooks," I managed.

"For a woman new to Vegas, you're showing up in the *most* interesting of places."

"Oh?"

"First that terrible tragedy at Binion's, then the hospital, then the airport...and now here. Funny how that works." He shifted his hard gaze to Kreios. "I don't believe we've met. Detective Brody Rooks, LVMPD."

He reached out his hand, and Kreios took it in a brief, hard shake, the action not a competition but not a sterling demonstration of camaraderie either. "Aleksander Kreios," the Devil practically purred. "But then, you probably know that already."

"One of the perks of the job." Brody shifted his gaze to me. "If your date will excuse you for a moment, I'd appreciate the chance to catch up. For old time's sake."

I shot Kreios a glare, but he merely inclined his head. "Of course, Detective. I wish you good hunting."

Good hunting?

Brody didn't seem to catch Kreios's jibe, or he didn't care. The detective reached for my arm, thought better of it, then gestured for me to precede him to the side of the room.

"It's not a crime to go to a party," I muttered as we walked.

"Give it a half hour and I'm sure you'll make it one," Brody snapped. "I don't want to arrest you, Sara, but you're making it awfully difficult." He jabbed his thumb at the cases. "Why are you here? And while you're explaining that, tell me exactly how you managed to show up on the arm of one of the sleaziest players in Vegas."

"Not anywhere close to being your business." Over Brody's shoulder, I could see Kreios clearly as he leaned toward the case in the center of the room. There was no mistaking his grin. Whatever buttons he'd pushed on Brody, he'd pushed them hard.

Brody noticed my distraction and also turned. Kreios saluted him with a raised champagne glass. "Christ," Brody muttered, his voice thick with disgust. "Who the hell are you?"

My gaze sharpened on him. The confusion and fatigue of the past two weeks coalesced into diamond-sharp pinpoints, whether ready to poke holes into this man or to jab myself, I wasn't sure. Brody shouldn't be here, not in this nest of Connected vipers. Not when SANCTUS and the Council were about to square off. And not where there was a big glass box of mystical mayhem that I suspected was about to be cracked wide open. "What I am is not breaking any laws. Remember that part? That's the part you should care about."

"Like I said, not yet." He didn't have to flick a glance at Kreios, but he did anyway. I didn't know what pissed me off more. That Brody thought I was sleeping with Kreios or that it was the one thing the detective could imagine me doing with him. Then understanding struck him.

"You're using your *gifts* for Aleksander Kreios? But how and why could he need you to find anyone? He's richer than God." It would have been comical if it wasn't so heartbreaking watching Brody play connect the dots. "You don't just find people anymore, do you? You find things. Expensive things. He's a collector." His eyes hardened. "And you're here to collect."

I widened my hands. "You're more than welcome to search me."

"Don't think I don't plan to." He stepped closer to me, and I sensed it again, the heady rush of desire that had barely begun blooming in my hormone-fogged brain over the last year of our work together when I was Psychic Teen Sariah, combined with the very real, very grown-up reaction to him now. "Look me in the eye and tell me you're not here to steal some of this gold, Sari—Sara. Because I *do* have the authority to arrest you, on suspicion of becoming a pain in my ass if nothing else."

I glared back at him. "I find things, Brody. Totally on the up-and-up."

Okay, technically about thirty seconds after I found something…I stole it. But, details.

He didn't back down. Instead he edged closer to me. "What aren't you telling me?"

More than he could ever imagine. "Back off, Detective. People are starting to stare."

To his credit, Brody didn't flinch, and he didn't move. "And what would your new friend think about me being this up close and personal with you, Sara? Would he have a problem with that?"

"Not in the slightest, I can assure you." Kreios had appeared at our side, so quickly and silently that I jerked back, though Brody's reaction was more natural. Kreios draped his arm over my shoulder, his touch once more electric, lighting my nerve endings on fire. "If you would be interested in getting up close and personal with both of us, Detective, allow me to give you my card."

"I know how to find you."

"Of that I have no doubt. But if you'll excuse us."

Without waiting for Brody's response, Kreios turned me back to the center of the room. "That was bracing." He slanted me a glance. "Do you want me to share with you Detective Brody Rooks's most pressing desires? Or can you guess?"

CHAPTER SEVENTEEN

We stopped in front of the nearest case. I shook my head. "If only you used your powers for good."

"Too boring. But here, this is interesting." He lightly tapped the case, his fingerprint-less fingers not leaving a smudge. "What do you notice?"

"A pile of old gold." Then I frowned, peering closer. "That's a wolf marking. At least on that one coin."

"The rest are similarly marked, but the artful tumble of coins makes it hard to discern." He nodded. "And this tiara. A truly fine piece wouldn't you say? Austrian, as it happens."

I frowned at him, then squinted at the gold again. "The placard says it was found in a basement, original ownership unknown."

"Let's just say that I've long had a personal interest in beautiful things." He gestured to another case, filled with a gleaming panel of intricately worked gold and amber shaped into a cross. "These all came from the same location."

I frowned at the ornate Russian cross. "But they're different sellers."

"Shell houses. Though no one is questioning it, not

this year." Kreios nodded. "This year, buyers are less choosy. Many of these pieces are reworked bits of old gold and jewels that were never part of the original pieces."

"But reworked gold is less valuable."

"Correct, in most markets, if that was the gold's sole attribute. It's not. Not here. Not among these people, this year." He pointed back to the original pile of gold. "It's a werewolf, if that helps."

It didn't. I frowned, searching back in my memory banks for a reference to werewolf gold. When I came upon it, I blinked. "No."

"Indeed," Kreios said with satisfaction. "I'm surprised it hasn't happened sooner. There is a great deal of stolen gold stored away in the coffers of the very, very rich. Gold that is now getting sold in the face of an immediate need for other things that money can buy. Perhaps protection, perhaps technology. Either way, this is a prime example of that kind of sell-off. Someone is off-loading their Nazi hoard at the Rarity. Quickly and completely. And these collectors know it. The savvier ones anyway."

"But anyone could see this, anyone with knowledge of the missing artifacts. It's in the open—even the general public got an eyeful today."

"People see what they want to see, sometimes. And sometimes they see what they're expected to see."

I stared at him. "Armaeus?"

He smiled. "Not this time." Kreios waved his hand in front of the case again, and a queasy shift of vertigo hit me, the sense of the seeing double. When I looked again at the gold, it seemed almost the same. Almost, but not quite. There were no marks on it anymore, and the tiara appeared strangely...plainer. "What was that?"

"Techzilla, Inc. again. A very sophisticated system. Unfortunately, illusions are my stock-in-trade, and the system does not work on me. Regrettable, truly. It's the closest anyone has come to success. I very much hope to meet the owners of the company soon."

I blinked at him. "You don't know them?"

"They must reach out to us first. One of the many failings of the Arcana Council's policy of 'look but don't touch.' Any research into intellectual property must be at the hands of willing volunteers. Quite tedious, as you can imagine. If Socrates had agreed to meet with us sooner…" He glanced up. "Ah. Jarvis Fuggeren has arrived. We should pay our respects."

"Why? Did someone die?"

"He has a weakness for fine scotch and women. Especially women who taste of fine scotch."

In my hand, my champagne glass swirled with a dark amber liquid. "I hate it when you do that." I took a sip, allowing the scotch to burn its way down my throat. "Okay, I don't hate it completely, but I still don't approve."

"Your brain is the most sensitive organ in the body. Who's to say an illusion appearing powerfully real is not, in fact, real?"

"You really need to work on your pick-up lines."

We made our way toward Jarvis Fuggeren. It was no easy task, as he was clearly the man of the hour. He stood next to the display containing the gold scroll cases, smiling for the cameras, answering questions in a jovial, expansive way. Yes, this gold had been in his family for generations. Yes, he was looking forward to allowing a new owner to experience the joy of possessing it. No, he didn't need the money—but neither did he need the gold.

This earned him a large laugh, and most of the crowd moved on, the Rarity's hired videographers gathering B roll and setting up shots with the other sellers.

I took a moment to survey the scroll cases, unable to keep from tensing up, though their power had clearly been muted by whatever Techzilla had done to the tempered glass. Up close and without their full power, the artifacts were nondescript, a set of golden scroll cases carved with Egyptian symbols. Pretty, yes, but pretty in the way that most Egyptian tombs were. You got the feeling that the good stuff had probably been emptied out of the slender cylinders long ago, and all that was left was a memory of greatness past. Still, even I could sense the long-ago importance of the scroll cases, and there was no denying that they were beautiful representations of Egyptian art. Old Kingdom, unless I missed my guess, and I rarely missed my guess. It was part of what made me so good at my job.

In another life, perhaps I would have been a museum curator or an art historian. A life where I'd finished high school in person and not online. A life where I hadn't spent five years with a flock of retirement-age RVers crisscrossing the country, one KOA camp at a time. A life where I didn't keep looking over my shoulder, expecting bad guys who never came.

By the time we reached Fuggeren, the level of the scotch in my glass had dropped precipitously.

"Kreios! They told me you would be here." Fuggeren strode forward and embraced the Devil, then turned his attention to me. "And leave it to you to monopolize one of the most lovely women in the room. You are?"

He extended a hand to me, and I grasped it, surprised at the flutter of energy that passed between us. Jarvis Fuggeren was a Connected.

Not of the highest order, nothing like Kreios and Armaeus. But he was powerful on a level that seemed almost…metallic, and my nerves started to jangle. Enhanced on technoceuticals? Was this the aberration Danae was so against, or was I simply too strung out to "see" straight?

"Sara Wilde," Kreios helpfully supplied. Meanwhile, I blinked at Fuggeren, trying to process what I was feeling.

For his part, Fuggeren leaned forward and bussed a kiss along my cheek. Whether he smelled the scotch or was impressed by my sterling personality, he certainly seemed happier for it.

"It is my absolute pleasure to make your acquaintance, Ms. Wilde. I feel that I must know you from somewhere, but how can that be?"

Kreios interrupted smoothly. "Sara has been gracious enough to find a number of artifacts for me on occasion. Gold plates, some jewelry, a bowl of uncertain provenance."

"Not uncertain to you, I suspect." Fuggeren eyed Kreios keenly. "And what are you interested in buying here?"

The Devil shrugged. "There is much to recommend itself. I find the preponderance of Nazi gold interesting, don't you?"

"The…" Fuggeren turned to the cases and paused, considering. I manfully tried to not roll my eyes as the two of them strutted for each other. The music had picked up and was now slightly irritating. It wasn't any song I'd ever heard before, nor was it Muzak or classical, exactly. It seemed to run together and around itself, growing louder, then softening out, impossible to track but equally impossible to ignore.

I left Fuggeren and Kreios to their posturing and wandered down the long rows of cases. The collection truly was a fine example of historical art, from the crowns and gauntlets of medieval times, to more classic statuary. Gold was a soft metal, easily molded and melted, and some of the pieces showed the wear of time. Others, however were pristine, and one particular set held my fascination.

Crafted in a pale, almost white gold, multiple torques and bracelets glinted from one of the lesser-positioned glass boxes. The filigreed artwork covering it seemed less form than function. The intertwining branches of trees, horns, snakes, and dogs linking up to become clasps and hitches, hooks and eyes. It all shone up from a rich emerald velvet so deeply green it was almost black, and it was arguably the most beautiful set of artifacts in the room, for all that it was off the beaten path.

"Lovely, is it not?"

If the man's presence hadn't made my skin crawl already, his voice certainly would have done so, and I schooled myself not to stiffen. His laugh showed me I needn't have worried about proprieties.

"I see my reputation precedes me. How nice that we can celebrate such fine artwork like adults, however, regardless of our personal differences."

I turned to him. Grigori Mantorov exuded unctuous arrogance, but there was no denying his charisma. I held out my hand. "I don't believe we've met."

"We have not, Miss Wilde. But you may rest assured your reputation precedes you as well."

"Unwarranted, I'm sure." I flashed him a smile, but something niggled at the back of my brain. A warning, a flash of alertness. Mantorov placed his hand in mine for a moment, yielding two insights. Connected, check. Enhanced, not even slightly.

"Not so unwarranted as that," Mantorov said. He flashed teeth slightly crooked and yellowed, an anomaly in his otherwise immaculate presentation. "You and I often go after the same things. I happen to get them more frequently than you do, and in greater supply."

I knew he wasn't talking about the typical cargo I found for clients, but about the young Connecteds who I recovered from the hands of dark practitioners. "I don't understand why you get them at all."

"Which is why you will never be quite strong enough to stop me, isn't it?" Mantorov turned to the case. "Similar to the druids in the wake of the Roman invasion. Those men and women were powerful, mighty. There was no reason for them to fall to their southern assailants, yet fall they did. You want to know why?"

"Why do I suspect you're going to tell me?"

"An educated audience is refreshing, I must admit. Allow me to continue yours. The druids had many powers, many skills. Their oral tradition was rich with abilities that were lost not more than a generation later. So they could have spoken the words of power, could have turned the tide. But they were afraid. They were not willing to put themselves up as gods among men, a model Caesar had already ably demonstrated, that even the monarchs of old before him had done. The druids were in service to a humbler divinity, a nobler divinity, perhaps you could say, but one who commanded them to always follow, never lead. And thus they were doomed to fail."

He leaned closer. I could feel the darkness encroach against my psyche. "Just as you are doomed to fail, Sara. I may call you Sara, yes? It's what so many of the children do."

I moved so quickly that I didn't realize what I was doing at first, grabbing Mantorov's hand and bending his little finger back hard enough to break, but not quite. Bone crunched and the pain that shot across the bastard's face was invigorating.

"I'm thinking you're not so different from the druids after all," I said, releasing him and patting his lapel. "You won't win this one in the end."

He straightened his tie, a little paler, refusing to massage his abused digit. But his eyes had gone flat and black, pieces of coal. "I will, actually. I'll always be the one willing to say the words that must be spoken. You and those like you will not." He glanced to where Fuggeren and Kreios stood, arguing like frat boys. I didn't feel up to explaining that Kreios was nothing like me.

The music swelled again in a sharp crescendo, and a cry of pain sounded from across the room.

Annika Soo stood in the middle of a knot of well-dressed partygoers, but the sneering disdain had been wiped from her face. Instead, her hands were at her ears, her lips pale and bloodless. She was staring at me—no. She was staring at Mantorov.

"I am impressed, though." Mantorov was next to me again. "Your stamina is stronger than I would have given you credit for. The others have already left. Annika, well, she always had a thing for pain. It's one of her greatest attributes. And Jarvis is no more gifted than a potted plant, despite his enhancements. As for Kreios, it appears he is more collector than Connected, though that is a pity. I had such higher hopes for him.

A liveried staff member helped a now almost incoherent Soo out of the room. She didn't make it, swooning before she reached the door, caught by another attendant. I scanned the room again. Brody stood at the door, scowling at Soo, then Kreios. Then his gaze swung to me.

"Now, I think," Mantorov murmured beside me.

As if the music's soundtrack suddenly lost its balance, the haunting streams intensified, and something deep inside my brain simply—shattered. I clapped a hand over the base of my skull, pitching forward, while around the room a dozen cases exploded outward. The lights blanked out.

Suddenly, the unadulterated power of the scroll cases billowed out toward me again, sending me to my knees, then flat on the ground. Screams erupted immediately and emergency lights swept on, weirdly amber. I clutched my ears, my lungs compacting, my brain desperately trying to explode out of my skull.

Around me, running footsteps and rushing bodies devolved into a macabre dance. I managed to roll to the side, and glass shattered again around me, other cases giving way. Those were not the important ones I knew, however. Those were not the targets of Mantorov's attack.

The scroll cases were.

"Kreios—" I tried, but the words were stuck in my throat along with my breath, and it wasn't Kreios in front of me at all, but the worn dress trousers and sensible shoes of the man I knew too well, once upon a time. Too well and not at all.

"Sariah—Sara. For Chrissakes." Brody leaned down and half scooped, half hauled me upright, trying to steady me on my stiletto boots, and gradually my sight cleared and I could breathe again. "What the fuck just happened to you?"

The police were evacuating the room from the two entrances, and I stared around blearily. Kreios was gone. Mantorov was gone. Fuggeren stood over his case, his fury evident despite his pallor, his shaking hands, his gasping breath. No matter what Mantorov thought, there *was* ability with Jarvis Fuggeren, and that ability was crippling him now.

But the scroll cases were gone.

Not only the scroll cases either. Samplings of the other gold had been taken as well, the careful stacks knocked over like children's broken forts. Enough from each of the cases to seem like it was an equal opportunity theft, but anyone with eyes to see would know the truth.

Brody shook me. "Please tell me you had nothing to do with this."

He sounded disgusted with himself, and I realized once the shock and vertigo were wearing off that something else had changed too.

"The music," I said, blinking hard. There wasn't any smoke, but I would have sworn there had been smoke. Then again, a few moments ago, I would have sworn a lot of things. "The music shut off."

"Total momentary power outage—or surge, something," Brody explained. "The entire casino went dark for about five seconds when the glass exploded.

Security team from Techzilla is going apeshit, but the grid reported no hiccup. It simply —happened. But when the lights came back up, the music didn't. Good riddance, you ask me." He shook me again. "I'm going to ask you again—"

"I didn't have anything to do with this," I said, shrugging him off. "Where's Mantorov?"

"Everyone is being evacuated and searched, held downstairs for questioning. You took a while to wake up."

I scowled at him. "You don't really think he's going to wait around for that, do you? That any of them are?"

"No. But you are."

"I've got places to go."

"The hell you do," Brody growled. "Don't make me arrest you, Sara. I've been ready to do it since the first moment I saw you."

"Remain there, Miss Wilde. There is nothing gained in drawing suspicion. I'll collect you when you're done." The words soared through me, firm and assured, at once invigorating and exasperating.

The Magician.

You owe me, I thought, very clearly.

"In more ways than you can possibly know."

CHAPTER EIGHTEEN

It took me another four hours to be released from the careful ministrations of the LVMPD. Jarvis Fuggeren had been at the station the whole time, taut and furious, and though he hadn't said a word to me, he hadn't had to. His stare had spoken volumes.

He wanted his artifacts back. He knew that I could get them.

If I recovered his property intact, there would be a bunch of cash dropped on my head. If I didn't, I got the feeling it would be a piano.

He wasn't the only one glaring at me though. I could feel Brody's scowl through the Arcana limo windows as he watched me be driven away, but at this point, he could get in line.

Once I arrived at Prime Luxe, however, it wasn't to meet Armaeus alone. Instead, the entire Council as I now knew it had assembled for the Welcome Home party.

Armaeus stood at the head of the conference room table, his face shuttered of emotion, but fury boiling off him in a palpable mist. Kreios, next to him, swiveled in his chair to scan the room, enjoying the show. The Fool perched at the far end of the table, and when I glanced at him, he waved. Armaeus's gaze snapped to me, but the Magician didn't move otherwise. It was as if he was caught in a thrall of his own making, or he was listening to a self-help CD that no one else could hear. Based on what I was seeing, that wasn't working out too well.

Eshe sat to the left of the Magician, her eyes also on me. I couldn't figure her out. Over the last few times that I'd been her oracle, she'd vacillated from being obnoxious to impressed to concerned, then back to obnoxious again. Now she stared at me as if I were a bug, which, frankly, was Armaeus's job. I could only be the in-house curiosity to so many people at once.

But it was the final person at the table who held my attention the most. Roxie Meadows sat in a low-cut cocktail dress of vivid electric blue, her face serene, but her eyes as curious as Eshe's—and all for Armaeus. She seemed to revel in his distress.

"Great, you guys have a quorum. Does this mean you can vote in the next board or something?"

My words roused Armaeus from his reverie. "Events are moving more quickly now."

"Events *you* put in motion." I didn't bother to hide my anger. "You failed to mention that. Kind of defeats the whole nonintervention thing you've got going if you decide to *herd psychics* here to tempt SANCTUS into striking. Are they already here? Is that what's going on?"

I hadn't heard anything from Nikki or Dixie while I'd been at the police station. Then again, it was two in the morning. Presumably even SANCTUS had to sleep sometime.

"SANCTUS is not in the city," Armaeus said, his sharp tone cutting across my thoughts. "They're not the problem."

"Yet," Roxie's musical voice sounded, and everyone else at the table jolted. How long had it been since she'd sat in on their weekly PTA meeting? Quite a while, I would guess. Eshe's face turned sour, and I relaxed. A whiny Eshe made everything all right.

Still, Roxie continued. "There have been more Connecteds entering the city, including the creatures of the northern lands. The city is full to bursting, Armaeus. SANCTUS would be foolish to miss this opportunity."

"We will deal with SANCTUS in the proper time," Armaeus snapped. "Theirs is not the greatest threat. They've never been the end game. As you well know."

Not the greatest threat? "So who took the gold?"

"Not Soo," Kreios answered. "She was nearly admitted to a hospital by the time she exited the Grand. It was possibly an agent of Fuggeren's, though if so, he's playing the outraged seller to the hilt." He shrugged. "Most likely Mantorov. After going peacefully along with the police, he never made it to the rooms where the questioning took place, and currently he's unable to be found."

"He's vanished," the Fool put in, waggling his brows at me. "Even Armaeus can't track him. It's been a wonder to see."

"I have my suspicions," Armaeus said tersely.

"But we don't have time for suspicions." Eshe also regarded me, her perfectly arched brows raised. "We have time for Sara to do the work for which she has been uniquely prepared."

That sounded like the High Priestess I knew and despised. I relaxed further. "Good to see you too, Eshe. Glad you're still creeping around."

"Miss Wilde." Armaeus's voice rang out crisply, and I turned toward him. "Grigori Mantorov is a mortal. As such, he cannot be brought down directly by a Council member. To find him, we require your assistance." He pointed to a spot on the table, where a familiar stack of cards caught my eye. "Your cards can guide us, or, if you would prefer to work with Eshe—"

"Not going to happen." I pulled out a chair and sank into it, leaning forward to collect the deck. It was my third favorite deck, but it'd been the one lying out on the counter in my hotel room, so I wasn't surprised Armaeus had found it. And it was pretty, which I needed, the hues a watercolor wash of the traditional Rider-Waite deck, but softer and with fewer crazy eyes than the original depictions. I shuffled the cards, feeling a few more of my kinks relax. "You know, you guys could have pulled a few cards while I was waiting, if you were in that big a hurry."

"Magic is a conversation, and Connecteds are called that for a reason," Kreios supplied. "There is a…knowing when the Council acts out of turn. An imbalance."

"This whole noninterference-kinda-but-not-really modus operandi is getting a little old." I frowned. "What happens if you throw caution to the wind and interfere? Do you get a time-out?"

The chill that settled over the room caught me up short. I lifted my gaze to Armaeus. His return scowl was wintry. "Perhaps better stated than you realize, Miss Wilde. More to the point, if we weaken in our resolve, so too weaken the wards we have set in place to ensure the balance of magic."

"Oh, please." Roxie's interruption was startling in its bitterness. "Like you truly care about the wards."

"Tick tock," Simon put in. "Mantorov left via private airplane at twelve twenty-four a.m., its flight manifest patently bullshit. He's going somewhere, though, and at speed. We'd probably do well to get there first." He turned to me, his eyes shining. "Madame Reader?"

I blew out a long breath. Shuffling the cards, I felt the combined weight of their stares. In more than one way, this was ridiculous. Assembled in this room was the most powerful set of Connecteds I'd ever seen, yet they needed me to read their cards for them. Not because I was better at it either. These people were at such a high level that not even Mantorov's audio blast bothered them.

My hands working the cards, I shifted my gaze to Kreios and Simon. "What was up with the musical bit? Mantorov did that, right? Why couldn't you guys hear it?"

Kreios shrugged. "My hearing at certain frequencies was damaged by my recent encounter in Italy. I do not know when it will come back, if it will come back. I did not hear the changing musical fluctuation."

"I recorded it from another floor, but not on a live feed," Simon put in. "I was blocking it to focus on conversations." He shook his head. "The recording ate itself. I'm trying to recover that."

"Miss Wilde," Armaeus prompted. "Shouldn't you be focusing?"

Not really, but I knew it would make him feel better, so I bent to the deck, clearing my mind of everything but the Connected who'd stolen the scroll cases.

Grigori Mantorov. No matter why he specifically

wanted the cases, I knew they would eventually be pressed into service of a campaign that involved the kidnap and abuse of the youngest and most unprotected Connecteds. I needed to find the bastard for other reasons than the Council and their money. Speaking of which…

"You will be paid, Miss Wilde," Armaeus, as always, was one step ahead of me. "We do not have much time."

I spread the cards out in a fan. On the run, I could pull a given card or two from my pocket or bag, or even find the cards extant in the world around me—signs, symbols, tats, playing cards on the street. But here, under the eyes of the Council, I craved the solace of a traditional read.

That didn't mean it wouldn't be fast, however. Reaching out with my left hand, I selected three cards in quick succession, laying them face up on the table. The first card was the Six of Swords, the second the Chariot. The third Judgment.

"Travel over water, followed by travel over land, but there's more to this…" I leaned forward, my right hand snaking out to pull another card, positioning it over the Chariot. I'd known the truth of the card before I'd turned it over. "The Magician." I glanced up at him. "You know where he's going, Armaeus, even if you don't realize it." I ran the symbology of the Chariot through my mind. "And this card is interesting for another reason. It's the sphinx. Those scroll cases were originally Egyptian. So were you. Kind of a nice coincidence, I gotta say."

He nodded, but there was a resolution in his eyes that unnerved me. He'd already known the truth. He'd simply wanted someone to agree with him. "And

Judgment?"

I considered the card. "Resurrection from the dead, the horn of the angels, a blast of trumpets, the biblical apocalypse, could be anything. But in this case…" I reached for another card, but Armaeus's voice stopped me.

"It is enough, Miss Wilde. I know where he's gone."

Everyone turned to him, allowing me to palm the final card and drop it to my lap. It wasn't that I was trying to be sneaky, but a card once drawn needed to be seen and understood. No matter if the Magician himself was speaking.

Armaeus hit a button, and beneath my cards—the whole length of the table in fact—the surface switched to a screen. The Fool knelt on his chair, leaning over in fascination as the map coalesced. I gathered the rest of the cards out of the way, keeping them separate from the final card in my lap. I needed to read it, but I needed to see this too.

"It is an ancient city in middle Egypt, or what's left of it," Armaeus said. "Now called El Ashmunein, it's known best as Hermopolis. Its ancient Egyptian name was Khemenu. The town that is left there is unremarkable."

"What, no temple?" I glanced up at him. Though I knew enough to get around, Ancient Egypt wasn't my thing. Wasn't his either, technically, but he'd lived there a lot closer to "ancient" than I had. "No museum? Where is he going?"

Armaeus shook his head. "There is nothing like that. Some excavated ruins, little more. At one point, of course, the Temple of Thoth in Hermopolis was considered one of the most powerful centers of worship in the Old Kingdom. Scholars would pore over ancient texts and create careful and exact oral translations of histories, all to celebrate the deity Thoth and his gift of language to the world. It was believed by many that the texts of the great library of Alexandria were merely the newest incarnation of works first held within the walls of the Temple of Thoth."

"Okayy..." I frowned at him. "And nothing remains of that temple today? Not even underground?"

He shrugged. "The temples were tragically destroyed during the Napoleonic wars."

Something in his voice pinged my Spidey sense. "Tragically."

He met my gaze. "And completely."

I looked around the room. Unlike in Armaeus's private abode, the walls of the Arcana Council conference room were *not* covered in cases containing priceless antiques and artifacts, also lost in antiquity. Or, at least, lost to a significant portion of society. "So sad that the library of Alexandria has bitten the dust too," I commented. "That leaves none of the ancient texts available for mortals to study."

"We have all suffered much through the march of time."

"We should go. We have to go." The Fool sprang from his chair, pacing the room as the plans for our departure consumed him. "There will be electronic signatures with those scroll cases. There have to be. If he's taking them to Hermopolis, then he thinks something will be triggered. Something *could* be triggered, with the right frequency. Makes sense. Thoth, god of language, scroll cases containing a script or actual parchment within that has a heretofore-untold language. It fits, it fits." He stopped and glared at us as if confused why we weren't moving. "We have to go."

I glanced down to my lap. Against the hemline of my leather skirt, the card gleamed up at me. The picture of a man striding into the darkness of an early morning, the cups of his past resting on the windowsill, symbolizing everything he was leaving behind. Not a happy card, not necessarily a positive card, but a card that was clear and obvious no matter where it landed in the reading. I held it up for the Arcana Council, then dropped it on the table. The Eight of Cups.

"He's right," I sighed as they studied it, feeling the ineffable pull of sadness the card always evoked in me. "What's past is past and done. We have to go."

"And I'm in, nonnegotiable," the Fool said immediately. He stared belligerently at us. "Kreios is currently deaf as a doorpost at higher magical frequencies, and he gets to go everywhere. Besides, I can track the electronic signatures of the scroll cases."

"Fine, I could use the help," I said. The fatigue was washing away from me, the same way it always did before an assignment. I turned to Roxie. "Dixie said you were her mentor, sort of a Welcome Wagon—before you joined the Council anyway."

She eyed me. "I was."

"Well, the Connected community in Vegas needs you again. Watch over them. I don't like the idea of SANCTUS loose in the city."

"Your worry is misplaced," Armaeus said. "The Rarity will continue, which is where SANCTUS's focus will remain for the time being. No one knew precisely what was to be shown, except for the scant few who got in today. Most of it remains." He paused. "I do not anticipate any action until solstice. That is when the full contingent of Connecteds will be in Vegas, and the Rarity will be in its closing hours. It is the perfect day for them to strike."

I nodded. "Well, great, but that doesn't give us much time. You keep me posted too, while we're gone."

"That won't be necessary," Armaeus said. "I'm coming with you."

"What?" Everyone in the room stopped and stared. Armaeus stood at the front of the room, his face eerie in its composure.

"The actions of the dark practitioners have been a thorn in the side of the Council for generations, Miss Wilde. Though they have not known it, their efforts to deepen and darken the world of magic, the creation of technoceuticals, and the development of practices involving the sale and trade of Connecteds for service and body parts have created an imbalance. An imbalance which we have sought to remedy as organically as possible. But it has been a war of attrition, and there is no question who is losing." He shifted his gaze to me. "There are simply not enough Father Jeromes and Sara Wildes in the world to counteract Mantorov or his ilk. And with the rise of SANCTUS, it has created even more of an imbalance."

I squinted at him, remembering Danae the witch's words, blaming the dark practitioners for the spread of technoceuticals—but not them alone. Could SANCTUS be involved as well?

Armaeus continued, inexorably. "This new situation is different. Before this past month, I did not know these scroll cases still existed. Before this week, I did not know that hands were moving in the market to force our more immediate action, an action which we have, perhaps, resisted too long. "

I let him spool on, but I held on to the word that struck me most out of his little speech.

Still.

He didn't know that the scroll cases were *still* in existence. Which meant he'd thought they were destroyed. Which further meant, based on his earlier comments about the Temple of Thoth, that he might very well have been the one who'd attempted to destroy them.

"What exactly are in these scroll cases, Armaeus?" I asked. "Why does it matter who has them and where?"

He turned to me. "The scroll cases, in and of themselves, are unimportant. Based on the images that Simon sent me, however, the ancient inscriptions on the side are not warnings not to partake of what is within. On the contrary, they are invitations. Not all gods in the faiths of this world believed that knowledge belonged solely in the realm of the deities. The monarchs and their advisors needed that knowledge as well, to rule their people." He waved a hand as if to include everyone outside the room. "To rule all people."

"And…the recipe for that knowledge is what's left in the scroll cases? Sort of an Evil Empire 101?"

"Not exactly." Armaeus's smile was thin. "For explanation, look no further than the ancient texts, starting with the Bible. 'And God said, let there be light.' Everyone focuses on the last part, never on the first."

"'And God said'?"

He nodded. "What resides—potentially—in the scroll cases is the language of the Highest Power ever to affect the world and all who reside in it. It is the language that brought the world into creation. The language that could bring it to its end." He tapped the table, displaying the ancient city of Hermopolis in high relief. "And the key to that language lies here. Grigori Mantorov is going to my home, Miss Wilde. I grew up amid the ruins of the Temple of Thoth, and I witnessed its final destruction. Whether he knows it or not, he has brought this conflict to my very door. And in such a way that I cannot ignore it."

"Bring on the cavalry," Simon said, slapping his hands together.

But Armaeus merely stared at me. "The Council has long allowed the affairs of man to cull the strength of magic. That is how it has been, and that's how it shall be, once this crisis has passed. For the moment, however, a different course must be taken. We must reclaim the balance between the dark and light, ignorance and knowledge, death and life. And we must do that while preserving the wards that have kept this Earth safe from an even greater threat for millennia." His gaze intensified. "It appears we'll be working together on this assignment, Miss Wilde. I trust that won't be a problem?"

"Oh, geez, not at all." I spread my hands. "I mean, hey, at least this time if a Connected dies in the line of fire, she'll have signed up for it, versus having been herded blindly to her doom. That's progress right there."

CHAPTER NINETEEN

There's no easy way to get to El Ashmunein, aka Hermopolis, aka the ancient Egyptian town of Khemenu. We flew into Hurghada Airport, south of Cairo, where we boarded another much smaller plane to avoid the five-plus-hour trip by car. I'd slept for as much as one body could possibly sleep without being in a coma, but though I was completely rested, my head still carried the residue of astral travel pain. I saw no reason to open my eyes while we angled down to the patch of dirt that apparently would serve as our landing strip.

Across the cabin, Armaeus watched me. He knew I was awake, and he knew that I knew that he knew. Things were starting off well for our first joint assignment.

"How long has it been since you've traveled to ol' Hermopolis?" I asked without opening my eyes. I liked talking to Armaeus this way. Much safer.

"I prefer the name Khemenu, named after the eight gods it honored. And not for many years." Which, with Armaeus, could mean a couple of centuries, but I let that go. "There is nothing left on the ground that will help us, if that's what you're asking. What wars have not torn down, the city's government has. They say it is for building materials or religious reasons or whatever other excuse governments use to destroy the past in order to build up the present."

That did cause me to open one eye. A smile flickered over Armaeus's face, quick and hard. "So if there's nothing left, what are we looking for?" I asked. "I don't recall there being any tombs opened up in this neck of the woods recently."

He shook his head. "Khemenu was not a city of death to the ancient Egyptians. It was one of birth. One of their principal creation myths was centered here. I believe Mantorov is heading here, in part, because of that myth."

I straightened in my chair, coming more fully back online. At the far end of the cabin, Simon snored lightly in his own chair, cradling his laptop.

"Creation how? What was their take on it?"

"Like many of the first civilizations, Egyptians believed in the concept of a family of gods that existed before the dawn of Earth and man. The Ogdoad was a system of eight deities, dual entities consisting of four pairs of gods and their consorts."

"Okay, makes sense." In the Tarot, four was the most stable of the Minor Arcana cards, so it wasn't surprising that the number showed up in a foundational creation myth. "Male-female aspects of the same element or whatever?"

Armaeus nodded. "Nun and Naunet ruled the element of primeval waters; Heh and Hauhet held sway over eternity; Kuk and Kauket were the deities over darkness; and Amun and Amaunet represented air, or that which is hidden. Of the four sets, Amun alone went on to have a role beyond the original

Ogdoad." He smiled. "According to the myth, these eight deities—water, eternity, darkness, and air—interacted, creating an enormous explosion. That burst of energy was released at a mound in Khemenu, originally called the Isle of Flame, causing it to rise from the water. At that point, the sun was born. There are conflicting stories about how, but one of the most popular was that a cosmic egg was created by the gods of the Ogdoad. When it opened, it revealed the 'bird of light,' an aspect of the sun god Re, who went on to create the world and everything in it."

"Fair enough. But there's nothing left of the buildings or this mound? No statues or obelisks or anything to point the way?"

He shook his head. "There are statues, of course. The city became an important center of worship of Thoth, and statues in his honor remain." He twisted his lips. "You can view them easily from the Christian basilica erected near the site of the old temple."

"Okay..." I thought more about it. "Water, eternity, darkness, air. Which all got together one day and combined to make an enormous explosion, resulting in an island of fire to add to the mix. So, water, fire, air, darkness, and, um...ternity." I scowled at him. "Do not make me utter the phrase 'The Fifth Element' twice. I'm not strong enough."

"All the elements necessary for a new birth—except one. The words to make it so."

"'And God said...'"

He nodded. "But Mantorov has the words now, or thinks he does. He merely has to locate the right place in Khemenu where the energies aligned once before, and say the words."

"Somewhere on the Nile, has to be."

"In a manner of speaking." He tilted his head. "How are you feeling?"

I instantly tensed. Having Simon along for the ride had proven to be the perfect chaperone for this trip, but the moment Armaeus's attention sharpened on me, my body responded. His touch was truly like a drug. A really good drug, with generally pleasant side effects so far. Except for that unfortunate total mind-numbing dependence part. Other than that, pleasant. "I'm pretty good."

He sighed. "Why do you resist me? I have been honest with you."

I almost barked the laugh. "You've not been remotely honest, but thanks for playing." I waved around the cabin. "This little excursion is the closest I've seen you get to an honest reaction since we've met."

He lifted his brows. "Do you believe so?"

"Tough to fake being pissed."

"And because I am not angry with you at this moment, you immediately mistrust what I say or do."

"I don't know what you are with me." I leaned forward in my chair. "You're my employer. We have a connection which you're happy to exploit, and I'm happy to let you. But the fact that you're able to put me back together again doesn't take away the fact that you're also able to take me apart. Don't think I'm not aware of that." I waved my hand around my head, as if warding off a fly. "And stop with the mental pressure thing, Armaeus. I already have a headache. There's no room for you in my brain."

He stared at me, exasperation creeping into his gaze. He leaned forward too, and I shifted back, trying to keep an exactly perfect distance between us.

Simon breathed out a deep, contented sigh. "I so love it when you two fight. It makes it feel like home."

Armaeus didn't move, didn't acknowledge Simon. "I won't assault you, Miss Wilde. That would void our arrangement, and I have no interest in doing that. However, I need you to be at your sharpest for what is to come." He grimaced. "To achieve that, I need more cooperation than you have been willing to give."

"Yeah, no." Still, there was no denying the pain rocketing through my brain. "I'll settle for slightly less agony, and slightly more sharpness, if you can do that while keeping your shorts on."

He didn't give me a chance to change my mind.

Moving quickly, he closed the last bit of space between us and reached his hand to my face, cupping my cheek and jaw. When I naturally shifted my head away out of some innate sense of self-preservation, his other hand came up, trapping me.

Light exploded inside my skull. My gaze was transfixed by the golden intensity of his eyes and my ears registered that he was speaking words, words I should follow, words I should track. But all I could see was the burst of light that seared through my brain and lifted me off my chair on a wave of electrical jolts that seemed likely to catch my hair on fire. Something caught my attention, and I dropped my gaze to his lips, lips that were still moving. Soft, sensual, incredible lips. They had roamed my mouth, my face, my body before, drawing a line of fire over and around and through me. And now they were whispering to parts of my inner self that typically didn't get a chance to chat back. Even my ankles practically vibrated with sensual promise, my entire body jacked up on a live wire of energy and want and—

He pulled his hands away.

I slumped in my chair, gasping. The Fool did too.

"Please tell me you're going to do that to me next," Simon breathed.

Armaeus ignored him, straightening. "The trip to the temple will be a short one. It's currently a barren wasteland, but beneath it—deep beneath it—flow the waters we seek."

"What, the Nile?" My voice wasn't working quite perfectly, and I tried again. "That seems a fair distance away from the temple ruins, based on the map I saw."

"The isle of fire erupted out of the water, but water was essential to the creation of it. The Nile is not a river that prefers to stay in its banks, and that was yet truer in the time of Ancient Egypt."

"Meaning?"

But Armaeus didn't seem to be listening to me. "Water is the source of all life in Egypt. It is the source of creation. It moves, and creation moves. It is not a fixed point. Regardless of where the river now flows, what we are more interested in is where it flowed during the time of the Old Kingdom and what aquifers it fed. "

I couldn't shake the idea that Armaeus was talking in a deeper, more resonant tone the closer we got to Khemenu, and I wasn't sure if that was a good or a bad thing. Bad, I suspected.

I drew in an experimental breath. There was no pain anymore, anywhere in my body. It had been replaced with an almost maddening electrical hum.

My gaze found Armaeus's again. "You did something to me that went beyond Excedrin Migraine, didn't you?"

"Do you feel better?"

Panic fluttered. How much had he seen? How deep had his touch gone? "I don't know how I feel."

"Are you in pain?"

"No."

"Then that's better, wouldn't you say?"

"I'm still waiting for my blast of mojo over here." Simon's voice was petulant, but it served to pierce the tension building between Armaeus and me.

The Magician regarded the Fool with amusement. "Simon's powers extend well beyond what he would have you believe. And," he said meaningfully, "he is not in any pain."

The Fool groaned. "So you all keep telling me. But so far all I can incarnate is mad code and naked teleporting." He sighed. "Not that there's anything wrong with that." He stood and stretched, then ambled off, muttering about the unfairness of it all.

"*Can* you do that to him too? That energy jolt?"

"I could, but it would not be necessary." Armaeus shook his head. "He doesn't need more electricity flowing through his veins. When he took on his role of Fool, he became pure energy. He recognizes the exchange in others, desires it the way that like appeals to like, but he doesn't need to expand his own current."

"So he's a mini Electro?" I let my gaze wander to where Simon had left his laptop. "No wonder he goes through so many computers."

"Where he fails is in recognizing the most profound of his gifts," Armaeus continued. "The Fool whispers in the ear of others, suggests the unthinkable, prompts the unexpected leap of faith. He is not meant to *do*, he is meant to compel others to do."

"Yeah, well maybe he enjoys being more hands-on."

"Like this?" He reached out and drifted a hand over my shoulder. Every nerve in my body leapt, as if aligning to a lightning rod. I was drawn instantly alert, short of breath, my heart pounding, my brain fully engaged.

"Stop it!" I twisted away. "That so has to be cheating."

"Not at all, Miss Wilde. I am not trying to provoke you. I am trying to prepare you. Your pain levels have exceeded my expectations, but by your own decision I cannot fully heal you. I work in a particular way, I apologize if that is not to your liking."

"There are so, so many things not to my liking, Armaeus. We don't have time to discuss them all. If you'd like, I can send you a bulleted list."

The Magician might not have been able to read my mind, but he wasn't an idiot. He knew I was outraged at what he'd done to the Connecteds. Unfortunately, he probably also knew I craved his touch like a choking man craves air. Because as Simon ambled back to his seat, his eyes on his cell phone, all Armaeus did was smile.

CHAPTER TWENTY

The ruins of the ancient city of Khemenu were not impressive.

As Armaeus had warned, the Temple of Thoth seemed to have been taken apart piece by piece, the good bits carted away while the remains were jumbled back together to give the approximation of what had come before. We'd moved on quickly from the large, quirky baboon statues of Thoth, Armaeus barely giving them a glance, and now stood in the center of…a whole lot of nothing.

More importantly, we were completely alone.

It was four a.m. local time. Clearly, no one was worried about whether or not we'd take another rock from the ancient burial site. But Mantorov wasn't here either, and that was more of the problem. Because no way did we beat him to Egypt, no matter how fast the Fool had pushed us. He'd had a several-hour head start.

Worse, Armaeus was acting exceptionally strange. Since we'd landed, he'd gone quiet, giving instructions to the local man hired to drive us to our destination in soft, unhurried words. He'd watched the bleak, dark city roll by, illuminated at very occasional turns. The place looked downtrodden despite being nestled in the fertile plains of the Nile. But while trees grew all around this space, the hill of dirt we were currently standing on was nothing but fine sand and rock dust. And still Armaeus stared, as if he was soaking in the awesome that was…dirt.

My hands twitched. "You want me to check my cards again? Now that we're here, we might have more clarification of the finer points on where to find Mantorov."

"He's here." Armaeus hunkered down to the ground, reaching out to pick up the shifting sands. He scattered the pile at his feet, watching as it got caught in the stiff morning breeze. "It's always been here, the power to create. And he has the key." He turned to Simon. "Are you ready?"

"There's not an electrical conductor within a million miles of this place," Simon grumbled, but he set his phone on the ground. And tapped another button. The device vibrated, then narrow pinpoints of light exploded from it, hued a ghostly green.

The luminous rays shot around the space in a building block of squares, an elaborate wireframe. For a moment, we all stared. Before us stood the fabled Temple of Thoth, in full reconstructed glory. Green walls shimmered in neon splendor. Enormous bird-headed statues stared out from its roofline.

Armaeus's gaze dropped to the doorway, set up high on the steps but off to the right from where it was expected dead center. He took several steps to align himself with it, then nodded.

The wireframe winked out. Simon was at his side, another device in his hand. "The charge is nonexistent here. Barely enough to register on the equipment."

"He found it. So will we."

"I don't know how," Simon shook his head, squinting across the bleak landscape. "There's no excavation here. Nothing but rocks and dust."

I scowled at the basilica and the outbuildings. "Maybe go down the well?" I gestured to the large cistern tip edging up out of the ground. "Gotta be deep enough."

"No." Armaeus walked forward, his hand outstretched seemingly to read the very earth. When he'd walked about twenty paces, he knelt. "This was the temple of my youth. The earth was good and plentiful, and the Nile gives birth to all things." He unhooked his water bottle and emptied it over the sand.

A stain spread. Slowly at first, then faster, fuller, with the earth soaking up more water than could possibly have come out of his bottle. Armaeus's lips were moving, and it was as if he could coax the ground to do his bidding. Then again, he probably could. These were his stomping grounds.

The sand gave way, rushing into the hole in the earth as stairs slowly emerged. Without waiting for the dirt to clear, Armaeus headed down.

Simon and I gaped at each other. "You think that hole is going to fill itself back in when we go down there?"

He stowed his device in his pocket and unhooked a flashlight. "I think it'll almost have to. Which is going to make getting out interesting, but hey, that's why we stick close to the big guy." Then he hopped down too.

I had no choice but to follow.

Fortunately, it was easy to keep close to Simon. Sand and dirt immediately flowed over us, pushing us down, so that by the time we reached Armaeus, we were practically jogging. The Magician half turned back to us and murmured another word. The flow of debris stopped, immediately coalescing into a wall of solid rock.

"Nice," Simon wheezed. I wrapped my headscarf around my face, trying to breath in filtered air. "Where are we?"

"Exactly where you should be, I should say."

The gun pressed into my neck was a shockingly cool sensation, but I choked anyway, freezing in surprise. Simon had a similar gun at his head, while the Magician remained in front of us, still and silent, though he'd turned back to face Simon and me. It took me a bare moment to realize why Armaeus wasn't moving, as flashlights flared on around us.

He'd been shot. And not by bullets, either. Four silver arrows were buried in his chest and torso, piercing the Magician in an eerily uniform pattern.

The men who'd loosed those arrows now stood with their bows discarded, automatic rifles apparently good enough for the rest of us.

But…why had they used arrows in the first place on the Magician, not bullets? And why was Armaeus so…frozen? Though blood gushed down the front of his shirt, his face was strangely serene. Granted, Armaeus wasn't much on showing his cards. Generally the more impassive he appeared, the closer he was to spontaneously combusting. Given his current state of Zen-like calm, we were due for a cataclysm of epic proportions any moment now.

And yet, he didn't move. He didn't speak. He only sort of…gasped.

Shallowly.

I forced myself to stare harder at him, though the sight of all that blood was impossibly wrong. Those were big arrows, two of them piercing his chest just inside his shoulders, two of them apparently shot through his kidneys. Armaeus was the Magician. He was immortal. But he could still be killed.

Fear unfurled inside me like a sickness.

"Good thing I had sentinels." Grigori Mantorov tsked, and then I saw the two men crumpled on the ground in front of Armaeus, clearly locals, the blood from their wounds already dried. "They warned me that you would be coming, and I confess I greatly anticipated this moment. I always did think there was someone else behind Kreios, bankrolling him. I simply never expected it to be a true servant of Thoth."

"I serve no one," Armaeus said. Even his words were too quiet. Too still.

"Oh, so you do speak. Excellent." Mantorov nodded to one of the men, and a frequency filled the air, causing my bones to vibrate. So did the arrows embedded in Armaeus's flesh. He scowled, his jaw clenched against the pain. "I need you to focus, though, dark priest. That is the purpose for this particular mix of base metals in these arrow points. As you are slowly bleeding out, you will remain stable. And I need you to translate for me."

"No."

"I don't, importantly, need you to be alive to do it. Your voice will still work as long as one of the arrows remain inside you. The Egyptians truly were onto something with their death rituals."

We were marched forward toward a bright rectangular opening at the far end of the room. I watched the dark pools spread across Armaeus's back.

He had to have known this was coming, right? The man read minds. He had to have known.

Mantorov pushed on. "Speak the words you were born to speak, then you may die in peace and comfort." He snapped another command at his men, and they lit four torches at each corner of the room, then doused their flashlights. As steady beams were replaced by flickering torchlight, we saw the ancient underground chamber of the Temple of Thoth the way it was meant to be viewed.

I stared all around me. The room was walled in gold. The burnished panels gleamed in the incandescent light. At the center of the room, a large table stood. On it were the scroll cases, still closed. I should have been glad that I could get this close without the cases leveling me. I could sense the wards Mantorov had wrought to protect us, like layers of heavy air. The man knew his magic and wielded it well. But something else nagged deep in my brain, where Armaeus's explanation lingered.

The original creation myth he had recited was born out of darkness, water, air, and eternity, he'd said. We were in an underground chamber, so yes, there was darkness, but very little air and no water. This setup didn't seem quite right for the creation myth. What would that mean?

"Speak."

Armaeus was pushed forward to the table, Mantorov reaching out to bear down on the edge of one of the arrowheads. Sweat dripped from Armaeus's face as he grimaced in pain. I'd never seen him so taxed, the veneer of his cool civility completely wiped away. It was as if he was submitting, purifying himself in the fires of his own destruction.

A bead of his sweat dropped onto the table, and I blinked. *Water.*

"Open them." Armaeus finally said, but his voice wasn't the rasp I was expecting. Instead, it resonated through the space around us with primal force. He was wounded, yes. But he wasn't quite dead.

Mantorov was no fool, however. "Open them yourself." He nodded to one of his men, and the man pushed the scroll cases toward Armaeus with gloved hands. Amped as I was, I vibrated with the electrical jolt when the Magician touched the cases. Simon, with his wellspring of kinetic power, felt it too. Mantorov straightened, but the other men around Armaeus didn't flinch.

Armaeus stretched his fingers over the hieroglyphs, so similar to the ancient markings of the Egyptians but fundamentally different to my eye, older, richer. I thought about the coinage I'd seen in the Devil's antique shop, how it had also looked similar to and yet different from so many different things. *Atlantis,* Kreios had said. Could that be possible?

I glanced around the underground cavern of gold, and decided…sure it could.

Armaeus spoke. The chanting rhythm of his words was heavy and hypnotic, but it didn't mask the sound that grew up from beneath him, a rumble of heavy earth.

No, not earth. Water. Small holes spat water from the corners of the room, and water leaked forth. First in a slow trickle, then stronger, until tiny streams began to slither across the room. *Sweet Christmas, not another freaking flood.*

Mantorov stepped forward and yanked one of the arrows out of the Magician. Blood sprayed, making my stomach pitch.

"Faster. I don't plan on drowning down here while you gasp and mumble."

Armaeus bowed his head and focused on the scroll case in his hand once more. But his energy had become erratic, unmoored. Four arrows, not three, were needed to ground Armaeus. Had Mantorov known? Had he deliberately destabilized Armaeus, or had he simply wanted to cause him pain?

At that moment, the first scroll case opened. Wind rushed through the cavern, putting out the torches—until nothing but darkness remained. Darkness and water and air. All that was left was eternity. From Armaeus's grunt of pain, I realized Mantorov must have yanked another arrow out of him. He stumbled forward, and I realized what was happening here. *Eternity.* The breaking of eternity was needed for the spell to work, and how better to evoke that eternal element than killing a man who should not die?

Flashlights flared on again, all of them trained on Armaeus.

"Heard rumors of this, of you," Mantorov said, eyeing him gleefully as the second, then third case snapped open. "Kreios was impure, his powers as dark and redolent with corruption as mine. He would be no good sacrifice to the gods. But you—you were their *servant.* Your immortality was a gift granted from them, not some elixir you forced down in the center of a screaming mob. *You* are a worthy sacrifice for me to make."

He shoved the Magician down until Armaeus's head was bowed over the final, smallest scroll case. "Open it!"

Armaeus's hands spasmed on the scroll case, and it

broke open.

A burst of roiling flame shattered the darkness, and all the creatures of Hell screamed forth.

Taking advantage of fiery chaos, I turned to the man beside me, who stood stupefied with shock at what he was seeing and hearing. I drew my hand back in a tight fist. The sound of my punch landing squarely on his jaw barely registered in the howling wind, but was far more gratifying than I'd hoped. Flames and sparks of electricity shot round and round the golden room. I vibrated with it, but Simon practically glowed. He turned to the man holding him and grabbed him by the throat. The redolent smell of burned flesh flashed through the air.

Armaeus and Mantorov still stood at the table. I dispatched a second guard, then turned, expecting Armaeus to be swept up in some kind of holy terror. But he wasn't. He was staring at Mantorov as if he'd seen a ghost. No, not *at* Mantorov… Through him.

My gaze leapt to the wall beyond the Russian, who now stood transfixed, his eyes wide, his lips peeled back. And the wall…moved. Cracks of light arced out from its surface, the very stones on the verge of evaporating.

An unearthly whisper shuddered forth, filling the space.

"You cannot hold me forever," it rasped, speaking through Mantorov's mouth. *"You cannot guard every portal back into the light. There are too many of them, Magician, and you are too few."*

"We will hold the line." Armaeus's voice had also changed—it was deeper, fuller. I turned at a sudden move to my right, then tackled a man fleeing down the room toward a far door—good to know, since that was probably the exit out of this hellhole—and worked his gun free. Except when I swung it back around, I didn't know where to aim. Mantorov was in the middle of some kind of epileptic fit, and Armaeus was...well, disintegrating.

"Eternity..." breathed the voice, but it no longer spoke through Mantorov. It came directly through the wall. *"It takes on a whole new meaning when you face it, doesn't it? You are weakening, Armaeus. Your strength ebbing away."*

The wall bowed outward from fine slits carved into the gold, and Simon cursed, his electricity going dormant while more burned skin filled the air with acrid fumes.

"Finish the spell, Magician!" Mantorov struggled upright again, regaining his capacity for speech. He wheeled toward Armaeus. "You cannot stop now!"

"It is no longer the time of creation." Armaeus closed his hands around the scroll cases. "You are forbidden!"

I could see light crackling through the bones on his skin and I stared, horrified. Armaeus swelled and seemed to come apart at the joints, pure light cascading from him as he worked to process the full weight of the magic he was wielding. Panic seared through me and I staggered forward, struggling to see whatever was coming through the wall.

And then I did.

Terror stilled the scream in my throat. In that moment, I was no longer in the subterranean chamber of gold. I was in my backyard, the wall of fire and pain behind me. And I was running, running, my eyes streaming with tears, my vision blurred, unable to escape the fire. It raged around me, and as I stared, a creature reared in the far distance. A blue dragon trapped on a field of red. Its wings spread wide and—

"No!" I cried before I fully realized what I was doing, and emptied a round of firepower into Mantorov's body. He jerked with the blast, toppling toward the cracking wall. For a moment, he gazed at me with all-consuming shock in his face, and then his expression morphed to fury as the man who'd stolen so many children had something stolen from him. Something he also could not get back, no matter how he tried.

"I cannot die!" he roared. "I cannot!"

"The hell you can't!"

"*Nigin!*" Armaeus's command overrode all the noise. The wall seemed to draw back into itself, sweeping Mantorov with it in a burst of white-hot fire. The scream of the dragon was the last thing I heard—and only then did I notice another, closer roar.

"Not this again," I groaned.

Water crashed onto us from all sides, swamping the room. Simon, closest to the door, was carried out in the initial burst before he started running of his own volition, screaming about stairs. Let no one ever say Simon wasn't smart.

"Go," Armaeus cried, half collapsing on the table in the center of the room. "Follow Simon."

"You first!" I waded toward him until I stood next to him in front of the smoking scroll cases. "Or I won't."

The Magician cursed something in an ancient language I couldn't make out, but when he turned toward the door, I swept the scroll cases into my jacket. I wasn't coming halfway across the blasted world to watch people freaking *disintegrate*, and have nothing to show for it. Those scroll cases contained answers. Answers I was more than ready to learn.

The water flowed at a higher intensity, pounding from the walls. I splashed the final few feet toward the door, turning around one last time to scan the room. Mantorov really was gone, I realized. The portal had swallowed him whole.

But something else was in the chamber that I hadn't seen before, something etched into the wall in sharp relief. I stopped and stared, despite the rising waters.

A dragon…with its wings spread wide.

"Miss Wilde."

Armaeus 's voice had the effect of a compulsion, and I turned around, suddenly aware the water was up to my thighs. This made running problematic, but the stairs beyond the far door beckoned, and I bent forward, racing for the exit.

CHAPTER TWENTY-ONE

We ended up at the bottom of the basilica's well. Sounds of continued destruction echoed through the passages.

"Can't you teleport or something?" I muttered, angling my flashlight up. "Or maybe call upon the Power of Grayskull at least, for some heat? I'm freezing my brains off here."

"I've summoned assistance." Armaeus leaned against the wall, his pallor evident in the dim glow.

"And I've had enough fire for one day, thanks," Simon's voice echoed from the far side of the shaft. He was shaking out his electronics, a fruitless task given the fact we were surrounded by fifteen feet of water. "I've had pieces of my body fried that are specifically designated fire-safety zones. You could have warned me, Armaeus."

"You had yet to tap your abilities sufficiently. It's good for you to start practicing." Armaeus's voice held a breathiness I recognized all too clearly, having extensive experience with getting my ass kicked. The guy was feeling his age. And probably those four arrow holes.

Simon groaned. "Well, it's not good for me to lose

data. I couldn't recreate that temple grid if I tried."

Armaeus stayed silent, and I eyed him, trying to gauge how much blood he'd lost. Not to mention the whole disintegration thing after he'd opened up the scroll cases.

Cases that he'd then pretty much left for dead. "So what was the deal back there? I thought you wanted to *preserve* magic in the world."

He winced, shifting against the rock wall. "Preserve the balance. Dark to light. Destruction, of course, is not generally the Council's stock-in-trade. When one element of magic grows to excess, however, the other must be bolstered. We can usually count on civil or religious conflict to destroy. But even when that destruction happens by accident, it is not our place to stop it."

"So you planned on leaving those cases behind?"

His smile twisted. "You have them, don't you?"

I shifted. "Well, yeah."

"So clearly I did not." Ignoring my scoff, he continued. "But your concerns are unfounded, Miss Wilde. There will always be magic in the world. It cannot be completely destroyed—ever." Armaeus shook his head as the great stone lid of the cistern above us moved with a loud scrape. "Magic is not contained in an object or a person. It is merely reinforced or channeled. Just as the waters of the deepest Earth transform into the crystal clouds of the atmosphere and return again as rain, it constantly transforms and regenerates. An endless cycle."

There was something important here, I knew it. Something I didn't want to miss. "So once magic is in the world...pure magic, or a pure magical entity...nothing can take it out?"

He hesitated. "Not without great cause. And great sacrifice."

"Which is not exactly a 'no.'"

A resounding scrape sounded above us, and hushed voices floated down. No one called out on either side, though, as a rope dropped into the dark space. I flicked the light up again, long enough to ascertain that no guns were being leveled at us. So far, so good. "Simon, you go first," Armaeus said, pushing the rope to him. "Can you secure the devices?"

"For all the good it will do us." Simon reached for the rope and pulled himself out of the water, wrapping his fists in the thick nylon as it was pulled taut. He swung toward the wall, bouncing off gently before getting his footing. Moments later, a second rope dangled down.

"Miss Wilde."

"Not going to happen." I grabbed the rope and stepped toward him. "Maybe you're not noticing the giant gaping flesh wounds you're rocking, but I am. Let me tie you up."

The slightest hint of amusement flared past his pain. "At last, now we are getting somewhere."

Still, he didn't protest as I made a makeshift belt out of the trailing end of the rope. At the last minute, eyeing the seeping mass of his back, I wrapped it around both of us, my chest to his spine. The scroll cases shifted in my jacket, like stolen beer cans after a midnight Stop-N-Go raid. I slid to the right to avoid bruising a rib.

"I could imagine a better configuration."

"Focus, Armaeus. I don't want the rope to make things worse. You may want to warn the boys upstairs that they'll be hauling up a heavy load."

The rope cinched tight, and I winced, feeling it constrict me against Armaeus's water- and blood-soaked clothing. My face buried into his back, my hands wrapped around him, I was surrounded by the scent of not only his blood, but cinnamon and heady spices, heat and fire and earth. My arms went naturally around his waist, my hands on his chest, and after a moment, his own hands came up, the warmth of his palms covering my fingers. He said nothing, his mental channel silent for once, but his hands cradled mine as if he was handling a rare and precious gem. The warmth he exuded filled me to the aching marrow of my bones, and I hung, limp and helpless as we were hauled out of the well.

I shouldn't care that he was hurt, I knew. He'd inexplicably brought hundreds of Connecteds into harm's way in Vegas. He was doubtless willing to sacrifice hundreds more to preserve his precious balance. He deserved to be hurt, deserved to suffer. And I shouldn't care. I shouldn't.

The ride back to the airplane in the Egyptian workmen's SUV was all but silent. Fortunately, we were almost off the temple grounds before the first geyser of water from the ancient temple room broke the surface. The Nile wasn't due to flood for another good two months, but hey, details. I'm sure the local utilities groups would come up with some way to spin the sudden deluge.

Simon watched a set of flashing lights crest the rise and raced toward the temple site. "Police? Really?"

The Magician's voice sounded like a long stretch of gravel. "They would have been summoned eventually. I simply moved up the timetable to encourage Mantorov's men not to return."

"Okay, but...will there be anything left for them to find?"

Armaeus shifted in his seat. "The chamber was completely sealed off from above when we reached it. By the time we left, it was not. The accumulated weight of thousands of years of debris will crash through the cracked roof. Water will mix with sand, filling the chamber with mud. In time, the waters will recede, and the chamber will remain, perfectly preserved. It will be rediscovered, at length, reasonably intact."

I frowned. "A length?" Dawn was starting to light the far eastern edges of the sky, and I could see the geyser now. It wasn't big, it wasn't strong, but for a land etched out of a desert, it was something of a miracle.

I sensed Armaeus's gaze on me, but I didn't turn his way. I couldn't look at him directly, at the evidence of his trial. I knew his immortality didn't preclude him from injury, or from death from deliberate action. But in all the jobs I'd worked for him, I'd never seen him bleed. I'd never seen him...vulnerable.

His words seemed more gentle when he spoke again. "I do not possess oracular powers, Miss Wilde, but it isn't too difficult a guess. The first rushed thought of the authorities will be of buried treasure and national historical value, but that will quickly cede to the realization that a fissure of the Nile has unexpectedly found its way to El Ashmunein, well away from the main line of the river. The god of resources and utilities has more power than Thoth does in this century. Undoubtedly, there will be the Egyptian equivalent of a media uproar, as the two sides draw lines quite literally in the sand, over how the land should be excavated and the fissure both preserved and exploited. If history is any guide, it will be quite some time before the chamber is reopened.

"And the bodies?"

"Mother Nature is notoriously unkind to those souls left exposed in her grasp. A significant amount of water poured into that chamber before sand cascaded down, and any ancient passages that remain will simply allow scavenging animals access to the bodies left in the open. The decomposition process will be swift and, with any luck, complete. At a minimum, it will simply remain a mystery once the digging commences and bodies are found." I could hear him shift in his seat. "We'll monitor the situation. If there is a need to intervene, we will."

Which, I suspected, would be at the intersection of maybe and never. Still, something in Armaeus's voice tugged at me. He'd been gutted by multiple arrows, but he was the Magician, dammit. Surely insta-healing was a perk of the profession.

Unless...

I braced myself and turned to him. "Those arrows. Was there anything special about them?"

"Special as in how?" The Magician's voice held a hint of warning, and I slid my gaze to Simon, who continued to mutter over his electronics. How much did the Fool really understand about Armaeus and the other Council members, and what they could or could not endure?

"They just seemed... super effective," I tried, keeping my tone vague. "I'm not sure, exactly. I didn't get a good look at them, what with all the blood gushing out of you. How'd you miss Mantorov being down there, anyway?"

Armaeus's chuckle was wry. "Now that is a pain

that will endure long after these wounds have healed. In my blind certainty of my goal, I knew Mantorov was close, but I did not stop to consider that the chamber had already been entered by more traditional means." He grimaced as the world around us brightened, dawn taking greater hold. "Those arrows were most likely found in the chamber. They were crafted by the Hyksos tribe," He tilted his head back against his seat, and closed his eyes. "Very powerful, very advanced for their time. Their weapons were considered superior during the fifteenth dynastic period. It is not surprising that they would have been adapted for use in defending the Temple of Thoth."

"Ah. So they didn't have any special properties to weaken you?"

"They possessed four large arrowheads that went all the way through me. That appeared to be sufficient."

"Sure." It all sounded very neat and tidy, without the obvious "because they're aliens!" subtext I subconsciously yearned for after too many hours spent on the History Channel.

Still, I couldn't shake the idea that Armaeus was hiding something. If only because he usually did.

He appeared to sleep for the rest of the car ride, then refused help or medical treatment when we arrived at the hop plane, and then again at the Council's private jet. When we had lifted off for the last time, however, he stood, making his polite apologies, and turned for the back of the plane where the sleeping chambers were.

Simon and I watched him go. Armaeus was barely out of sight before the Fool turned to me. "You ever see him this messed up before?"

I shrugged. "I haven't known him that long."

"I have." He peered to where Armaeus had sat. "Blood dried a long time ago, but dude's still stiff as a pole and not in a good way. It's freaking me out."

"It is?" I frowned at him. "You don't seem freaked out."

Simon laid a hand on his chest, his face alight in the artificial glow of his work table. Now that we were back on Armaeus's private jet, Simon had all the comforts of home—including a workstation fit for a tech god. Before him on the table was the completely dismantled digital reconstructor, its components laid out in exacting precision. "I hide it well. You should go to him."

Returning my gaze to the back of the jet, I sensed the pull and rightness of Simon's suggestion. Then I realized who it was *making* the suggestion. "Stop that." I narrowed my eyes at him. "You're trying to create trouble."

Simon grinned. "In this case, the trouble's already there. I'm simply trying to help it along. Keeps things interesting," he continued, answering my unasked *why*. "I'm immortal, you're not. There are a limited number of adventures you're going to be able to have in a given lifetime. Why not go after them to the fullest? Seems a waste of heart and brain and lungs and bone otherwise. Life's so dull if you don't take chances."

His words resonated with me on a soul-deep level, but then, Simon's biggest fear in life appeared to be getting bored. When an eternity stretched before you, I supposed your perspective changed.

A rustle against my mental barriers brought up my head. Simon blinked at me, his face betraying confusion. I was officially off Eshe's payroll, and Kreios couldn't throw his will as far as Armaeus could. Which left no one but the Magician rooting around in my head.

Except he wasn't rooting, exactly. The tendril of outreach was far more tenuous than that. Almost unconscious. Like a hand that crept out in sleep, seeking the comfort of connection.

I scowled at Simon. "Are you doing this?"

"Doing what?" Real curiosity gleamed in his gaze.

I tapped my temple.

He shook his head. "I completely got the short end of the stick in terms of mystical powers. Influence and teleportation is great, but talking inside somebody's brain? That trumps it every time. If I can pick up those skills, I'm totally applying to Arcana U."

"You can do that?"

He grinned. "You never know if you don't try." With that, his gaze dropped back to his exploded device. "Now go check up on the old guy already. His pain is making me twitch."

I couldn't tell if I was being manipulated or not, but there was no denying the frisson of pressure stirring in the base of my brain. I hauled myself out of my seat, wincing with a million aches of my own. Shucking off my jacket with its treasure of gold scroll cases, I thought twice about leaving the cases alone. I liked Simon, sure. But that didn't mean I trusted him.

I slipped into Armaeus's sleeping chamber and dropped my jacket and the cases on the seat next to the door. As with everything else on the jet, the room was ridiculously luxurious, several times larger than any cabin needed to be. A single, full-size bed centered the space, open on both sides. The room was dark but not soundless: the rushing sounds of the ocean flowed out of speakers, bathing the chamber in a lulling cadence.

Beneath it, I could hear Armaeus's labored breathing. Decidedly less lulling.

"How bad are you?" I asked into the gloom.

"Return to the main chamber, Miss Wilde. This is not your concern."

CHAPTER TWENTY-TWO

"You're going to be a really obnoxious old man, you know that, right?" I moved forward, gradually making out Armaeus's figure. His clothes were laid neatly on the chair beside the bed, and I paused there, picking up the shirt. Four ripped holes stained with dried blood remained on both the front and back. "You keeping this as a trophy?"

"The positioning is useful to note. The wounds were not debilitating, and yet achieved significant blood loss in minimum time. What was the goal in…that…" His voice dropped off at the end. "I need rest, Miss Wilde. If you can stop your interrogation for the moment, I would be happy to engage with you at a later time."

He needed more than rest, though. And I knew *what*, suddenly. As well as I knew my own body—the body he'd healed more times than I could count, even if it was sometimes against my stated wishes. The magic wielded by the Magician was not the sly subversion of the Fool's manipulation, nor the blatant sexual trigger of the Devil's illusions. It also wasn't the arcane purity of the High Priestess's spell-borne sight. The Empress's ability was to make something out of nothing, a gift that clearly brought abundance to her door, though I'm not sure what else had shown up alongside it.

But Armaeus was different. He was the most powerful Arcanan I'd encountered, and his abilities were the most primal. They centered on the most primal of functions too.

I sat down on the bed, and everything tensed—not just Armaeus's body either. The entire atmosphere around him turned electric with awareness and adrenaline. "Miss Wilde."

The words were almost panicked, and a trickle of power surged up within me, fast and sure. I wasn't going to bang Armaeus in his sickbed. That was something between us that could not be broached easily, and this was not the time.

But that didn't mean I couldn't help him now, when he needed it most.

"We don't know what we're walking into, back in Vegas," I said, leaning over him as my hand trailed up his arm. The energy in the room warmed, then began to dance, and the lights dimmed further. I moved the coverlet aside and winced at the bandages on Armaeus's chest and across his abdomen. They'd been applied with force and precision, but the blood was beginning to seep through. The silver arrows were not simple weapons, no matter what he'd said. They sapped him of his ability to self-heal, or at least delayed it significantly. "I need you—the Council needs you to be at your best."

And so did the Connecteds back in Vegas, since he'd sicced SANCTUS on the city. Whether he wanted to or not, Armaeus was going to help save them. Right after I saved him.

"I will heal."

"Neither of us has time for that. Let me help you."

"You're not strong enough."

I cringed. He was right, of course. When I'd seen him practically explode with ancient magic in the temple room, I'd grasped a whole new appreciation for a Council member's psychic abilities versus a mere Connected's. But I was the only one available, and one made do with what one had. "Oh, yeah?" I countered, my words a light tease. "Maybe you should stop underestimating me."

"You play…a dangerous game, Miss Wilde."

Armaeus's voice was a bare rasp, but there was no discounting the undercurrent of energy within it. An energy that had been missing before. Which meant what I was doing was working.

Granted, I had the sensation I was handling pure radium without a hazmat suit, but with any luck, I wouldn't deal with the fallout until my body was likely to fail on general principles. Those last few years of life probably weren't going to be worth much, anyhow.

Armaeus's laughter rumbled, and I smiled. "Someone's feeling better, if you're trying to read my thoughts again."

"You open the door, I will walk through. Always know that."

"I'll take my chances."

"As you say." Beneath my hand, his skin became warmer, almost uncomfortably hot. I skimmed my fingers over his chest, pausing over his heart. It beat frantically against his rib cage. The cadence of its fury was too fast, too hard, but as heat radiated from Armaeus, I could see his body loosen, the corded muscles in his arms and legs losing their tension, relaxing. I could feel the blood rushing through his veins, feeding his muscles, warming him and diminishing the pain to a smaller and smaller force. In its place, the sensual coil of need writhed up, filling him with a different kind of heat. The forces of creation existed in the very center of Armaeus's being. This was the power the Magician wielded. This was why his every move was a sensual threat. The most basic of creative energies formed the very core of his ability, and he'd had several lifetimes to hone that ability to perfection.

I couldn't do what he did. But I could, at least…do this.

I leaned forward, pressing my lips against his collarbone. The heat index of Armaeus's skin jumped to about a million and three, nearly singeing me.

"Enough, Miss Wilde. Stop."

The command was in my mind, and a warning. I hesitated. In the past, Armaeus had pushed through my own protestations without hesitation, overriding my caution when he'd high-handedly decided that his brand of healing was faster and more efficient than any other.

Right now, efficiency seemed to be a good idea.

I spread my fingers wide above his bandage. In my mind's eye, the rent muscle and skin fused together, cauterized by the power of his deep wellspring of magic. Directed by my touch.

"I'll stop, I promise," I whispered against his skin, getting used to the heat, the power beneath my fingertips, the whorls of sensation exploding in my brain and along every nerve ending. "I'll stop right after I do *this*."

Before I could lose my nerve, I lifted my body over

his, angling my head down to cover his mouth with my own. The moment our lips touched, a flood of heat burst from Armaeus's midsection, searing through me and setting the entire room ablaze in a crackle of electricity. Armaeus's arms were around me in an instant, the cry ripped from his throat an agonized growl, and he crushed me to him, fusing us into one being.

Power ricocheted between us with enough force to pulverize my brain cells, but somehow I held on to him. He snaked his hand up to the nape of my neck, locking my lips against his. His tongue slipped into my mouth, tasting and exploring, as if he'd never kissed a woman before and might not ever again. His body was on fire, leashed back with a ferocity that did nothing to hide his rock-hard shaft buried into my belly. He rolled over and pressed me into the bed, and I realized—belatedly—that he was completely naked other than his bandages. Which were only over his chest and abs. My clothes would ordinarily be sufficient barrier, except they were in danger of going up in smoke, and I found I didn't care—couldn't care—though as Armaeus finally pulled away from me and stared down, hard, at my face, I could feel the pricks of hysteria pinging at my brain, darkness encroaching on all sides of my vision and pushing in on me, threatening to swallow me whole.

Armaeus's eyes were dark and fierce, the gold no longer pale but blazing with intensity, his skin flushed with power, his mouth open, his breathing hard. His body moved against mine with primal ferocity, and I realized my hands were no longer cupping his face, but trapped in his grasp, pinned to the mattress. Without speaking, he lowered his mouth to mine again, hungrily assaulting my lips, dragging his mouth over my face, my chin, the hollow of my neck, my collarbone. My core swam with heat and need, and the darkness loomed closer, heavy with threat.

I fought it back. I had control here, no matter that Armaeus's fists were locked around my wrists, that his breathing was wild, almost panicked. When he lifted himself again, I flicked my gaze south. Though the abdominal wrap held, the upper bandages had slipped from his chest, and perfect, pure skin gleamed around two new scars visible on his pecs, scars that glowed white.

I lifted my eyes to his. Stark, raw power greeted mine, and the darkness edged closer. "Feeling better?" I managed to keep my voice steady, though my own heart was racing.

Armaeus drew in a shaky breath, awareness coming back to his eyes, his fingers loosening on my wrists. He lifted his body off mine, and I instantly felt the loss. "That…was unwise," he said. The coolness of his tone was almost laughable in the face of his rock-hard body, still vibrating with desire. He rolled to the side, facing me, but his arms caged me. He wasn't quite ready yet to let me go.

As the darkness receded again, I realized I wasn't quite ready to leave him either.

"It worked, though," I said. "You're stronger."

"I'm stronger." We stayed there for a long moment, adrift in a turbulent sea. Then he steered us into more predictable waters. "You'll be returning the gold scroll cases to Fuggeren this morning."

I released the breath I hadn't realized I'd been holding. "That was the plan, yep."

"For a fee, I suspect."

"That's generally how it works." I shrugged in his embrace. "I'm happy to give him dummies, if you think he'll buy it. I assume we need the real deals to fight SANCTUS."

He paused a beat too long. "As you say." Then he moved, winced. "We will need but one of them. The smallest. I can make a passable replica, though. He'll likely never notice."

"Then my conversation with Fuggeren will be very productive." I shifted my gaze back to him. "Can anyone else speak that language?"

"Yes." He smiled. It wasn't a good smile. "The others, however, are not a threat at present. Fuggeren can maintain possession of the scroll cases, or sell them at his leisure, and we'll have full access to Fuggeren, or to whomever he chooses as his buyer. Make sure you give Simon the cases before you hand them over."

"You don't think Fuggeren will sweep for bugs?"

"I'm counting on it, in fact. But I doubt he'll sweep inside. The scroll cases will be delivered intact, sealed, and in pristine condition. The same cannot be said, unfortunately, for Mantorov. That will take some explanation."

"I don't think anyone will miss him."

"True." Armaeus's gaze flickered. "*You* must be more careful, however. You should not have attempted to heal me." He shook his head, his gaze roaming my face, the crown of my head, before coming back to lock on my eyes again. "I was hurt more than I'd anticipated, and the recovery came upon me slowly enough that I didn't harm you or, worse, consume you."

I frowned at him, not really wanting to consider the ramifications of "consume." "I don't know, your healing seemed kinda fast and furious from my angle, just saying."

His brow arched. "I was able to maintain control."

"And so was I." I pushed him back, and he fell away. "I get that you're the all-powerful one, but don't miss the important part here. I did this." I gestured at his body. "You needed it, and I gave it. And both of us—well, one of us—kept her clothes on. Win-win."

His eyes were dark, too dark as his gaze shifted to meet mine. "And how do you win?"

I kept my emotions on careful lockdown. What he didn't know wouldn't hurt either of us. "Well, number one, I got the whole contact high. I suspect I'll start feeling the results of that power infusion any moment. Number two, I know you'll compensate me for going above and beyond."

"And compensation was your main goal?"

"Compensation is always my main goal." I lifted a finger. "But I don't need your money, Armaeus. Not this time. I need your honesty. Tell me the truth: did you drive all those Connecteds and wannabes to Vegas to draw SANCTUS there?"

His mood turned instantly stony, which was enough answer for me. I rolled to a sitting position, a little too grateful for this new surge of anger, burning off the last of my desire that refused to yield. "Why? Tell me why, when you're all high and mighty in your noninterference, would you *manipulate* innocent people to toddle into your tailor-made trap?" I might have yelled that last bit, but Simon was smart enough not to come running.

Armaeus scowled at me a long moment. When he spoke, his words were clipped. "SANCTUS has been building in power for decades, but over the past year, its activities have stepped up markedly."

"Yeah, well, so have the activities of the entire black market. Why do you think I'm so desperate for every job that comes my way?"

"This is different. SANCTUS is poised for a strike, but there has been no reason for its sudden influx of power. The balance of magic is as it ever was. We could have gone another several months, another year without them striking."

"And that would have been bad, why?"

He leveled his gaze at me. I held up my hands. "Oh no, no, no. You're not laying this one on me."

"You agreed to remain in Vegas for the duration of your work with the High Priestess, but I needed you to understand the full extent of what you might accomplish. You are, arguably, a wild card in the war on magic. You don't know your own abilities."

"I know my own abilities just fine, thanks. I find things. That's what I do. That's all I do."

"You find things, yes." Armaeus had somehow edged closer to me. I remained seated on the bed, but he leaned forward, crowding against me in the small space. "But that's *not* all that you do. Your abilities under the influence of the Pythene gas outstripped any of our expectations. And as Eshe intimated, the gas has dispersed from your system, yet your abilities remain."

"But they're still a variation on finding stuff," I hedged.

"Your ability to manifest as an *illusion* convincing enough to handle a corporeal object and shoot men who believed they were being shot until the illusion lifted, is not a variation on 'finding.'"

I opened my mouth, shut it. Tried again. "Okay, you have me there. But I was in the middle of the entire Council on that excursion. Between you, the Devil, Eshe, and the Fool, something was bound to give."

"Perhaps. And perhaps something else will give, as you say, should you be tested further."

"Are you *trying* to piss me off here?" I glared at him. He was every inch the bronze god, gorgeously perfect despite the tattered bandages hanging off him, and every bit as impersonal. "Connecteds aren't yours to 'test,' Armaeus, any more than they're yours to use as bait. I don't care how long you've been creeping around this world. They're humans."

Another lifted brow. "I'm human."

"Kinda not really, no." I crossed my arms. "And some of the people waiting back in Vegas for the apocalypse or solstice or whatever aren't even *skilled* Connecteds. They're right at the fringe, open to what's out there without fully grasping it. Still others have abilities but no idea how to use them. They're not prepared. They're not combatants in this little war you've set up, they're victims. I simply can't understand how you could have justified summoning them this way."

His gaze didn't waver, and after another beat, I connected the rest of the dots all on my own. "You bastard."

He shrugged. "You have a history of not leaving behind those who cannot fight for themselves."

"Yeah, well, guess who I *do* have a history of leaving behind—"

A sharp rap came at the door, and without being asked, Simon opened the cabin and peered inside. His delighted smile turned disgusted when he saw my comparative state of dress to Armaeus's undress. Then he noticed Armaeus's chest, and his brows went up.

"Glad you're feeling better. Now if you two are done cat-fighting, we're about to land. And despite some of us having immortal powers, the captain is adamant that we all be strapped in our seats for the event." His gaze traveled between us. "Unless you'd rather be strapped into the bed?"

CHAPTER TWENTY-THREE

"Thank you for your willingness to meet at the station, Miss Wilde."

Brody's words were clipped, formal, and I shrugged, glad I'd had the foresight to shower off the dirt and muck of Khemenu before dialing up Fuggeren. Brody had picked up instead, and had tersely explained that he'd been assigned to a special task force in charge of protecting the gold show. The Rarity had opened to great fanfare despite the attack at the gala, and all the pieces other than the scroll cases had been recovered within hours, spread around Vegas like Easter eggs.

Distractions.

Now I turned from the gleaming gold scroll cases and faced the two men. It was already three o'clock, but Fuggeren looked like he'd come out of the dry cleaners ten minutes ago, his skin and hair as perma-pressed as his suit. He smiled at me, and I could almost hear the money landing in my bank account. I'd impressed him. He was a good man to impress.

"You had no difficulty reclaiming the pieces?" Fuggeren asked, earning him a scowl from Brody. "They appear to be barely handled."

"I didn't. Thank you for the use of your transport and pilot." We both knew I hadn't used his resources, but with any luck, Brody didn't. Fuggeren inclined his head.

He was right too. The scroll cases had gotten more than a spit shine from Armaeus. They'd been transfused with enough Magician mojo to make them practically glow from the inside. Even the smallest one, the fake one, looked better than the original, though all of them were once again dormant. As if the nervous energy that had knocked me across the storage room at the airport had finally been burned off completely, and now they were napping.

I narrowed my eyes on the cases. Had Armaeus done something more to them than he'd told me? I hadn't had time to inspect them myself, nor had I any facility with the ancient script. How would I know?

"Where's Grigori Mantorov?" Brody's words recalled my attention, and I smiled into his scowl. H knew he was being lied to, but not how, exactly.

"I suspect he's in Egypt," I said. "I was lucky enough to intercept his courier en route to the temple site in El Ashmunein. Fortunately it's a long drive from Hurghada Airport. I had ample time to catch up."

"He wasn't with the cases?"

"Not that I noticed."

Brody's glare would have made me uncomfortable any other time, but I was still buzzed from my mile-high healing session with Armaeus, and not likely to come down anytime soon. I also needed to get the hell out of the station and back to Nikki. She'd been radio silent while I was out of town, but my phone had been blowing up since I'd landed, asking me to please get to the chapel already. I didn't think she was about to propose.

"Detective Rooks, I plan to make a commendation to the mayor regarding the conduct of you and your staff throughout this happily brief investigation." Fuggeren's words made Brody blink, and he refocused on the man. "Without your support, my property would not have been returned to me so quickly, and the Rarity Gold Show would not have gone on without a hitch. Further, we would have drawn undue attention and speculation to a city which does not deserve it for anything other than the most positive of reasons."

Brody didn't lighten up. "I'll need to file a report."

"And I'll substantiate any appropriate version of the case that helps you the most," Fuggeren said. His words were light, and surprisingly, Brody didn't bristle. Instead he leaned back, considering the man.

"You don't need to do me any favors, Mr. Fuggeren."

"On the contrary, I do." Fuggeren smiled, and in that smile wasn't simply a man worth billions, but the favored son of a long line of billionaires. "And you'll find I always pay my debts. Miss Wilde." He turned to me with a speculative gaze that noted every crease and wrinkle in my shirt, every scuff and bruise on my skin. It wasn't a lascivious assessment, because Fuggeren wasn't interested in me as a person. He was interested in what I could do for him. I was getting used to that kind of scrutiny these days, from mortal and immortal alike. "I hope to have the pleasure of working with you in the future."

"I look forward to it." I stood, and the men followed suit. Fuggeren leaned in to shake my hand, then bent quickly toward me, as if to deliver one of those European kisses to the cheek that I was so terrible at reciprocating. When he neared my face though, his words were low. And definite.

"I assume you have kept the smallest case for a good reason. I look forward to its return when you are finished."

Then he straightened, smiling again broadly. I grinned gamely back. As we both turned to the door, Brody gestured for me to remain. "I'll need you for a moment more, Ms. Wilde." His glance wasn't lascivious either, more was the pity. I definitely preferred lasciviousness to officiousness in my cops.

I loitered in the conference room while the two men made their good-byes. It hadn't been an official meeting with suspects or persons of interest. It hadn't been recorded. We weren't in a room with a two-way mirror, either, which was probably a good thing. I always ended up staring at myself in those things.

"Thanks for waiting, Sara." For once, Brody didn't stumble over my name, and I found myself a little wistful about that. It had become the one piece that linked us to the past, to a time when life maybe wasn't a whole lot better, but it was a whole lot simpler.

He gestured for me to sit. When I didn't, he sighed. "We're on the same side, remember?"

"The same side?" I couldn't keep the edge out of my voice. Brody did that to a person. Especially to my person. "Then explain this charade to me." I flicked my hand at the room around us. "You asked me to come down to the station to meet with you and Jarvis. I did. But you didn't record the conversation, and you didn't video it, from what I can see. It wasn't observed. So why, exactly, are we doing this here? What do you have to gain from it?"

His eyes betrayed his amusement. "You think I'm doing this for my personal gain?"

"Well, it's not like Fuggeren gives a shit about being in a police station." I folded my arms. "While I make a habit of avoiding them."

"Yet here you are, being a good citizen, showing your cooperation with local law enforcement."

I narrowed my eyes at him. "Don't patronize me, Brody."

"Then don't be an idiot." He'd taken a step closer. "I've taken a lot of heat for some of the crazy-ass shit that's happened in this city over the past few days, and I expect to be taking a lot more. The least you can do, while you're here anyway, which we both know isn't for very long, is to keep me informed of the worst of what's to come."

My gaze sharpened. He couldn't mean what I—

Brody's irritated wave cut that thought off. "No, Sari—Sara. I don't mean with your goddamned cards. You want to use those, that's on your own time. I'm not mixing that into police business, not anymore. But you've got ears, you've got eyes. You're in tight with Nikki Dawes, and she is a hell of a lot more than the natterclack she puts herself out to be."

Natterclack? Still, I nodded slowly, trying to follow Brody's words. "You want me to be a snitch?"

He rolled his eyes. "Sara, are you, or the people you hang out with, doing anything wrong?"

"Not at all."

"Then why would I need you to snitch on them? I need you to tell me what's coming that may *harm* them. God knows Dixie Quinn has been running to me for the last two years every time one of the Connected community gets so much as a hangnail. Surely you can provide information of a broader scope if you hear it."

"From what I understand, that's not the real reason Dixie was running to you."

As soon as the words were out of my mouth, of course, I regretted them. Brody's brows shot up, his lips twitching into an almost-smile. "Why, Sara, I didn't know you cared."

Which was bullshit, and we both knew it. But it also allowed him to take a step closer to me, until we were almost nose to nose. The heat of the man enveloped me in a way that was nothing like the kinetic, overpowering energy of the Magician. This was much more subtle, yet stronger too, a magnetic draw I couldn't fight at this range any more than I could fight gravity.

"So tell me, is that 'caring' the reason why you're staying…or is it the reason why you're determined to leave the city the first moment you can?"

"I don't want to have this conversation with you."

"It's not a conversation, it's a question." He kept his body loose and easy, in marked contrast to mine. "It'd be helpful for me to understand exactly why you're hanging around, and where things stand between us."

"Um, they don't stand anywhere, Officer Brody—Detective Brooks," I amended quickly. "We worked together ten years ago in a purely professional capacity."

He nodded, his face not betraying any reaction to the blush chasing over my face. "We did. But we're not working together professionally now, are we?"

Wait, what?

Somehow he'd gotten closer to me. "I specifically don't want to work 'professionally' with you, Sara. I want you to share information with me as a concerned citizen, yes. But you are nowhere near being a subject in this or any other case at this point, nor are you acting in any official police capacity. You can leave the city at any time. You probably should leave the city, in fact. The woman I met two weeks ago was planning on it, I know that for sure. The question is...will you or won't you?" His eyes were the color of a winter day, clear and unworried, and despite the intensity of his glance, he didn't seem jacked up, didn't seem invested in the answer, didn't seem—

"Miss Wilde."

So not the time.

"Why do you think I should leave the city?" I blurted the words before I could stop them, and it was Brody's turn to smile, the little half smirk that he'd used so many times with so many people while I'd watched him, starry eyed with teen idol lust.

"Doesn't matter what I think. Will you or won't you?"

"No. I mean, yes. Yes."

"Sounds like you haven't made up your mind on that."

"This isn't a good time."

He shrugged. "I can wait."

The double meaning of his words dropped me into another rolling wave of confusion. He could wait. He had waited, sort of. Or at least he'd remembered me, from all those years ago. Remembered the girl I'd been or tried to be. I didn't know if that was a good or a bad thing. A bad thing, I was pretty sure.

"There's been an intriguing development, Miss Wilde."

Not. Now.

"I said I could wait."

I blinked at Brody, my brain trying to balance the conversation in my mind with the one in front of me. Despite my sense that the Magician wasn't pulling my chain, I shoved Armaeus out of my consciousness. Brody was a different story, though. He wasn't using magic. Not any sort of magic I could ward against, anyway. And he was definitely pulling my chain. But I wasn't going to react like a kid anymore to that. I was grown-up. Grown-ups did things differently than teenagers, I was almost sure of it.

"It's none of your business whether I stay or go," I huffed, very adultlike.

"Nope."

"So why do you want to know?"

"Other than I might possibly lose a good CI?" He shrugged, his flinty blue eyes betraying nothing. "Call it professional curiosity. The kind of work you do, the kind of people you know—we're going to run into each other, Sara. I like to know what to expect."

My inner teen stared at him, gape-mouthed. I tried not to follow suit. He really…didn't give a crap. "But you…" I blinked, my mind rushing through all the years, all the daydreams, all of the completely ridiculous fantasies I'd made up in my head about this man, this stupid cop who really had just been working with the snot-nosed kid from down the street, her value all in her cards and her visions and nothing…

Well, not completely nothing. "You *kissed* me." He had too. When he'd first seen me two weeks ago, seen me and known it was me, back in his life after ten years in the wind, he'd pulled me into his arms, and—

Had that simply been an *interrogation technique*?

Outrage blasted through me as a loud rap sounded at the door, which immediately opened. A uniformed cop stuck her head in. "Sorry to interrupt, Detective, I didn't want to forward it to your voice mail." She glanced down at her clipboard. "An Armaeus Bertrand is on the line for you."

"For him?" I blurted, and Brody's head swiveled around to me in surprise, once again all cop.

The woman nodded. "Says there's been a development in the Rarity theft he wanted discuss with you. He was…" She straightened a little, blushing. "He was, ah, most insistent."

I stared at her. The woman had to be pushing sixty, and she was as pink and wide-eyed as a kid. Then again, Armaeus was pushing nine hundred. So to him she *was* a kid.

"Thanks, Nancy," Brody said, and the woman straightened further. Maybe surprised that Brody knew her name, maybe surprised that she had a name at this point. The Magician could do that. "Patch it through to my cell phone?"

"Will do." She left the room, and Brody turned more fully to face me.

"What is your relationship with Armaeus Bertrand, exactly? Does he know you're here? What's his involvement?"

I narrowed my eyes. It was a reasonable question. Armaeus had not been at the Rarity, and Brody wouldn't know that he was connected to Kreios, necessarily. But at the moment I wasn't inclined to do Brody any favors. "He's a client. I work for him." Brody's mouth turned down, and I pushed it a little more. He wanted us to be all business? Fine. This was my business. "I find items of interest for him."

"Items like the gold scroll cases?"

"On occasion, sure. But those weren't his scroll

cases. They're Fuggeren's. So Fuggeren was my client on that job." Granted, Armaeus was my original client and Fuggeren the tagalong after the fact, but details.

"That's pretty—" Whatever comment he was about to make was cut off by the racket of his phone. He pulled the device out of his pocket and thumbed it on. "Detective Rooks."

I turned to leave, but he held up a finger. I offered him one of my own and was out the door.

CHAPTER TWENTY-FOUR

"He's on to you, you know."

I sat with Nikki at the SLS outdoor bar, scanning the pool area. By the time I'd hooked up with her, she and the rest of the visiting Connecteds had decamped from the chapel in search of cooler territory in the face of the scorching afternoon. The SLS pool was packed, but the crowd wasn't your typical college or twenty-something crush. It was like the entire Midwest had emptied out of their RVs and into the SLS, and everyone was waiting for the church fair to begin. "Brody. He suspects you're a lot more than what you seem." I decided not to mention the word "natterclack."

"Yeah, well, that'd be the detective part of Detective Dishy." Nikki took a long pull on her bourbon and soda, squinting into the sun. Today she wore a white miniskirt paired with red canvas platform high-tops, white knee socks banded at the top with red stripes, and a faded Converse all-star tank top artfully cut to show off her industrial-strength bright red sports bra. Her auburn hair was in pigtails, and her star-shaped sunglasses took up the top half of her face. "He say anything specific, or did he just get really low and growl, 'I'm on to her, you know'?"

I smiled, relaxing for the first time all day. "I think he knows you're not just another pretty face is all. He hasn't taken the time to dig."

"Tell him I'm an open book. Anytime he wants to riffle my pages, he knows where to find me. Dixie's had her chance at him, and you aren't grabbing that low-hanging fruit, so to speak. Somebody's gotta."

"I'll let him know." Armaeus's call had been to inform Brody that more of the Rarity gold had been recovered at the Luxor, hiding among the kitsch. I knew this not because Brody had told me, but because Armaeus had mentally mute-conferenced me into the phone call as I'd stalked out of the station house. Way better than Skype.

That was no more an "intriguing development" than a Tinder breakup, though. So either Armaeus wanted me out of Brody's mitts for his own reasons, or he had some other development to inform me about, and he needed me in the clear to do it. Either way, he hadn't uttered another peep, so I'd decided to check in on the crowd at SLS.

The solstice celebration had technically started earlier today, but there remained way too many of them. "What are they all still doing here? I thought the Rarity was winding down."

"It's in its final day, with the triumphant return of Fuggeren's scroll cases, though the savviest connoisseurs are convinced the ones on display now are fakes. No point tempting the gods by putting them out there a second time to grab. But remember, these people aren't here for that. They're still waiting for some kind of Psychic Rapture, which they're convinced will be at sundown, tonight. We've got a whole parade planned down to the Bellagio fountains, where their visions told them they'd have the best view. We tried to talk them down from it, but nothing doing. It's nuts." She eyeballed me. "They think you're someone special, by the way."

I frowned at her. "What do you mean?"

"Their visions." Nikki waved a hand. "Some of them have seen you, seen you do great things. Bathed in light, shining through a storm, the whole nine yards."

"Armaeus is behind those visions, Nikki. Roxie wasn't lying about that."

"Some of them, sure. But not all of them, babe. You got skillz, I'm telling you. Sooner or later you've got to own that."

"I've overreached myself before." I shook my head, shoving the old memories away. "I'm not going to make that mistake again."

"Child, you—"

"Where are the witches in all this?" I interrupted her. "I haven't heard anything from them since they crashed the diner. Do *they* still think all hell's going to break loose?"

"I don't think so. Danae and the gang have been nose to the bedrock for the past three days. I'm not much on my ley line configurations, but they're pretty sure that the city's grid will hold. Hold what, they're not saying, but hold."

"Maybe SANCTUS knows that Armaeus got a hold of the scroll cases and they've called everything off." I blew out a breath, taking in the crowd. "There are just so many Connecteds here."

"More than we imagined possible. More than Dixie can handle, you want to know the truth. She's beginning to sound like a camp counselor off her meds." Nikki shook her head. "Those who don't know better are all abuzz with excitement. The ones who do know better don't know whether to get the hell out of Vegas or stay. If it *is* the Rapture, no one wants to be left behind, you know? Not when the deep end of the ocean is hella more dark than it's ever been. And Roxie has returned to the fold with a vengeance, dispensing her little gems of wisdom to the masses pretty much every hour, on the hour. At least up until this morning. Then solstice hit and she had everyone rapt with attention—except then she warned them all that the real celebration wouldn't be 'til, you guessed it, sundown."

I looked at the sky. Sundown wasn't all that far off. "She say anything useful?"

"Nothing we can hold her to." Nikki shrugged. "She's keeping them here, which I'm against, but she's keeping them happy, which I'm all for. Still, for someone incarnated as recently as the seventies, something's...wrong with her."

I quirked her a glance. "Not like you to judge."

"I'm not talking her plastic surgery. She just—bugs me. I don't know if she's scared or got something up her sleeve, but she feels off to me."

I considered that. What I'd been able to find on Roxie Meadows hadn't been super conclusive. While she'd been huge in the sixties and seventies, the party stop for musicians and celebrities from all over the world, her flamboyance had simmered down markedly with her accession to the Council. Part of that was because of her discretion, what with the whole anti-aging thing she had going on, but I agreed with Nikki. There was something more there. "Anything more from the Devil?"

"Not a peep. He's not anywhere, Eshe isn't anywhere. It's like a storm is rolling in, but we don't know from what direction, or whether to bring our umbrellas or snow shovels."

I slanted my gaze to the east, at the far horizon. I couldn't see it beyond the towering Arcana Casinos. In the waning day, the trans-dimensional homes of the Council were almost indiscernible, the bare shift of a shadow or refraction of light. They were there, but they served merely to make me feel more insulated, not less. Not insulated, exactly. Trapped.

Nikki wasn't a mind reader, but her next words nailed it anyway. "It's like we're waiting for the other shoe to drop, and it's going to be square on our heads."

I nodded. "The Rarity's big closing bash and auction happens this evening, and it's solstice, and everyone here seems wired for sound. Part of me wants to lock them all down, but part me thinks they'll be safer in the open, mingling with un-Connecteds. Safety in numbers and all."

She nodded to the floatie-and-fairy-wand crowd in the pool. "We couldn't lock down this crowd without the National Guard. The alcohol started flowing at six a.m., and really hit once the official solstice mark was passed. It's giving a whole new meaning to the last man standing. I don't know if they're scared or excited or simply that desperate to drink the Kool-Aid."

"Technoceuticals?"

"Not that we can tell. But that shit has so many variants, who would know?"

"Where's Roxie now?"

"Turtled up. Dixie was supposed to meet with her after her big speech, but the old girl split. Her assistant called instead, said Madame was indisposed and not feeling well, and needed to recover. Put off Dixie until next week."

"By next week, it could be too late."

"My thoughts exactly."

"So we should go to her house and get her, right? See what's really going on?"

She grinned. "My thoughts exactly."

Before we could move, the waiflike blonde that Dixie had befriended, Naeve, came rushing around the corner. "Aura reader, heads up," Nikki breathed.

I wasn't too worried, but then the woman stopped in front of us, panting with excitement. "Have either of you seen Dixie?" she gasped. "I—her cop friend, the cute one? He's been—"

Her gaze swung to me almost before the words were out. Nikki's hand nudged mine, and a wave of pure ease and detachment washed through me, a total instant Zen massage. The woman finished, and I blinked at her, trying to hear her voice over the rush of birdsong and ocean breezes.

"Injured?" I frowned. "Really?"

"Well—that's what I heard." Naeve stumbled back a step, tilting her head. "You know him too, right?"

Nikki snorted. "I don't think any warm-blooded woman in Vegas doesn't know Detective McHottiedom." Dixie sashayed around the corner, and Nikki glanced up, casting a lazy glance over her bourbon. "There's Dixie now, if you want to give her the news yourself."

"Oh! Yes—" The woman turned and dashed off, and Nikki removed her hand from mine.

"What the hell was that about?"

"Which part?"

"Was she trying to provoke a reaction or is Brody really hurt?"

"If he was, you really think *that* child would have picked up on it? No. She's purely an aura girl." She eyeballed me. "She was trying for yours, big-time. Dixie isn't known for being subtle, so ordinarily she'd ask you straight out. But this Brody thing has her tied up. She knows there's still something between you two beyond the whole Sariah Pelter business, and she doesn't understand what."

"There's nothing between Brody and me. She can have him whenever she'd like."

"Yeah, we're all believing that." Nikki drained her glass. "But, we can let that bucket of crazy simmer for a while. Instead, let's go see what Roxie has cooking. Stop off first at the hotel, so I can spruce up, 'kay?"

"I think you look great."

"Well, that's certainly true." She cocked a hip. "But I have the perfect thing for skulking through expensive houses, and I'd hate to pass up the opportunity."

We stood, and Dixie strolled up to us, happier than I'd seen her in a while, if still harried. The aura-reading elf had skipped merrily on her way, and I felt a small pang in my chest. If Dixie was super into Brody, who was I to horn in on that? I had my hands full with Armaeus anyway. And about six jobs lined up in the queue. I needed a romantic entanglement like a hole in the head.

"Nikki!" Dixie fairly bounced, her smile including both of us. "I'm glad I caught you." She was straight-up Stepford wife today, in a sundress and tennis bracelet, her pedicured toes peeking out of strappy sandals and her hair bigger than Texas. "Tell me you've got a plan for the parade up to the Bellagio?"

"You mean the *best party ever*? Why yes, yes, I do. Starts at dusk, rocks till dawn."

My phone jangled in my pocket, which startled me. I didn't know I was carrying a phone. "Sorry," I said, taking the opportunity for what it was worth. I held the phone to my ear and stepped away, toward the main exit of the SLS.

"Miss Wilde! I'm so glad you picked up. This is the front desk at the Palazzo. We've left several messages on your room phone."

I frowned. "Um, I've been out of town for a few days. Is there a problem with the room—the bill or anything?" Armaeus had been putting me up at the Palazzo for long enough, I supposed. Probably time for me to check into more economy digs.

"No, not exactly," the clerk said, recalling me. "You've had a package left for you at the front desk, and it's… Well, we think it'd be best if you retrieved it."

"A package?" Had Nikki been ordering from QVC again? "I'm sorry. I hope it isn't spoiling or anything."

"No, no, nothing like that. It would be best if you could fetch it, though." The man's voice was strained, and I shrugged. I scowled over at Nikki.

"You didn't order anything into the hotel, did you?"

She thought about it. "If the Thunder from Down Under has shown up, they're definitely mine."

I rolled my eyes. "Meet you there."

She waved me on, she and Dixie head to head, and I made my way through the sun worshipers to the front of the SLS. The walk to the Palazzo wasn't far, even in the blistering heat. By the time I reached the front lobby of my palatial hotel, however, I was wringing with sweat. Forget Nikki's change of clothes. I needed one.

I made a beeline for the front desk. "Hi, I'm Sara Wilde in room—"

"Miss Wilde, thank you." The clerk beamed at me. "I'm so glad you picked up my call."

"How'd you get that number, anyway? It's, ah, a new phone."

"Mr. Bertrand provided it to us. I do hope that's all right?"

Armaeus's telepathy of an hour earlier filtered through my memory. A "development," he'd said. "How long have you had this package?"

"A day or so. But it—well, you'll see. Please come with me."

I moved into the space behind the counter, through the door into what appeared to be an extended coat closet. At the end of the narrow passage, the corridor branched off in two directions. The desk attendant turned right. "We ordinarily keep residents' packages under lock and key until they request them. We scan everything, of course, for electronic or other explosive devices."

I stared at him in horror. "Do *not* tell me someone sent me a bomb here."

"Oh no!" He blinked at me. "But it's, well…odd."

We rounded the corner, and I could understand what he meant, immediately.

The package was a metal box, a padded envelope sealed with packing tape at its top. And it was humming.

"Ahhh…" I bit my lip. "You've had it scanned for a bomb?"

"There are no electronics inside it whatsoever. We

were going to call someone from Techzilla if we couldn't get hold of you today. It's not causing any harm, but it's…a little unnerving.

"Yeah, I can see that." As I approached the box, the humming grew softer, stopping when I stood right in front of it. Beside me, the man's eyes goggled.

I smiled brightly at him. "Well, hey! Looks like it's happy to see me. I'll take it upstairs."

"Will you—would you mind letting us know what's inside?"

I blinked. "I thought you scanned it. Don't you already know?"

He shrugged, his cheeks reddening. "That's the thing…nothing. There's nothing inside it at all. It's, well, an empty box."

As it turned out…not exactly.

I was still considering the thing—definitely not touching it—when Nikki sailed into my room thirty minutes later, double-checking herself at the door.

"Doll, what in God's creation is that? And where has it been all my life?"

I grimaced, leaning back on the sofa seat as she strode farther into the room. "That," I said, "is a crown originally worn by Genghis Khan, which I acquired for a client who was most insistent that it was going to be the answer to all his dreams. Unfortunately, said client is not answering his phone, or his text, or his e-mail, and there was nothing in the box besides this thing, in all its Mongolian glory." Nikki stepped forward. "Don't touch it," I held up my hand. "At least not directly. The last time I did, I woke up an entire army of bad guys."

"And it's here because…"

I sighed. "Apparently, there's been a development."

CHAPTER TWENTY-FIVE

The Magician wasn't answering his phone either, and after another full hour of trying to raise my client in Ulaanbaatar, we gave up. Stowing the helmet in the hotel room safe proved a nonstarter, since it instantly started humming again. Loudly. In fact, anytime I got more than fifteen feet away from the thing, the humming kicked up.

After much discussion, we ended up stowing it in a messenger bag, which Nikki refused to carry since it didn't go with her outfit. Besides, she reasoned, she was already packing a gun. She didn't want to weigh herself down.

We had barely enough time to visit Roxie before the Connected parade was due to hit the Strip. At that point, we'd need to be back at Ground Zero, with every Council member reporting for duty along with Armaeus and his scroll case of doom, just to be safe. And again, maybe the crowd of revelers would work to our advantage. Maybe SANCTUS would decide that solstice night wasn't the best time for Armageddon, given how many un-Connecteds would be caught in the crossfire.

Maybe.

As we tooled up the curving drive toward Roxie's, however, something was definitely off. There was no one in the guardhouse, no sprightly valet to come out to greet us. The place was deserted. As in deserted, deserted. Shouldering my messenger bag, I stepped out of the car with Nikki, and we moved up the palatial steps with increasing speed.

"This isn't good." Nikki stopped me with an outstretched hand, then proceeded up the last several steps without me, the gun that had been tucked into her waistband now out and up. I had my own gun hidden in my hoodie, but my fingers were already tingling.

The front door stood ajar, and there were signs of forced entry. Based on the blank screen of the security system inside the door, the electronics in the house were disabled. Nikki shot me a glance. "You going to call Brody?"

"Hmmm." I weighed my options. "Prolly should." He'd wanted me as his informant. It was probably to my advantage to play along. And yet…

"It'd be bad if he was in a meeting, though. Or on a date." Nikki edged the door open a little more, her eyes glinting with excitement. "Maybe you should text. Or Facebook him, maybe."

"Text." I nodded. "I bet he keeps that on silent unless he's getting pinged by official channels." I keyed in the address and my suspicion of a break-in, downplaying the latter to a "possible." Then I glanced back to Nikki with wide eyes. "Gosh, in the absence of official instruction, I wonder what we should do?"

Nikki laid a hand on her chest, her inky-black T-shirt and jeans perfectly offsetting her army boots, her auburn hair pulled back in a ponytail below her SWAT ball cap. "Roxie is our friend. We're very close."

"It's only to be expected that we would check on her."

"She could be hurt. Or drunk. No one should drink alone."

Despite the banter, our voices were tight, our movements precise. We entered the house without touching anything with our hands and edged the door nearly shut again behind us, both of us tense and alert. The place had the same feel as before—creepy mausoleum of the strange—but it screamed abandonment, too.

"Staff?" I murmured.

"Nothing feels dead here." Nikki shook her head. "Place is a ghost land." We moved into the theatre, passing the sign advertising five-dollar card readings. Nothing remained on the stage. Not the table, not the crystal ball. The rest of the tour of the house proved equally perplexing, until we stopped in the front room again. I scanned Roxie's scrapbook pile. Something made me look twice at the overstuffed volumes, and I paused, frowning down.

"I wonder..."

The Connecteds of this world were a sketchy lot in many ways. As a fringe group living on the edge of society, they sometimes had very good reasons to make friends in high places. And sometimes even better reasons to make friends in low places. "Roxie became a Council member in the seventies, right?"

"Yup."

I pawed through the stack of scrapbooks to get toward the bottom. The further back they went, the thicker but less glamorous they were. By the time I reached the 1970s, the book was heavy with old tape and bristling with news clippings, playbills, and fading photographs. Roxie hadn't been a member of the Arcana Council then. She'd been a grifter searching for a score, and she wasn't too choosy about who she made it with, if these pictures were any indication. Most of her photos had been taken on the arms of guys who looked like they were little more than thugs.

How much had she gotten in return sharing her gifts? So much profound magic in the world was seemingly granted by objects or conferred by spells, and people were always willing to believe something.

I paged through at a rapid clip. Roxie had made the rounds with starlets, musicians, politicians, and mobsters, each account more breathless than the last. Her face changed too, over the course of one year in particular—fuller, richer, more beautiful. Something had shifted in her, something important. I paged back further. And then I found it.

"Son of a bitch," I breathed. I pointed at the picture, and Nikki squinted down.

"Is that Jerry Fitz—no, way too young. Then again, that family tree has gotta be crooked all the way down to the roots. Fitz's dad?" She shrugged. "Well, she wouldn't be the first to rub shoulders with a bad guy. He's about as ugly as his kid was."

"Not him. The guy next to him."

Nikki frowned and leaned in. "Dude in the suit? Never seen him before."

"I have." I rocked back on my heels. "He's a lot older now, and he's upgraded to robes. That's the future Cardinal Rene Ventre. I don't know what he was doing in nineteen seventy six, but currently he's the head of SANCTUS." I stared at the picture again, memorizing it. "He was probably a foot soldier back then. He had to be somebody to be in that picture with her, considering where she ended up, and given that Fitz the younger was in bed with SANCTUS for at least a little while."

"That's not Fitz, though, that's his dad." Nikki shook her head. "She might not have known this Ventre guy at all."

I took in Roxie's wide, hard smile. "She might not have known what he was going to become, but she'd already had a lot of hard years in the grift logged by the mid-seventies. She knew how to spot someone important. Someone powerful. And some alliances, once formed, might be hard to back out on. No matter where your life took you later." I focused again on the elder Fitz, thinking about all the pills his son had been hyped on, all these years later. Had the technoceutical market already been in full swing all the way back then?

"Speculation." Nikki pushed out her lower lip. "All we know is that Roxie went to a party where she was schmoozing it up with Fitz's dad, and a very young, very green future cardinal was in attendance too. Doesn't mean she *wasn't* cutting deals with bad guys, doesn't mean she was."

"And if she did...and she subsequently was elevated to the Council..." I grimaced. "I don't know how that works. The Council is about balance, dark to light. But if everyone knows you're working with the bad guys? That's not going to make you super popular at the dinner table."

"Then again, she lived up here, not down on the Strip. So maybe she knew she wasn't welcome."

"But if you're the Council, and you know you've got a traitor in your midst, wouldn't you want to keep a closer eye on her? Pushing her away seems kind of dumb."

"Dumb—or playing the long game. And let's face it…their long game is a lot longer than most."

At that moment an ear-splitting shriek sounded through the house, like the whine of a laser cutting through solid metal. My inner ears revolted, but Nikki responded far worse, the sound driving her to her knees in full collapse.

I flailed for my messenger bag and pawed through it, even as another burst of pain scorched my brain. The only thing I could think of—*the helmet*. The Mongolian crown. Whatever it was, I needed something to cover my ears. No matter what kind of crazy came along as a gift with purchase.

I shoved the thing on my head, and the pain suddenly…stopped.

That Genghis Khan was all right, I decided on the spot. Though I could hear the psyche-shredding noise on the outside of my helmet, it no longer crushed me.

"Oh, Sweet Mother Mary…"

I wheeled around. Nikki was sprawled on the floor, her long legs akimbo, her arms cradling her head. She was trying to wedge herself under a coffee table with questionable success. Her pain was as outsized as her body, and I stumbled over to her, dropping to one knee. I pulled on her shoulder, then jerked back, narrowly avoiding her elbow check. Using all my strength, I dragged her from the table, and she came around, fist flying.

"Ow!" My head rang with another sound, but it was Nikki who bounced back, grabbing her fist with her other hand, white with shock. "You hit me!"

"What *is* that?" she wailed, shaking out her hand.

"Here." I wrenched the crown off my head, nausea swamping me. I yanked off her hat and pushed the helmet over her ponytail. It wasn't a perfect fit, but she shuddered anyway, sinking back to her knees.

"*ThankyoubabyJesus,*" she moaned.

I wasn't doing so well, though. The sound assaulted me from all sides now, riddling my bones. Worse, handling the crown was freaking me out. The last time I'd touched the thing, an entire phalanx of death-masked bodyguards had come crashing down on top of me. I hadn't thought too much about them since leaving Mongolia, but my client had gone radio silent. Was there a reason?

I knew I needed to move, to escape, but without the crown to shield me, I couldn't do anything but sink to my knees, my arms wrapped around my head, vibrating with sound.

"Sara—Sara!" Brody Rooks came pounding up beside us, catching me with one arm and hauling Nikki to her feet with his other hand. I blinked at him, trying to focus. "What the hell is wrong with you two? Why weren't you waiting outside?" Pause. "What in God's name is Nikki wearing on her head?"

Nikki moaned beside me, and I tried to focus on Brody. Not terribly easy, though, since there were six of him. "Can't you hear that?"

He frowned at me. "Hear what?"

The sound threatened to cleave my skull in two. Twisting away from Brody, I jammed my hands over my ears. Only then did the sound dim enough for me to breathe, but barely. Nikki twisted away from both of us, stumbling back. At that moment, a new variation to the sound pounded through me, scraping at my lungs, my bones. Taking me apart and putting me back together again.

"What time—what time is it," I gasped. "Has the sun set?"

"What?"

I staggered to the side, then attempted to move past Brody. He barked commands to the men and women who'd somehow appeared behind him, then his steady arm wrapped around me, propping me up.

"What is wrong with you?" he hissed again. But at least he was moving now, hustling me toward the door, as if he thought I'd magically recover when I got outside. I knew I wouldn't, though. I knew the sound would just get worse.

I was right.

"Nikki," I gasped.

The stream of curses behind me verified that Nikki was being helped out by the boys in blue as well. Her hands were on either side of the crown, though whether she was trying to remove it or hold it steady, I wasn't sure.

"Talk to me, Sara," Brody growled. "I don't know what's happening to you. Do you need a hospital—both of you?"

"No." I turned toward the Strip's skyline. It gleamed merrily in the distance, the image-on-image exposure of the Arcana Council's homes flickering like found video over top of it. Of all the casinos, this time it wasn't Prime Luxe or Scandal that flared the brightest, it was a fragile fairyland castle, soaring over one of the most elegant hotels on the Strip: the home of the Empress.

And before that casino, steam roiled and churned, smoke without a fire.

"Sara!" Nikki's voice sounded wrenched out of her

body, and I turned as she pulled away from the cops, reeling toward me. In her hands, she held out the Mongolian crown, her eyes wide with stark pain, her entire body trembling. "Take this—go. You'll... It has to be you, not just Armaeus. Saw it—you have to go!"

Without thinking, I grabbed the crown and jammed it on my head. Nikki collapsed back into the arms of two powerfully built policemen, out cold. I winced. She'd hate missing that.

I turned to Brody, grabbing his arm. His eyes practically bugged out of his head at the sight of me wearing my fancy Mongolian helmet.

"I'll explain on the way," I said, pulling him toward the knot of police cars. "Take me to the Bellagio."

CHAPTER TWENTY-SIX

By the time we got there, it was clear that something seriously screwed up was hitting the Strip. The streetlights had shut down, rendering traffic an impossible snarl. Horns blared and drivers raged all around us. Brody had long since ditched his vehicle, and we were approaching Las Vegas Boulevard on foot from a side street, angling over and into the complete logjam of traffic.

All the mirror-bright Jumbotrons were flashing up and down the Strip, though, streaming several times faster than their normal rate. People in the streets were alternately fixated or running for their lives...

Or on their knees screaming in pain, their hands clamped over their ears.

Most of them I didn't recognize, of course. A few of them surprised me. The ones I did recognize even if I didn't truly know them—hadn't seen any of them until earlier this week—made everything clear.

Connecteds were falling like flies.

No wonder SANCTUS hadn't had a problem with wreaking judgment in the middle of a crowded city. No one but the psychics were being hurt.

Judgment.

My mind flew to the card I'd drawn in the Magician's conference room not two days ago. In the rush and tumble of finding the scroll cases, I'd forgotten it, but here it was, in full living color. The Judgment card depicted an angelic being soaring high above the Earth, blowing a horn. At its call, those who were blessed would rise up, while those who were not…

Another piercing tone rent my eardrums despite the crown, and I winced, staggering against Brody. This wasn't the Rapture. It couldn't be. This was more like a Daft Punk concert gone horribly wrong.

"I get it, I get it," he muttered, sounding like he had lockjaw. I tried to focus on him.

"You can hear that?"

"I'm not deaf, Sara. I heard it as soon as we turned onto the Boulevard. I don't know why it's making everyone flip out, but someone is clearly on the wrong end of a sound-system board and can't shut it off. Gotta be some sort of electric malfunction in the grid, but if it's not, if it's a weapon, then it's a damned effective one. At least for about a third of this crowd."

"It's a weapon." My words were lost as he muscled us forward, his arms steady around me. He half pushed, half dragged me toward the Bellagio. I could see it primarily because the fairytale castle soared above it, lighting the way. We'd made it as far as Caesars Palace when I heard my name called out.

I wheeled to the side. Simon sat in a souped-up double cab monster truck, which was parked unceremoniously on the lawn in front of Caesars. Beside me, Brody bristled. "Who the hell is that—is he the one doing this?"

It was a reasonable assumption. Both of Simon's

cab doors were open, revealing a veritable forest of electronics. But Simon himself looked like he was barely hanging on. He was plastered against the back of the cab, writhing in pain, his hands jammed to his ears.

"Sound emission," he groaned, shaking his head as we ran up to him. "I thought I had it contained, but it kicked up too fast. My abilities—tied to inner ear." A new whine sang out over the Strip, and he sagged against his truck cab. "You're going to need to do..."

"Oh, *Hell* no." I took one look at the war room in his truck and made the decision easily. I yanked my helmet off and staggered back as the full assault of noise hit me. But I straightened and drove forward.

"Here," I said, thrusting the crown at Simon. He stared at me blankly but didn't protest when I fitted it over his head. It looked a lot more at home over his skullcap than Nikki's ponytail, and Simon's shoulders straightened, his gaze snapping to mine.

"What is this thing?"

"Use it, but watch out. Anyone run up to you wearing a Mongolian death mask, he is *not* fooling around."

Confusion blanked his features, but I didn't have time for explanations. He'd figure it out. Another blast of sound had him diving for his controls, while I fell back against Brody. The detective had swiveled his gaze back to the Bellagio too, apparently not as interested in playing traffic cop as getting to the bottom of the disturbance. I couldn't blame him. A torrent of steam billowed up in front of the elegant casino. I staggered forward, and Brody's arms went around me again. Despite the pain in my head, the solidity of him against my body felt right. It felt good.

Then another blast of sound jerked me off my feet and almost sent us toppling. "Christ, Sara, what is your problem?" Brody gritted out, sounding pissed. "It isn't that bad."

"Not for you it isn't." I braced myself against him. "Remember the sound at the Rarity party? Annika Soo toppling over like a sack of potatoes right before all the cases blew? This is that. Times a million."

No one could accuse Brody of being slow. "Son of a bitch." He stared at me. "The Rarity was a dry run."

I couldn't respond coherently to that, but it didn't matter. Brody hauled me along and I held on to his jacket, my eyes swimming with tears. Gradually the pulse lessened, shifted, and I was able to lift my head again without the threat of hurling. I was one of the few, though. We moved through the crowd, and visibility got a lot better, mainly because so many people were collapsing right and left. Like Nikki in Roxie's mansion, they were taking shelter under cars, under each other, or in the flimsy protection of their own folded arms. The people in the cars weren't faring much better. It wasn't the metal in Simon's helmet that was providing him protection, but something else. The stones? The magic left over in the crown itself? Something.

I didn't have time to puzzle over it. The final knot of people gave way, and at last we were at the Bellagio. With a glance, the reason for the steam became clear.

The dancing fountains of the Bellagio Casino were an attraction known the world over. Placed in graceful lines and arcs throughout the pool, the fountains were timed to shoot streams of water against the backdrop of a precise selection of music, perfectly calibrated to both soothe and delight watchers, from toddlers to octogenarians.

That wasn't what was happening now.

Geysers blew and swirled, moving water as if it was being dredged up from the depths of the Earth. Instead of a happy spray, the fountains were like a desert-born hurricane, localized barely within the edges of the pool.

A black van had been pulled up onto the sidewalk in front of the Bellagio, nothing special. It didn't have the letters SANCTUS emblazoned across its panels, or a pope hat, tails, and dagger symbol. It wouldn't have necessarily been all that out of the ordinary, except for the mini satellite dishes perched at its top. The whole effect made it look like a high-end cable or media news network van.

The back doors of the vehicle were open, and Armaeus stood behind it. Next to him, Kreios stood at his ease, holding Roxie. The Empress sagged like a wilted flower in his arms, and I couldn't tell if he was being solicitous or keeping her from escaping. Either way, she wasn't going anywhere fast. Eshe wasn't nearby that I could see, but then sight was becoming more of a problem the closer I got.

Armaeus's voice sounded in my head, scoring me with pain. Only he wasn't talking to me.

"You dare. You dare to come into my home with your petty tricks, to paint a damning mark upon the most gifted of this world?"

For all his righteous fury, he wasn't doing anything to stop said damning mark, and Brody winced beside me as my fingers dug into his arm. I squinted, trying to see Armaeus through the crowd. His voice sounded ragged, beneath his anger. Too ragged.

"What's happening?" Brody gritted out. "The

sound just amped up about six times."

I managed a bleary glare around me. The Connecteds remained definitely affected, but their reaction had taken on a new character, almost an excitement instead of pain. They were quivering like tuning forks. And they were all angled toward the black van.

I blinked. Even *I* felt better, sort of. Stronger. More alive. And about to come out of my skin.

"It's—the van. SANCTUS," I tried to say. "Need to—get—"

"I know. We'll get you there."

When I tried to take a step and failed, Brody practically picked me up, pushing me forward. From this vantage point, I couldn't see all the men Armaeus had transfixed in front of the Bellagio. The ones I could see, however, weren't doing so well. Their weapons lay on the wide concrete sidewalk in front of the fountains, smoking and twisted. And the men themselves had their hands slapped over their ears, writhing in agony.

I straightened a little, frowning at that. They weren't reacting the way they should be. The Connecteds in the street all seemed to be rallying, but these men…

Armaeus stood between the back of the van and the Bellagio fountains. His hand was held high like some modern day Moses in front of the roiling water. He wasn't commanding the seas to part, however. Instead, he twisted his fingers toward the van, and the pitch of the electrical tone jumped several more notches. *"You – are hunting – the wrong prey."*

The wrong prey? I pulled myself up, using Brody as a human prop. "Don't do anything stupid, Sara," he managed. "I don't feel so great all of a sudden."

I glanced at him. I felt ...actually a lot better. With the elevation of the tone's pitch, something new was rolling through me, something that couldn't quite be classified as pleasure but was a lot better than the cocktail of pain that had been ramming through my system up to that point.

Behind me, the worst of the screaming had stopped too. Progress.

But Armaeus... Armaeus was on his last legs. Four equidistant flares of red shone on his torso, and though a haze of magic beamed from him, creating a shield, within that shield he looked gray with fatigue. The smallest scroll case was open at his feet, and he was bathed in its waves of energy. But were those waves helping or hurting him?

We cleared the remaining several feet and came around the end of the van. Brody and I seemed to be the only non-Arcana Council members still coherent.

Armaeus paid no attention to us. His focus was on the back of the van, and renewed fury swamped me when I saw what was inside. A screen showing a room full of black-robed clerics glowed from the van's interior. Men I knew. Men I'd seen, while spying on them via astral travel. But these men, these SANCTUS elite, weren't amorphous images anymore. They were real.

And they'd done enough damage for one lifetime.

I surged forward in Brody's arms, memorizing their faces. Each of them had the blood of hundreds of people on their hands. Possibly more. Many of them children. So much needless death. So much needless agony for them to repay.

They were apparently putting a down payment on that bill right now. They sat transfixed in their chairs, gripped in the Magician's thrall.

"You must...pay." Armaeus shook his head hard as I stared at him. Had he picked up my thoughts? He rallied. *"You must see the truth of what is worth fearing."*

The sound flowing out of the van grew worse again, seeming to set my bones on fire. The vehicle was clearly some kind of transmitter, except Armaeus had taken the controls. And now he was faltering.

Beside me, Brody moaned, and it was my turn to hold on to him. "Hang in there, big guy," I muttered. Then I reconsidered. "Or give me your gun." He'd commandeered mine before he'd let me in his car. Blasted cops.

His answering laugh was sharp with pain. "Not a chance."

Armaeus's exultant words thundered out. *"See the truth!"*

With that, he turned, and the scroll case at his feet burst forth with light. I knew what those cases had been built for. I knew the language they contained. Language Armaeus now held in sway.

And worse, or better...I could hear that language too. It filled my mouth and ears, a benediction begging to be spoken. It filled my heart and soul, a fury begging to be unleashed.

Armaeus threw his head back as his hand shifted again, and the sound was so loud, my molecules seemed to come apart. *"You would—"*

A voice boomed from the Bellagio fountains. *"You will fail!"*

No sooner had the Magician turned to the raging water than he faltered, going down on one knee. I did break free of Brody then. For I could see what lay beyond that watery curtain, billowing with fury. I could see what watched with unholy frenzy, twisting and roiling back on itself. I could see what Armaeus had ensnared and what he meant for it to do.

I could see.

I jolted forward, racing for the ring of magic crackling around Armaeus.

"No!" Brody staggered away from me, dropping heavily to his knees, then collapsing to the ground.

Armaeus wrenched his hand in a sideways motion.

The world was split in two.

I caught the flash of a robed figure, the light in its hands falling away. Water gushed out of the Bellagio fountains, churning, roaring. And there, within the waves, a monstrous creature thrashed.

It was a dragon. A blue dragon, trapped on a field of red.

CHAPTER TWENTY-SEVEN

I knew a dragon when I saw one, of course. And I'd seen this one before. I should have been prepared when it slid forth from the water and raked the world with its serpentine gaze. Its wings flared. Its snout lifted. Fire leaked from its mouth.

But I wasn't prepared. Not by a long shot.

Fear swept through me like a tidal wave, rendering me mute.

I was the only one, though.

The screams that began were most noticeable because of their depth. It wasn't the women who started screaming first. It was the men. An ancient, almost primeval cry of terror that struck at the most basic of their protective instincts. The awareness that this, they could not take down with spear or club or bow. This, they could not vanquish. This, they could not drive back.

To this, they and all they held dear…were char.

The dragon opened its mouth, and the roar that issued forth was destruction and death, power and demand, and endless, oppressive servitude. It was a world swept with pestilence and pain in the service of but one true master, all talents and treasures bent to serve this one higher being.

A being of storm and loss.

"No!" Whether I spoke the word in the ancient tongue of the gods or in my own, the dragon heard me. So did Armaeus. Both of them turned their attention on me, and I was lifted in the vortex of their focus, struggling to breathe.

Armaeus looked like I'd never seen him before. Filled with an unholy fire, he appeared several sizes too large, still marginally human but somehow spilling out of his body and occupying the space around him. His chest bled freely, blood streaming from him in crimson flames. Kreios stood beyond the edge of our protected circle, his post with the Empress abandoned. She lay like a crumpled rag doll to the side. But Kreios didn't add his power to Armaeus—he couldn't. He was on the outside.

Only I could stand.

And once more, I gazed out over a field of rage and fire and saw what was staring back.

Llyr.

An ancient and terrible dread filled me. I knew this creature, and it knew me. Though it had made no move toward me at the time, I'd seen it in a flash a decade ago when I'd watched my own home go up in a ball of fiery death. I'd caught glimpses of it in the years since, the blue dragon trapped on a field of red. I had known it was there, shifting in the darkness, but had no reason or understanding as to why. But it knew me, knew me and wanted me as its own, just as it wanted the world as its own.

As the world had been once, and was fated to be again.

My bones turned to water.

The Magician kept speaking, but I couldn't hear him any more. Couldn't hear his incantations, his protests. I was trapped in the eye of Llyr, and my very blood slowed in my veins, agony coursing through me.

"You feel it, don't you?"

That wasn't the Magician speaking.

I centered my attention on Llyr. It was staring right at me. Its gaze was bold, challenging, but it did not strike me as male or female, or sexual in any way. It was an entity made up of pure energy and pure malice, and I was nothing more than its tool.

But I could be an *extraordinary* tool.

"I will give you riches and power beyond your imagination," it whispered, its words slipping along and through and over and around Armaeus's, even as the Magician exhorted the leaders of SANCTUS to cease their battle on Connecteds and take up arms against this foreign threat. Llyr's words were spoken aloud though, not in my head. I could hear them. The dragon was here. In this world. And it meant to stay. *"I will return in triumph and glory, and you will be my general."*

"No," I managed, my word barely a whisper.

"You cannot deny your nature, no more than you can deny your parents. Or do you still not realize who you are, Sariah Pelter Wilde? Or who you were?"

The creature lunged forward, though it remained constrained in the boiling waters of the Bellagio fountain. Still, I stumbled back. My breath caught. My lungs burned. My eyes swam with blood and gore. In Llyr's gaze, I saw death—death and pain, in that order. Surrounded with all the riches in the world and too broken to enjoy any of it.

"The limits of your life would be swept away. I would

give you what the Council would not. I would give you truth. I would give you past and future. You are far more like me than you know. Far more than you can imagine. Far more than your mother's daughter – or your father's."

That caught me. An image of my mother flashed before my eyes. How many years had it been? Would I ever get the truth of why she died? *How* she died?

"You are asking the wrong questions."

The statement was so familiar, I was yanked out of my reverie. The creature's maw opened, and what sounded like laughter emerged, laughter and rending fire. The flames licked along the sidewalk, setting aflame the Connecteds closest to the water. That woke them out of their stupor, and their screams galvanized the others.

Without thinking, I stooped down to the concrete and lifted the scroll case to my face. Power suffused me, and I could see the bones of my fingers separate, the yellow pulse of flame and energy bursting up and out.

"You're not meant for this world," I cried, holding the scroll case high. "You shall not rule!"

"I will – "

"No!" I steadied my hand and spoke the words of binding, words I didn't know, couldn't understand. But it was as if by positioning myself as a prism for the magic within the scroll cases, the word of creation would do the rest. My very blood caught fire then, my hair melting away, my eyes going wide, and still I didn't falter—I couldn't falter. There was no money in the world that would stop a creature like this. There were no jobs I could take on, no riches I could steal. But I would be damned if this thing broke through on my watch to take its due of the Connected. "No. You will *not!*"

The dragon recoiled. Its scream was not one of pain or anguish. It was not of the wrongfully accused. It was not even of madness. It was intelligence and knowledge, and deep, abiding fury.

More words flowed through me in the ancient language encoded within the gold scroll case, a language so secret it did not rest on tablets or papyrus, but was inscribed on the very air.

All at once, the water reversed direction and rushed again toward Llyr, beating back the creature which was putting an enormous clawed foot on the sidewalk. The concrete buckled beneath the dragon's weight, and it punctured the slab like it was Styrofoam, its talons wedging a deep groove as Llyr was dragged back toward oblivion.

But I wasn't finished yet. I was lit on fire, electricity sparking off me in every direction, my body suffused in a flowing robe that wasn't my clothing but the arc of power that coalesced around me, bending the magnetic field in such a way that the deep underground currents of energy-infused ley lines beneath Vegas reverberated with power, shuddering throughout the city and far beyond. And I spoke the language that had no words, the slipstream of its images and form blending within me into a dance of deadly power.

The water burst even more forcefully against the dragon, ensnaring it bodily within the bounds of the Bellagio pool. Llyr wheeled back as if struck by an unseen hand. Its wings spread mightily, tripling its size, but the power facing it was too great, too focused.

Another shadow flashed across the gap between worlds. The watery veil thickened, rendering the image of the dragon blurred, harder to see. A hazy image of a robed figure flickered again, hunched and hastening, his lamp shooting a brilliance so bright that it could be seen across the dimensions.

Then it vanished, and the portal with it.

The dragon's scream resonated along my nerve endings as it finally fell back into the hole from which it had been summoned, and was gone.

Llyr was gone.

The roar in my brain would not subside, however, and I turned—without thinking, with only knowing—and hurled the golden scroll case into the SANCTUS van.

The resulting explosion rocked the whole of Vegas, a burst of magic so powerful and sure that it traveled all the way across the planet to find the seed of evil buried deep inside those who would root out magic for good. Found it and blasted it to nothing within its squalid hole.

A part of me traveled with that burst. Traveled and witnessed, understood and reported, a million fractured images coalescing as one.

For a long, frozen moment, silence blanketed the Strip.

My knees buckled.

Slowly, far too slowly, I fell.

And face-planted into concrete.

The city rushed back to life, as if exhaling a collective breath. Above and around us, the lights of the Jumbotrons flickered and blared once more. From somewhere a horn sounded. At a far distance, a siren wailed.

A strong set of hands held me and pulled me to my feet, steadying me.

"Well done, Miss Wilde." Armaeus's voice was

grave, resonant with the power he'd thrown. The irises of his eyes had gone from golden to completely black. He seemed otherworldly, staring down at me. I was pretty sure I saw smoke wafting from his ears. The bloody rents in his clothing were gone, the material clean, perfect.

"What…what just happened?"

Armaeus straightened, standing away from me. The smug smile I was so used to had returned to his face. "So many…fascinating things."

Around us, everyone stirred. The men beside the van stumbled to their feet, looking like they'd been hit with baseball bats. They blinked around owlishly, fear spreading across their faces. The van itself smoldered, a warped husk of twisted metal. The Connecteds in the street and surrounding the Bellagio fountains milled around with equal confusion. To my magic-amped eye, the world spit and spun with arcing lines of power, a bristle of electrical wires dancing with too much charge. But the un-Connecteds didn't see this. Couldn't see this. Even the Bellagio's famed reflecting pool had returned completely to normal, dancing with happy abandon in the reflected lights of the city.

My gaze dropped. Well, not completely normal. Four huge gashes marred the cheerful white concrete of the fountain area, extending backward toward the pool before ending right before they pierced the low wall.

The SANCTUS paneled van smoked and steamed beside us, but it was no longer held in a thrall of magic. It seemed almost normal, actually.

Right up until a golden scroll case rolled out of its open doors, then bounced across the sidewalk toward me.

No one noticed as I picked the case up, stowing it in my hoodie. Everyone was chattering, Connected and otherwise, most in knots with each other. Other than the shattered concrete and the smashed van, the rest of the world was acting like the last hour had never happened. Traffic rolled forward, people were talking, walking—like animatronics wound up and set to movement on the Strip.

"Sara." Brody's words were less of a plea than an irritated snap, and I turned to him, reflexively reaching for his hand to pull him to a standing position.

"Jeez, Brody, I'm sorry, I—"

When our hands touched, I froze, my eyes going wide.

"It's okay." Brody's own momentum carried him forward, and he shook his head. "I have got a bitch of a headache, though." He frowned. "Why the hell—how the hell did I get downtown? I thought we were meeting at Roxie Meadows's house." He glanced down at his hand, which I was still holding—now with both of mine. "Um… You okay, Sara?"

"Sorry." I dropped his hand as his gaze swung to the smoking hulk of a van. "The sound came from there?" he asked, wincing as he took his first step. "Shit, my head hurts."

He faltered, and I grabbed him again, taking his full weight. He smelled like heat and ash, and I couldn't deny the zing of awareness that went through me. Except what I was feeling this time wasn't the simple rush of pleasure and anxiety and hope and doubt that Brody's touch had been exciting in me pretty much since I'd hit puberty. This was something else entirely.

Brody was a Connected.

"Not exactly, Miss Wilde." Armaeus disentangled me from Brody and stabilized the detective, eyeing him fully in the face. For his part, Brody blinked at Armaeus as if he couldn't fully see him, still shaking his head. "The purpose of the SANCTUS attack was to wage a sonic blast at a specific frequency which they knew to be harmful to Connecteds."

"Cardinal Ventre and Roxie," I said. "They were working together all this time. She chose his strength over the Council's in the end." Nikki and I had been right about that much at least.

"The initial pain you experienced was the result of their efforts, yes. It was," he nodded, standing back from Brody, apparently satisfied that the detective wasn't going to crumple. "Neatly done."

Brody's brain came back on line, bristling as his last synapses flared to life. "So where is Roxie Meadows, exactly?"

Armaeus gestured to a small knot of people around the fallen woman. She was moving, at least, but moaning. Weakly. Brody headed off for her without a second glance to me.

I frowned. "What did you do to him?"

"A harmless adjustment." Armaeus dismissed my concern. "What SANCTUS did not seem to recall, and of course the Empress had no interest in explaining, is that a slight alteration to the pitch they'd chosen would produce an effect quite the opposite of what they intended. Instead of destroying the sensitivities of Connecteds, it augmented them, the same way it had augmented Roxie's abilities all those years ago. In some very special cases, Connecteds will find themselves altered quite dramatically."

"Dramatically?" I watched as Dixie emerged from

the crowd, her face alight with wonder. "Like how dramatically?"

"Those Connected with a moderate level of ability are now masters. Masters are now savants. For a short while, even the dilettantes and fringe practitioners of the Connected community will experience heightened awareness, astral travel, lucid dreams, visions, and coincidences that cannot be easily explained away."

"So they got their Rapture after all."

"In a word, yes." Armaeus nodded. "It will seem as if a psychic renaissance has been visited upon them. The rush of power will show them the pathway to greater understanding, if only for a while."

I grimaced. "Everyone?"

"Everyone within the enhanced magical boundaries of the Las Vegas power grid. As it happens, that includes several very powerful Connecteds. The Deathwalkers will find themselves enhanced to a level they will find virtually intolerable, as they will not consider it organic to their own abilities."

Despite myself, my lips twitched. "Danae, too?"

"Danae especially," he said. "Annika Soo remains within the city, recovering from the first blast she received at the Rarity gala. Now she will have another level of augmentation to manage. We will be watching her very closely. Monsieur Mercault arrived this afternoon, in a coma." Armaeus tilted his head, his gaze fixed on the horizon as a smile ghosted across his lips. "He is no longer in danger, however. Which means that answers will be forthcoming regarding the assault on his home by SANCTUS, and just how deeply he is mired in the network of dark practitioners."

I gaped at him. "You think you're going to turn

him to your side?"

Armaeus's glance back to me was sardonic. "I am on no 'side', Miss Wilde, but that of—"

I held up a hand. "I beg you. Don't say it."

"Very well. But Mercault, Soo and Danae should all prove very interesting to watch, over the coming days." His gaze rested on me, and though he was speaking normally—as normal as Armaeus got anyway—his eyes remained far too dark.

A sudden, irrational concern gripped me. "You were augmented too, weren't you."

"I needed to be." He waved back to the fountain. "Calling Llyr to show his face is not the act of an acolyte, at least not for an acolyte who wishes to keep control of the portal."

"That's where Mantorov screwed up, right? He didn't have the power—you did. And the portal took him because of that.

"Grigori Mantorov knew a great deal, and knew enough that he did not wish to channel Llyr of his own volition. He drew me there, anticipating correctly that I would come for the same treasure he craved. The language of the ancients."

"...And God said..."

He nodded. "A language not written for this dimension but which transcends it, accessible to the trained who speak it with power." His smile twisted. "Or who possess the ability to use it without training."

I ignored that for the moment. "Now what? Brody is a Connected, Armaeus. He wasn't before."

"He was—somewhat," Armaeus said. "You cannot augment what is not there. He is an able detective, and his success is doubtless in part due to what he would call intuition. That is what was augmented, in a pure psychic sense."

"Yeah, well." I frowned as Brody and Dixie stood staring at each other, lost in conversation. "He's not going to start levitating or anything, is he?"

"Is that truly your concern?"

"Nope, he's not my concern at all." I shifted my gaze back to the Magician. "I thought you were injured. Failing."

"And again you came to my aid." His expression softened. "Your raw power was at the surface, waiting to be tapped. In the moment, I judged it would be more effective than mine. Llyr has faced me before. Old foes know each other's weaknesses. You, however, he underestimated."

"Not by a lot." He'd missed the mark on fame and fortune, maybe. But not when it came to my parents. That had been spot-on. Too spot-on.

I felt a familiar pressure in my mind.

"Cut that out, juice head," I snapped. "I've been amped up too, you know. Which means my wards are stronger."

"And yet…" He stood closer to me. Way too close. "Were you to allow me, I could also help you push past boundaries that you have heretofore been unable to break, make connections from which your own mind has barred you. In the time we have remaining under this influence, it is something to consider."

And maybe, just maybe my brain wouldn't break anymore. Maybe, just maybe, I didn't have to be afraid of what Armaeus would find if I let him in.

Then I seemed to hear the rest of his words.

"Ahhh… Time we have remaining?"

"The effects of this sonic blast cannot be sustained. Worse, they can only be replicated with a sound emission once every several years. Otherwise, repeated exposure to the sound produces lesser and lesser results."

"So Roxie's greatest con was well-timed, back in the seventies."

He nodded. "If she had not ascended to the Council, her abilities would have faded as well. The sonic amplification would have run its course."

"Like a drug."

"Exactly like that." He gestured to the crowd. "At this moment we are—all of us—under the influence of a drug."

"There goes my future in the military." I squinted at the men in the van. "What about them?"

"Those truly not possessing psychic abilities will be unfazed, but the majority of those involved with SANCTUS turned to the group, ironically, because of their psychic abilities and their repressed shame over them. Now they will feel a great rightness within them that should feel like a wrong. It will send many of them to prayer, some to defection from their faith-based beliefs, and others will simply expand their understanding about what is possible in this world."

"They've become the enemy." I liked that. I liked that a lot.

Traffic parted enough for a tow truck to lumber onto the sidewalk, aiming for the crushed van. The SANCTUS drivers were being checked out by EMTs at this point, a cluster of cops standing off to the side with Brody. "You're going to let SANCTUS's minions go?"

"They will be cited for failure to control their vehicle." He shrugged. "After that, there will be no recollection that they did anything other than jump the curb to avoid a pileup on the boulevard. It can be very challenging to drive in Las Vegas."

I watched Dixie and Brody helping Roxie to her feet. She was crying. "What's her deal? She should be in clover."

"Not…exactly." Armaeus shook his head. "The Empress taught SANCTUS how to build their device. She helped them test it, perfect it. She knew what she was doing, and what it would cause. She simply didn't expect it to be calibrated directly for *her* at any point."

I thought about the variation in the wall of sound right after I'd given Simon the Mongolian crown. "You calibrated the sound to affect the Council?"

"Not the Council—her. As a result, she is no longer Connected. She can no longer be a member of the Council, now or evermore. No amount of artificial enhancement will allow her to regain her abilities to the sufficient level. She'll return to her normal timeline of life, and pass when her days on this Earth are complete."

"No more a…" I turned back to the Bellagio. Sure enough, the fairy-tale castle that had soared above it like something out of an overblown Disney movie was gone. The space above the Bellagio was empty blue sky.

"Sweet Christmas," I breathed. "Is there a severance package?"

"Wealth. Health. Beauty, according to her definition of it. The things she most wished for in this life, her deepest dreams and desires, will be granted to her."

"Kreios." I widened my eyes. "That's why he was here. To know her desires when her abilities were swept from her."

Armaeus nodded. "In addition, she has a story her

mind can accept and build upon. In Roxie's case, she was a grifter before her exposure to augmentation transformed her into something more. Her recollection will be simply that she was a very...successful grifter. A stage queen of the seventies, except her stage was in Vegas, and her life became extraordinarily comfortable because of that."

I stared at the weeping woman. "She doesn't seem comfortable."

"Change never is. When her mind clears, it will be easier for her." He said the words matter-of-factly. There was no warmth in his voice, no basic human compassion. Then again, Armaeus wasn't human, exactly.

Still, something didn't add up. "But you changed the frequency to build *up* the Connecteds, after you zapped her. Why didn't she gain it back? Hell, Brody is walking around glowing like a night-light now. Why not the Empress?"

Armaeus's smile was dark, darker than anything I'd ever seen on him, which was saying something. "I guess you could say it was magic."

A flash of bright blue caught my attention then, running through the crowd.

It looked like a man.

In a Mongolian death mask.

CHAPTER TWENTY-EIGHT

By the time we got to Simon, he was perched in a crouch on top of his truck. Not in the bed of the truck, on top of it. Surrounding him were thirteen figures in long tunics and pants, sporting masks of wolves, demons, tigers, bulls, bears, and birds of prey. They practically shimmered with purpose, straining toward him without breaking the circle of deference that Simon had somehow circumscribed around himself.

Armaeus peered thoughtfully at the creature nearest him. He lifted a hand, and the man froze, allowing Armaeus to draw his finger along the top edge of his mask. "This dates from the eighth century. That's well before the time of Genghis Khan's crown."

"Well, apparently these guys get around." I frowned up at Simon. "What are you doing up there?"

"I'm thinking," he snapped. "I tried taking off the crown and tossing it to them. They threw it back."

I looked from him to Armaeus and back. "How do we get them to go away?"

"I don't think we do." Simon glanced down to me. "Where'd you get this thing, again?"

"Um…found it?"

"Well, I get the strong feeling that these guys want

it to *stay* found. Whoever you handed it over to didn't want them hanging around, so…now they're here. They want someone to follow."

Armaeus's lips twisted. "They are not unlike many in this world."

"Not helpful." Simon stood, his hands going out in a soothing gesture. The watchers moved as well, echoing his movement, never edging closer.

"Sir." A uniformed officer stood at the edge of the sidewalk and stared up at Simon. From his perspective, Simon had to look stoned on a full selection of drugs, each more trippy than the last. "Is this your vehicle? It can't be parked on public property." He frowned at the circle of death masks. "Neither can they."

I blinked, and realized that the world had gone on while we were recovering. Traffic was moving smoothly again on the boulevard, not counting the extra-large number of EMTs on the scene. Now Simon's hyper-tricked-out monster truck was…noticeable.

"I, um, got run off the road earlier." Simon huffed out a breath. "I haven't been able to get my vehicle started."

"Is that why you're on the roof, sir? Wearing that helmet?" The officer's voice sounded pained, and he took another step forward. "If you can't remove your vehicle you'll be cited and it will be tow—"

In an elegant, flowing motion, the death mask closest to the officer turned, drawing his arm down in a graceful arc.

The cop hit the pavement, out cold.

"What the—" I dropped into a squat and crawled over to the police officer. He was breathing, with no apparent injuries, his heartbeat steady. He was actually…snoring.

I squinted up at Simon as he hopped off the roof of the truck and landed lightly on the ground. "He's not dead."

"Of course he's not dead. They were protecting me."

Was it my imagination, or did Simon's chest look a little fuller now? He pulled off the helmet, sighing. "But really and truly, I can't accept this. You'll need to find a…um…"

The creatures were kneeling. Now to anyone walking by, Simon was holding a helmet and staring at a crowd of supplicants, while a passed-out cop lay at his feet. That couldn't be good. Simon frowned at Armaeus. "Do you speak, ah, Mongolian?"

The creatures lowered farther, and a soft, murmuring chant lifted around us, ethereal and eerie.

Armaeus folded his arms. "It appears they are pledging fealty to you, Simon. They do not want to return to their homeland. They want to follow you to yours."

"Mine! What am I going to do with a posse of undead?"

"Anything you would like, it would appear."

Simon frowned, looking from the men to his helmet. "What if they're assholes?"

"Every friendship has its challenges."

Simon sighed. "Fine. Tell them I—"

Before he could get the words out, the creatures lifted their arms and backed away, bowing.

My head started to hurt. "What in the…"

At Simon's feet, the cop was stirring. Simon set the helmet into the truck's bed, then squatted down. "Officer? Officer! Are you all right?" he shouted loudly. "Do you need me to call an ambulance?"

Armaeus drew me away. "I think Simon will be able to manage from here."

"But the—"

Armaeus gestured almost lazily to the street. Standing at the curb were thirteen men, lined up at attention. Their bronzed skin linked them, some of them as young as Simon, some old, with whisper-white hair and deep furrows bracketing their eyes and mouths. They wore long, brightly colored tunics over dark loose pants, and they watched Simon without speaking, their gaze intent, their smiles wide. None of their masks were in evidence. Still, even in Vegas, they stood out. "Seriously? They're human now?"

He eyed me. "They were never anything but. The abilities of the human race exceed modern imagination, but not that of the ancient seers. You, out of everyone, should know that."

"I guess." We were walking past the Bellagio again, where the enormous claw marks were—

Armaeus waved his hand.

—magically gone.

"You get off on doing that, don't you?"

"People see what they expect to see, Miss Wilde."

I stared at the dancing fountains, and at the empty hole above the grand casino, where a fairy-tale castle once stood. And blinked again. The castle was gone, yes. But the space wasn't empty. An enormous glittering glass foolscap soared above the Bellagio now, shimmering in the spray of the fountains.

I grinned in spite of it all. "That was fast."

"An improvement, I should say."

I couldn't argue. Especially since the place would be populated by sort-of almost real live people. "So, now you need a new Empress?"

I sensed him glance toward me. "Are you interested in the position?"

"That would be negative. Getting benched seems pretty extreme."

"What happened to Roxie is not common and was brought about by her own hand."

"Yeah, no." I waved him off. "I'm good. But that gets you down to...what, five? You, Kreios, Simon, Eshe—and the Emperor, right?" I swiveled my gaze to the grey stone castle above Caesars. Like the Empress's palace, I'd never seen any sign of life there. "Does he ever come out of his hole?"

"I suspect he will shortly." It was impossible to read Armaeus's tone. It was neutral, almost bored. But I'd been around him long enough to find that worrisome. "The Council has but one governing rule, Miss Wilde, beyond the balance of magic. And that is not to weaken the Council. Roxie sought to do that. Whether out of malice or spite or simply because she thought she might gain power because of it, does not matter."

"And...what, the Emperor did that too?"

"No." Armaeus shook his head. "The Emperor is, perhaps more than any of us, dedicated to the balance of dark and light magic."

The dots connected all on their own. "He's the dark, isn't he?" I stared at the monolith. "That's why you don't want him here. Roxie was dark too. Eshe, for all her bitch face, is neutral. Kreios is dark, but sort of like chocolate is dark. " I frowned at him. "What are you?"

"None and all. As head of the Council, that is my lot."

"Somebody's gotta do it, I guess. And Simon?"

"Light." Armaeus's mouth twitched into a tired smile.

"So with Roxie gone, you're out of balance. You're going to need to add some true darkness of some kind."

"The balance does not have to be exact. Roxie was not that dark. She was vain and petty, but her augmented magic was strong. The evil did not outweigh the good that she wrought until the very end."

"Okay, but who else is out there? Death, the Hierophant, Hanged Man, Hermit? Maybe Justice, if you want to get technical about it. The rest…I don't see as people, so much. The Lovers, I suppose. But that's two people, right?"

I thought about the robed shadow that had flickered in the maelstrom. "Who's seated currently, and what holes do you need to fill?"

Armaeus didn't answer, and silence stretched between us. Eventually, we reached the Luxor, and I stared up at Prime Luxe soaring above it, all metal and crystal and fierceness. It suddenly occurred to me that I didn't live there. My home was at the Palazzo at the other end of the Strip. And that wasn't really a home either, I supposed. It was… I didn't know what it was, suddenly.

Time to go. "Well, have a good evening. It's been fun."

Armaeus turned to me. His eyes continued to glow with that eerie half-light. "Are you sure I can't tempt you to continue our conversation?"

I thought about Nikki. Hopefully the cops had taken her to the hospital, where she was being tended to by strapping young doctors. I thought about Simon and his baker's dozen of personal guards, turning on all the lights in the Foolscap. I thought about Brody and Dixie—leaving together, both of them aglow with the surge of power that Armaeus had fed into them.

"How long will it last?" I asked again, shoving my hands into the pockets of my hoodie and nudging the now dormant scroll case. "The augmentation, I mean. The power surge. How long until everyone goes back to normal?"

He glanced back down the Strip. "The effects will vary. For the Connecteds with at least moderate innate ability, it could last several days. For those unfortunate enough to be at SANCTUS headquarters when you threw the scroll case at the screen, the effect will likely last far longer."

"Yeah, well. They had it coming."

Armaeus's lips twitched. "With today's actions, SANCTUS will be in disarray. Some will not be able to handle their newfound psychic abilities. Some will far better than they would prefer."

"Which makes them like the rest of us. And the people here in Vegas?"

"Impossible to tell."

"Right." I thought a little bit more about Brody and Dixie. I glanced again at the spires of Prime Luxe.

"My offer to extend our conversation stands, Miss Wilde," Armaeus said quietly. "I assure you, I only wish to talk."

I nodded. "I could use a good talk right about now.

CHAPTER TWENTY-NINE

The Magician's penthouse living room was bathed in soft light when we reached it, the dim glow accentuating the magnificent view of the Strip. He crossed to the bar, and the familiar sound of thick-cut crystal glasses clinking together should have helped unwind me. Instead, it kicked me up another notch. I pulled the scroll case out of my hoodie and set it carefully on one of Armaeus's shelves.

"Miss Wilde?"

I turned, and Armaeus was beside me. His eyes now practically gleamed with the unholy fire of the power surging through him. He handed me the scotch, and I took it, taking a sharp swallow.

"Kreios was unaffected, right?" I asked. "He seemed pretty much normal, anyway. What about Eshe?"

"Eshe was in deep meditation at the time. She knew the confrontation was coming, and she wanted to take advantage of it in her own way. She seeks to maintain her hold on the enhancement long enough to undertake her own oracular attempt—not solely to be able to guide someone like you and interpret what you see, but to view the world with her own eyes. If she can reach a transcendent state to seek out the answers she craves, she will no longer need intermediaries. As to Kreios, yes. He appeared unfazed by the blast. That bears further study. He was also unsurprised that he was not affected, which, frankly, is more curious still."

"He's psychically deaf?" He'd said something about that after the Rarity attack, but was it true?

Armaeus wasn't convinced either. "Or so he would prefer us to believe." He rolled his glass in his hand. "The Fool was unaffected because he was protected by the Mongolian crown."

"What about me?" I couldn't help but ask. "Because I sure as hell felt it when the pulse was set to 'pulverize,' and, obviously, I was pumped up enough to hold that scroll case without singeing my skin off. But I don't feel different now."

"It's a very good question." Armaeus set down his glass, untouched, and took mine from my hand. He tilted my face up to the light. "Your eyes remain the same. Your energy does not appear to be affected."

"Oh?" I struggled to keep my voice steady. It'd been a long day.

"No." He drew his fingers along my chin, the pressure sending excited whorls of sensation skittering along my nerves. I knew he was aware of my physical reaction, but for once, he disregarded it. "You spoke directly to Llyr, which was very dangerous, and quite foolish."

"Llyr." I repeated the name. "You knew I was looking for him all this time, didn't you?"

"Not until you brought his image to me scrawled on a bar receipt." His gaze met mine. "As I said then, there has never been a Council airplane with Llyr's symbol inscribed on it. We have done our level best to eradicate all imagery related to it."

I stared. "But I saw it— "

"Yes. Which shouldn't have been possible. The fact that you did is another piece of the mystery in which you are mired, Miss Wilde." He paused, letting the moment play out. "You saw him long ago, as well, I suspect. The day you left Memphis."

I met Armaeus's gaze, knowing what he wanted. Though he'd been responsible for bringing the Connecteds into harm's way, that hadn't technically voided our deal. Our deal had been that, if he helped me *protect* the Connecteds, I was to give him a piece of my mind. Literally.

But now I wanted that too. Whether it was the influx of power or the adrenaline from a job well done, the idea of exploring my past didn't bother me at this precise moment. I needed to know, to understand. And Armaeus could help me.

"How long would it take?"

He shifted closer to me. "But an instant. I swear that would be all that I need."

"Fi—" Armaeus bent toward me before I could finish the word, and covered my mouth with his. Instantly, my mind shuddered and balked, the scene racing before me ripped whole cloth from the fabric of my past. Breakfast alone at the table. The note, the touch of wrongness on its page. The surge of fear, of needing to run, to escape, to fly—the race to get out of the house and into the yard, falling, running, slipping, until everything went up in a surge of smoke and fire and sound—all around me. And then I saw—I saw...

Armaeus broke away, and I sucked in a huge breath, swaying in his arms. He scowled down at me, his face like stone, and a surge of all that leftover grief and fear and rage welled up within me, so strong I nearly choked on it.

"What?" I gasped, searching his eyes. "What?"

Armaeus blinked, then apparently could truly see me again. An emotion I'd never seen before crossed his face. It was almost...tender. Full of wonder.

Annnnnd... Something inside me broke.

"Kiss me again, Armaeus," I whispered before I could stop myself. "Now, before all the pain returns. The questions. I want more. I want it all."

He went very still. "You're not yourself."

"Aren't I?" I stood up on my tiptoes and brushed my lips against his. There was no fear this time, no wall of self-preserving terror. Instead, I needed the Magician, more than I'd needed anything in my life. Needed Armaeus's hands on me, his mouth on mine, his heat surrounding me. Needed something to penetrate to the icy-cold core of my emotions and thaw the pain that was gnawing at me, turning me dead inside. "Please."

Armaeus's war with himself took about three point five seconds. "I will do this because it is pleasure, and healing, and pleasure and healing are what you most need."

That sounded conditional, and I wasn't about conditional. But as Armaeus dragged me into a rough embrace, I didn't care. With a swipe of his leg, my knees buckled and I fell to the floor, his body covering mine as he ground me into the thick carpet. And his mouth was everywhere. On my mouth, my temple, down the curve of my neck. His fingers tangled in my hair, pulling my head back, exposing my collarbone to his questing lips. My back arched instinctively beneath him. He brought his left hand around and pushed my tank top up high on my chest. Then breath hissed from my lips as his fingers closed around the weight of my breast, kneading it, rolling the nipple in his hard fingers, teasing with both pleasure and pain.

"Yes," I moaned. "Yes—that. Please." I strained toward him. His mouth met mine, and I drank him in, surrounded by his heat. Power shot through me, exotic and sure, filling me up.

For a moment, we hung suspended together, out of time and space. I pulled back, and his eyes transfixed me. In that moment, I felt the awesome power of him, yes, but also the endless ache of enforced isolation that had stretched across the centuries of his long life. Isolation that fed and honed his abilities, but that also held him apart from the most basic tenet of his powers. The wild, primal magic that I could feel if only…if only…

I let him in again for the briefest moment. Felt the long, searching tendrils of his mental touch slip over and through my mind, seeking out the broken places, probing, testing...

He snapped back, and yet another emotion flashed across his face that I had never seen before. At least not on him.

Jealousy.

Carefully, deliberately, Armaeus pushed me away, creating more space between us. "I meant what I said to you, Miss Wilde, when we first met." His voice had taken on a dangerous edge, his eyes once again glittering. "Do you remember my words, precisely?"

I floundered for a response, out of my depth. "That I was irresponsible?"

As I watched, his face cleared of all emotion, returning to his coolly civil mask. When he spoke again, his words were quiet. Detached. "That when you want me, truly want me, then I will be waiting for you. But I will not have you turn to me when your mind and your heart are filled with confusion over someone else." With a smooth, graceful motion, he regained his feet.

Wait, what? I scrambled upright too. "What are you talking about?"

"You should know that your concerns over Detective Rooks are unfounded. He has no carnal interest in Dixie Quinn." Cool eyes flicked over me. "At least, not anymore."

Embarrassment shot through me. "I don't care about who his—how do you know that?"

"We've already ascertained that there are very few minds that are not completely open to me, in all ways. Except yours."

"It's kind of rude."

"You're not curious?" Armaeus lifted his brows, the frost of his anger shimmering between us. "You don't wish to know what the innermost thoughts are of those who are thinking about you at this very moment?"

Yes. "No!" I scowled at him. "You'd really suck to play hide-and-seek with."

"You do want to know."

"Not from you I don't."

"Very wise." His smile had turned hard. "The value that I bring to you is not one that is born of trust. You have other options for that, if trust is truly what you seek."

"I know I'm little more than a science experiment to you," I spat, my filter completely shredded at this point. "You've never told me anything unless it could help you meet your own selfish ends."

Armaeus's laugh was scoffing. "You are a *part* of my selfish ends, make no mistake. And I will not rest until I understand everything about you." He peered at me, then nodded once. "Very well, Miss Wilde. Though you cannot bring yourself to ask, I *will* show one piece of what you truly seek, when all the distractions are cleared away."

He held up a staying hand when I unconsciously moved toward him.

"No. Do not touch me. I will not have you confuse this for anything more than what it is." His gaze went distant, piercing me through. "Look . See."

Something in his voice would not be denied. I stared into his gaze and saw beyond the eerie dark gold eyes, into the wealth of knowledge and history that was hidden there. And I saw more.

A blue dragon, trapped on a field of red.

Staring back at me.

The unearthly power of the creature stretched toward me, but I was wrong, I realized suddenly. Llyr *wasn't* staring at me, exactly. It was staring at something between us. The barest shadow of a robed figure, holding aloft a—

"You pierce the veil so easily…" Armaeus murmured. "You see so much."

I blinked at his voice, the image slipping away. "Who's in there? Who is that with the dragon. The man… He's in robes of some sort?"

The image nagged at me, even as it faded. A shadowed figure…a wavering light. Then the connection closed completely, and Armaeus's cold, dark eyes once again held mine. And I could recall nothing but the dragon. Llyr.

My head throbbed again, not painfully, but I held my hand up to it to ensure my brains weren't falling out with the blast of knowing I'd just received. The essence of a god who'd once walked this world and nearly destroyed it. "Llyr. What is that, Welsh? The only Welsh god of that name I've heard of is nowhere near that powerful."

"That's by careful design." Armaeus loomed over me. He was darker, more intense. He swelled with a power that wasn't fully his own, I knew. But that didn't make it any less effective. "Llyr in many ways was the founder of the original Council. We were built to balance his abilities."

I stared at him, finally refocusing. "You threw him *off the planet,* Armaeus. That doesn't seem super 'balanced.'"

"It was not supposed to escalate to that. But when he resisted our attempts to constrain his power, he unleashed the forces of the elements. Mortals were caught in the balance, drowning beneath the waves he stirred."

"Whoa, whoa. Waves. Do not even."

"There are records of a great flood in almost every culture with a written record, Miss Wilde. Surely you do not think they were all fabrications?"

"Well, no, but I don't recall the part where a giant blue dragon flapped his wings and caused the waters of the Earth to rise. I would have remembered that."

Armaeus shrugged, but his energy did not dissipate. "Why now?" I asked. When he didn't speak, I prodded. "All of this. Llyr. SANCTUS. Why is everything happening so quickly?"

"SANCTUS, in one form or another, has been emerging for centuries. Over the past few years, however, they have expanded their operations dramatically. Through a power not of their own making, they are shifting the balance of magic. When that balance is upset, the veil between the worlds grows inconsistent. Where it is weak, Llyr is strong. And he can't be allowed back into this world." He held up a hand to forestall my question. "The 'magic' of Llyr isn't magic. It's domination and force. It is not a power that allows anything else to exist. The darkest of your dark practitioners that you rail against, those creatures who feed upon the weakest of the Connected, who drink in their power and exploit them... They would be his most minor foot soldiers."

I nodded. I'd seen Llyr, experienced his strength. I knew Armaeus was right. "So that's why you wanted to show him to SANCTUS before, you know...I barged in?"

He shrugged. "In part. SANCTUS could easily destroy the Connecteds of limited power, bolstering the dark practitioners until they destroyed all that was light. The trouble with that scenario, however, is that dark magic alone would remain. And a world built solely on dark magic is more unstable than a world slightly unbalanced. The veil would weaken. Fall away."

"You fought him, didn't you." I stared at him. "You've confronted Llyr before."

He met my gaze, his eyes too cool. Too distant. "Llyr was banished from earth long before I—"

"Not then. After. That's why you're so determined to keep him contained. Something happened and he almost broke through a second time. Except you fought him. Kept him trapped beyond the veil." I felt the force of rightness to my words, their truths winging through me. "I'm right, aren't I? And to make that happen…you gave up something. Something important."

Armaeus's words, when they came, were bleak. And barely a whisper. "The balance must be preserved. The world must remain whole."

A cold fear pierced my heart, but I held his gaze. What had he sacrificed to keep magic in the world? What would he give up to maintain its balance?

Who was the Magician, really?

"Could you… Can you show me, then?" I whispered. "What you feel, what you see? What this balance looks like, in a world filled with magic?"

Armaeus went still for a long moment. "Why?"

I didn't trust myself to explain that. Not yet. Not ever, most likely. "Humor me."

Without speaking, the Magician moved to stand behind me, his arms crossing over my body, pulling me close. The act was strangely intimate—not sexual, exactly, but deeply, utterly personal. He bent his head until his lips grazed the crown of my head. "Do not close your eyes, Miss Wilde. See ever out, not in. Understand?"

"Sure." I was surprised at how my voice trembled, but the world had taken on a new cast. As I stood in Armaeus's embrace, it was no longer the vivid neons and floodlights of Vegas's Strip, but layers, endless layers of energy, dancing and weaving. Some wavelengths were wobbly, some were strong, some dark, some light. It was a silent orchestra of power, and it was all moving for me.

"Who would you see, what would you see?" Armaeus's words were quiet, almost soundless. "What is the energy that is the true driver of the world?"

"Possibility," I whispered.

"Possibility. Mortals of pure potential, stretched to their finest purpose. Like you have been stretched. Like I would stretch you again and again, for you to grow in your abilities, protect whom you would protect, and for you to be who you were truly meant to be. To claim your birthright." His breath hushed over my hair. "If you would but accept that it is yours to claim."

Mine to claim?

When I would have instinctively moved to escape, to flee, his body held me still.

"Look and see, Sara," Armaeus murmured, and my whole world filled with his words. "See and know. Where is your strength, what is your future? What lies in wait for you, ready for you to grasp?"

"I don't know— "

"I think you do. I think you have for a long time." As if in spite of himself, he shifted closer, drifting another soft kiss over my hair. The frisson of electricity his action caused was unmistakable, crackling with promise. "You must accept the truth for what it is."

I gazed over a city now more familiar than my own muscle and bone. Whether it was a holdover from the scroll cases' ancient magic, or Armaeus's touch, or the sweet combination of exhaustion and exultation that I had stood in the path of danger and found the strength to hold firm—to protect those who could not protect themselves, the world in front of me simply wasn't the same. I wasn't the same.

I'd taken a simple job for a simple purpose and set in motion an inescapable change deep within myself and in the world around me. Change I'd never expected. Change I needed more than I'd ever imagined.

I stared into the lights of Vegas and came to an unnerving realization.

After all my years of running…I was home.

THE WORLD OF IMMORTAL VEGAS

Want to learn more about each of the Arcana Council members and other details about Immortal Vegas?

Visit http://www.jennstark.com/immortal-vegas/ for a full introduction!

COMING SOON FROM IMMORTAL VEGAS

Ready for Sara's next adventure? BORN TO BE WILDE will be released in February, 2016!

BORN TO BE WILDE

The past has a way of catching up with you.

If there's one thing that Tarot-reading magical artifacts hunter Sara Wilde has never been able to track down, it's the truth about her own past. But now a powerful new threat to the psychic community will take Sara back to where it all began: the last job she worked with Officer Brody Rooks as "Psychic Teen Sariah," the job that destroyed her life and sent her on the run. Because the enemy she fled all those years ago has returned… with a score of demons as his personal army.

Worse, Sara's infuriating mentor, the dangerously seductive Magician, is pushing her to stretch her abilities and explore the very deepest reaches of her magic. But every demand draws her further into the spell he's weaving around her. And every challenge tests her vow to keep him at arm's length.

From the glittering chaos of Las Vegas to the Lost City of Atlantis, Sara must risk everything in a quest for vengeance that grows darker and more twisted with every step. To succeed she'll have to face the truth about her past, her abilities...and the impossible, unstoppable attraction she has to the Magician. A truth that will reveal her ultimate role in the war on magic.

Life is full of surprises when you are Born to Be Wilde.

BORN TO BE WILDE
Available Feb. 2016

AUTHOR'S NOTE

The cards that appear at the opening of this book were the ones drawn by Sara during a pivotal reading in the story, before she, the Magician, and the Fool head to Egypt. Here are the three basic interpretations a Tarot reader might give to someone pulling these cards:

THE SIX OF SWORDS

Things are about to improve. You're moving away from your problems and into smoother waters. You may travel overseas, and the future could be unknown, but the further you get away from past difficulties, the better you will be able to embrace a new adventure.

THE CHARIOT

You're on the move! Ambitious, determined and ready to create your own destiny through your actions, you are assured of victory if you focus on your goals. You may be on a physical or spiritual journey, but if you follow your path with joy, you will reach your desired destination.

JUDGMENT

A spiritual awakening causes you to release the past and start anew. You're being put to the test and you succeed, or you're being judged in some way and you are considered worthy of moving to the next level. You now have the ability to transform yourself or a situation into something new and better.

ACKNOWLEDGMENTS

Wilde Card was truly a labor of love, and would not have been possible without so many wonderful people. Thank you to Elizabeth Bemis for being the best friend a girl could have, as well as for your book formatting, graphics and my site. Sincere thanks also go to Gene Mollica for the photography and cover design/illustration for Wilde Card, and to Linda Ingmanson and Toni Lee for collaborative and above all thorough editorial skills. Any mistakes in the manuscript are, of course, my own. Kristine, your critique was flat out amazing as usual, and I'm so lucky you put up with me. Lindsey, thank you for your editorial and strategic insights. Dana, you will never know how much your enthusiasm and feedback matter—thank you! Finally, to Geoffrey, thank you for your vision, insight and guidance, every step of the way. It's been a *Wilde* ride.

ABOUT JENN STARK

Jenn Stark is an award-winning author of paranormal romance and urban fantasy. She lives and writes in Ohio. . . and she definitely loves to write. In addition to her "Immortal Vegas" urban fantasy series, she is also author Jennifer McGowan, whose Maids of Honor series of Young Adult Elizabethan spy romances are published by Simon & Schuster, and author Jennifer Chance, whose Rule Breakers series of New Adult contemporary romances are published by Random House/LoveSwept and whose new modern royals series, Gowns & Crowns, is now available.

You can find her online at **www.jennstark.com**, follow her on Twitter **twitter.com/jennstark**, and visit her on Facebook at **facebook.com/authorjennstark**.

Made in the USA
Monee, IL
13 August 2020